Greater Expectations

Trish's Story

Jacqueline Gillam Fairchild

For Jerry

Greater Expectations: Trish's Story

Copyright

Library Cataloging Data:

1. Dating Agencies, 2. Romance, 3. Roadside Diners, 4. Veterinarians, 5. Modeling, 6. Nature Magazines, 7. Shopping, 8. Photography 9. Make Overs, 10 Self Help Books

Library of Congress Control Number: 2018909503

In praise of Estate of Mind:

"I love your book! I love your book so much that I have to argue with myself about how many chapters I can read in one sitting because I don't want to finish it! What an inspiration. After the first few chapters I I cleaned my entire porch (Some years I haven't used it at all) and have lunch there on weekends while I read. I love the characters, your descriptions are fabulous. I can't say enough good things and just wanted you to know. Thank you for writing this absolutely delightful book. When I finish, I guess I'll just have to read it again!"

Bonnie Mason
Community Business Development Manager
Barnes & Noble, Inc

In praise of Creating Memories:

Take three lonely elderly ladies, add a ditzy young woman from a New York advertising firm, and a Californian race car driver, mix in some magic and put them all in a remote, Midwestern town. POW! Romantic, funny entertainment for everyone.

I categorize this book as romantic, comedic fantasy because it has a little magic from Scotland. There are several laugh-out-loud scenes in here, as well as funny one-liners.

Beach reading? Yes! Fun read on a snowy night? Yes! The novel goes down fast and easy, like a slice of rum cake.

Andy Zach-Author: *My Undead Mother in Law* and *Zombie Turkeys*

Acknowledgements:

For Linda Hartman,

Nancy Waktins, Sally Lariviera

Colleen Simpson, Jacqueline Gerber

Rik Hall, Sean Flannagan

And Judy Morgan

Endorsements:

"Jacqueline is one of the most creative and interesting persons I have ever met."

J. Peterman
iconic catalog entrepreneur,
TV character and author

Introduction

Jinx stooped to pick up the newspaper as she headed to the door of Fairchild's Ltd., her tiny English shoppe, she owned with her husband Jefferson. The newspaper slipped out of her hand and fell open. Stooping once more to grab the paper, she noticed a bold ad on the back page of the first section. Quickly she gave the paper a cursory glance before stuffing it in her canvas tote.

'Greater Expectations

Tired of being let down and disappointed?
Impossible to meet that perfect companion?
Call us today
Greater Expectations
A Dating Service that lives up to its name.
$1-800$--555 D$-$A$-$T$-$E'

"Hmph," Jinx thought as she clicked open the lock. Absently she let herself into Fairchild's, flipping the 'closed' sign to 'open'. Her husband Jefferson turned on the lights, which automatically turned on the CD player. Jim Hart sang about how hard it was to find love. His voice drifted over the shoppe as Jinx started turning on the decorative lights over by the Popsicle colored cashmere sweaters.

She stopped to refold one and then noticed the Cadbury's chocolate bars were a bit disheveled. Of course Jinx had brought her standard healthy lunch of chopped broccoli and a boiled egg. As a matter of fact, it was the same lunch she'd brought the day before--literally. She snagged a roll of McVities Digestive biscuits. Were they getting too old to sell? Only one way to find out … And maybe a pot of Yorkshire Gold tea to dunk them in, just in case they needed dunking that is …

Jinx moved on to tidy up some new lavender soap that sat on a crystal cake stand. Jim Hart had switched to singing about looking for love in all the wrong places. By the time she ended back up at her computer behind the counter, Jim Hart was singing about being all alone. She looked at the newspaper ad again sighing, thinking of all her lonely friends and customers.

Chapter 1

Dev stood by his desk and scrolled down the computer—bored, all the same, one after another. Faces, albeit pretty, stared at him. Messages, all the same: 'Single girl looking for Mr. Perfect.' Dev didn't feel perfect. He wasn't perfect—far from it. Why didn't any of them say 'Looking for ...' and he couldn't put it in words? If he could, he wouldn't have such a hard time looking ...

***

Trish looked out her ice frosted window, and concentrated. But how could her window be frosted, it was summer? She looked closer, leaning in. She saw her reflection, wearing that camel cashmere coat she'd seen at Nordstrom's that was the same color as her honey hair--fabulous.

Next to her stood the most drop dead gorgeous man she'd ever seen. He had an arm around her, protectively. The look in his eyes was tender yet sizzling at the same time. His hair was almost the same color as Trish's; sun streaked a bit, as though he had been some where warm. Why he was wearing that wool top coat she'd just seen in Barney's! Handsome and great taste in clothes!

"Wait! Why am I concentrating on his clothes--or my clothes for that matter?" Trish looked closer, "How superficial am I?" Then she sighed, knowing she wasn't, not really. She was a fashion devotee sure, but well, clothes weren't everything ...

"How about that look?" She couldn't explain the feeling it gave her. He was looking at her like she was a dish of strawberry ice cream. "I don't think, well, I'm pretty sure, no one has ever looked at me like that before."

And it made Trish soften to almost a puddle. She reached a finger up carefully to the ice crusted window just to touch their reflections.

And the frosted window with the handsome man dissipated. Just like that.

And turned into her steamy bathroom mirror.

Trish was no longer wearing the million dollar cashmere coat. She was wearing her ratty bathrobe.

And the man? The man who had reduced her to a shimmer of herself? He was gone! Gone was his sexy look. Gone was his expensive Barney's coat. Gone was his look that said she was his.

Gone.

All gone.

And Trish was back, in her bathroom.

***

"Caffeine! I'll just sit here for a minute with some strong caffeine and clear my head." And Trish sipped the scalding brew of Yorkshire Gold tea, letting it seep into her system. "What was that? Was that way back? When I was younger?" But Trish knew it wasn't. She hadn't looked younger; it wasn't her carefree high school days or her foolish college days--or even later.

"No, it was now--right now. But why did I look younger?" And then Trish sighed as her tea took effect. "Maybe I didn't look younger; maybe I just looked happier ... glowingly happier."

And for the life of her Trish wasn't sure if it was that new Lancôme cream she was using or ... or, well, she knew. She couldn't kid herself. It was the look of being loved and loving. She swiped at a stray tear, refusing to give in. "I'm not unhappy. I'm not. I have a great career. And of course I have my friends ..."

Trish flipped through her closet and pondered, "What should I wear ..." She went back and started over settling on a black pencil skirt. Short--but not too short; stylish, well 'stylish like'. The skirt had been stylish when she'd bought it a couple months ago. At the same time she purchased a tiny black cami with glitter straps; subtle--well not too subtle. One wanted to be noticed when one was out.

When one went out ...

The cami lay in a drawer forgotten. Well not really forgotten, just not worn. And now the skirt was trudging into the office, with a modest blouse, white of course, tucked neatly into its waist band. And the four inch heels with the glitter toes to match the glitter straps were napping in their box. Okay hibernating.

Trish stepped into her black pumps — well they had a hint of a heel and some ever so guarded style. "Hmmm," She looked at the scuffed toes. "Probably time to go shopping ..." Then she sighed, "For more conservative pumps — to wear to work." Trish grabbed her beloved Chloe bag and ran out the door. "Who says I never go out?" Then she sobered. "Of course, I go out — to work. But work, well, it is work. And it doesn't count. Not really. It wasn't out 'out.'"

Trish was glamorous--tall, leggy, blonde. She was a style-- a style that had always been popular--a style that worked like a formula. "It had worked for me ... hadn't it?" She stopped, catching a quick glance of herself in her car windshield. Even in her business clothes she had style, and yes it had worked.

Worked so well for so long she'd just taken it for granted. "No rush. No sweat. No worry or effort for that matter." And no real notice as it started to taper off. "Oh heads still turn, occasionally. True they are older but so am I," She admitted it. Yet it didn't matter if she admitted it or not, there was a younger crop out there. "And they have my style, they are using my formula."

"And they are getting my results."

**

Trish drove absently to work. She passed a young mother pushing a baby stroller and for one split second Trish wondered why that woman wasn't at work. "Oh yeah, a baby ..." And then she sighed.

She drove past cookie cutter houses in a cookie cutter neighborhood. Something she normally picked on with her usual sarcastic streak. But today she looked closer. "One house, two cars, one woman, one man ... is that so much to ask? Don't lots of people have that?" And she knew they did. That's how the system went--the pairing off and living happily ever after. She heard someone yelling from one of the cookie cutter houses. "Well maybe not all happily ever after. Still ... that person had their shot at it." And Trish realized she hadn't.

Had her shot that is.

She thought back to earlier days when she felt it was all before her. "Well it was all before me, I was starting an exciting career – which I still have, actually have perfected. And it was like a playground. Not quite college playground where everyone was my age, and all I had to do was just show up for class and smile ..." And she thought, and decide what to wear, and who to go out with--or who not to go out with. Because men had been like Kleenex back then, another one always popped up.

And after college the working world had been exciting.

She was exciting.

Men flocked around her, though not quite like college. College they were all her own age, and well, she knew there was more out there. So, she tossed them away, disposable-- gone. But the working men, well that was different. That frivolous feeling was gone.

Yet the working men, who she was attracted to were also just starting out. She had no idea where they were actually going. And she didn't want to wait around to find out. In case, well, in her own rude way she knew, in case they weren't really going anywhere. So again, she didn't take any of their attention seriously.

No, she had plenty of time.

Trish worked hard, actually loving her job in Human Resources, and time just dissipated. And along with time the men. On an occasional quiet evening she would wonder about this one or that one from years ago: where they were, who they were with. And then she knew, maybe she'd had her shot.

And wasted it.

Unintentionally, of course, but wasted none the less. No one had told her there were expiration dates on, well, finding someone. There weren't. "Of course there weren't." But then again, she woke up one day to find things had changed. The playing field she knew so well had changed.

And no one had warned her.

Even if she hadn't been caught unaware it might not have made any difference, because it just was what it was. Trish wasn't old. Old was, well, it wasn't Trish. No, she wasn't old.

Just older.

***

Trish left her car at the employee's parking lot at Caterpillar International and headed in. She was in the business of placing people in jobs; she worked in Human Resources. "I don't know why we don't just call it personnel like the old days," She complained. She never saw people--or not many. Since Caterpillar International employed thousands of people around the globe; Trish saw a lot of applications.

Her job was to sort them in slots for potential jobs, and then grade them by what she read. How qualified or unqualified. Many applicants knew where they wanted to work, but many others just knew they wanted to work for Cat.

Trish looked at these uncommitted applications and tried to figure out what stack they should go in, if there was a hint of potential for one of the millions of categories they could fit in.

She had a high-powered job with a lot of responsibilities, but the bottom line was, Trish evaluated pieces of paper, and placed those papers in piles; piles for the next person to evaluate in a more detailed way.

Handed to her, sorted, and handed over. No human contact, well almost none--certainly none with the names on the applications. Trish liked her job. Her analytical mind thrived on interpreting future employee's applications. But when all was said and done, her world was her job.

But before it all began each day, she did have a tiny bit of social life, albeit with two other women — her friends who also worked at Cat International. They met for breakfast.

They called it their 'Power Breakfast' because they were supposed to, but actually it was a time for them to all meet, gossip a bit, and start their days reassured they had each other--she had friends: Maggie and Pandora.

***

Maggie worked at Caterpillar International, in accounting. Maggie loved her work, or should she say her computer screen. "I love making numbers come out right on my screen; endless columns of numbers, representing whatever, from budgets, and planning figures, to reviewing failed budgets, and non-successful projections."

Maggie's was a world of numbers--numbers on a screen. She was good, okay, great, at what she did. Maggie thrived on what she did. Had done it so long it was now second nature--long enough that she was better than good--she was a pro. Still, she was in an office, with papers and a computer ... for hours, days, weeks, years. What else did she have? The bigger question was what else did she have the energy for?

***

Pandora had been a Home Ec major back when Home Ec was still a subject. Somewhere along the line the courses were dumped, and Pandora found herself kitchen help. She also worked at Caterpillar International--in the bowels of one of the many restaurants that fed the endless stream of employees. "I

8

love to bake and I love people, so the job had originally seemed ideal for me, well at least the baking part. Probably Trish had sorted my application to a pile that read 'kitchens'."

Now, years later, Pandora found herself in the sub--basement kitchens in her corner making one thing: oatmeal cookies. Not just any oatmeal cookies. These were bars with raisins or milk chocolate chips, and cinnamon. "They are heavenly--the milk chocolate taking your average oatmeal cookie one step further. The bar shape allows for more chewy surface and in fact is simpler, quicker, and hence cheaper to make."

Pandora ought to know. That was all she did--day in and day out. Her hair and clothes smelled like warm cinnamon and oatmeal.

By the time Pandora realized what working for a mega company meant, she was already dependent on the benefits. Pay in the kitchen was relatively low, variety--nonexistent. "I am a cog in the machine. A cog that makes oatmeal bars. Eight hours a day."

It didn't help that the surgeon general, and Caterpillar's physicians, said oats lowered your cholesterol and blood pressure. That oats were the perfect food blah blah blah. That only meant more people ate oatmeal bars--rationalizing they could have dessert, or a snack, and oats at the same time.

The restaurants, and cafeterias, often had left over Key Lime pie, starting to go a bit oozy, or Turtle Cheesecake, totally wonderful yet unpredictable as to its daily consumption, slowly crusting up. "But my oatmeal bars area sell out day in and day out."

And Pandora used the oversized Hobart mixer, and made batch after batch that she passed on to a baker. Who then passed them on to a slicer and then divided them--some to be wrapped in Syran wrap by a wrapper for the coffee shoppes, and some left for the restaurants and cafeterias.

Intelligence, who ever that was, wasn't sure how long the oat craze would continue, so Pandora remained alone, minding her batters, spreading them in her pans. "I can make them in my sleep except when I sleep, I dream of people--not oatmeal bars." Pandora knew she was buried.

***

Trish and Maggie had been old friends from high school. They reconnected when they realized they worked at Caterpillar. And they met for breakfast at one of Caterpillar's many food facilities before they started their days. Somewhere along the line they met Pan, and Pan joined them for breakfast.

Today was like all the others. Trish sighed heavily, "Hi guys," And plopped down, her morning newspaper dropping with her hand bag on the table. The paper had split open to the back page of the first section.

Pan went to move it, and started to read, "Hey Guys--listen to this:

'Greater Expectations

Tired of being let down and disappointed?
Impossible to meet that perfect companion?
We have the answer right here
Call us today
Greater Expectations
A dating service that lives up to its name.
1--800 − 555--D--A − T − E
We accept all major credit cards.'"

They all laughed, "Perfect companion?" Maggie just shook her head, "I'd like to meet any one, perfect or not. All I ever meet are stacks of reports, lists of numbers."

"How about me? Anyone interesting is simply a name on an application. I fantasize over those names, and it still does me no good," Trish lamented.

Pandora shook her head in agreement, "I'm never let down or disappointed, because I never meet anyone to disappoint me. It's isolated down there in my corner of the kitchen."

"Aren't there any cute dishwashers or head chefs?" Trish asked, knowing she never saw applications for kitchen help.

"No. They're all old--very old, and women. I think they've been there since Caterpillar started. What about you Maggie? Aren't there some cute bookish types up in accounting?" Pandora was sure there had to be someone up there.

"I wouldn't know. My area is so isolated, and I work for that mean widow Mrs. Bernardo! And I pass my work on to a spinster Miss Wood. No, I haven't seen any accountant types," and Maggie just shirked, accepting it all.

The three girls continued to be-moan their lack of social life, joking in a way, yet there was a tinge of seriousness to it all. Serious, because they knew it was true.

"Why if it wasn't for our breakfast meetings together, I'd have no social life," Maggie whined, making no attempt to hide her disgust. Actually, Maggie had given up on a social life, and decided life wasn't all that bad; far from ideal, of course, but she had just learned to accept her situation--not that she couldn't complain with the best of them. But in her heart she knew it was all theatrics. There was no social life for her--period.

"I volunteer at the hospital and at my church," Trish started, "And all I ever meet are other volunteering women!" And in her heart she had to admit she started volunteering to meet men, and ultimately just kept going, finding she liked it. It was not only rewarding, it was something to do, somewhere to go. And eventually she had gotten amerced and well, liked it.

"I hate to think back to the days I had plenty of places to go …" But Trish had somehow squandered those days, and they had evaporated when she wasn't looking, or maybe when she was clawing her way up the ladder at work. It didn't really matter. Those days were in the past, and all the girls tried to live in the right now.

Their gazes all fell back on the ad. "It seems so, uh, impersonal to join a service," Maggie started slowly. She didn't

11

dismiss it though. "And does it say we're desperate to even consider it?" And Maggie wasn't desperate, or at least she didn't want that label. She was, well, maybe 'established' was the word. Yes, she was established. Still the ads intrigued her. They lit something up that was buried, and Maggie wasn't even sure what it was.

"But I wonder what the applications are like," Trish mused. "Heaven knows I see enough applications--I've learned to read between the lines." Absently she ran a hand through her mane of long blonde hair, ruffling it up a bit. "Maybe they are male versions of us; career people with no real outlets to meet each other."

"It doesn't say what it cost, but I'm sure there's no way I could afford to join. I make the least of us down there in the kitchen," Pan stated it like the fact it was. No one said anything. It was just a fact.

Maggie shook her head, "Any extra money I have goes right to the nursing home for my mom. I told her to get nursing home insurance." Maggie couldn't let go of that fact.

Trish turned beet red, "My VISA is so over the limit that I probably live on far less than you two, regardless how I dress." Gingerly she touched her Tissot watch and sighed. Of course, shopping wasn't a substitute for living ... And no, she didn't live to shop. And then with a sigh, Trish realized she did shop to escape, to indulge, and to be out. Well maybe she needed more avenues of going out ...

"Hey, we don't even know what it costs. It could be cheap ..." Pan volunteered wishfully. "And besides none of us said we want to join up. Come on! What kind of men sign up for these things?"

They left for work laughing about Greater Expectations and the men who joined.

***

Trish headed home. "Back to my empty apartment ... plenty of time to try that new nail polish color and maybe sort my shoes." She said it with humor but in her heart she knew the truth. She had no one waiting for her. No faithful dog ready for his walkies, no bored cat still interested enough to demand her attention to get fed. "I'll grab a yogurt, and maybe start looking at my shoe collection …"

But Trish knew that was because there was no one to hurry and change clothes for and meet for dinner--a romantic dinner, or no one to make a dinner for, "Like I cook! Ha!" Yet she knew she would cook, or at least re-heat, so she and this mystery man could have a quiet evening in. No rushing out of a restaurant by a waiter anxious to fill the table again.

The idea of a quiet dinner with maybe a little soft music, where she could listen to someone's day, and forget her own. Where she could gaze up into his kind eyes; see love, lust, or both. It hardly mattered if she cooked or not, if she had someone to come home to, she'd figure something out.

Suddenly her yogurt sounded awful. And her apartment looked like a shrine to a woman who shopped--shopped to fill her time, her lonely time … and bought clothes with nowhere to wear them.

For the first time in a very long time, Trish had to face her true feelings. And those feelings said … well she wouldn't admit it. She'd admitted too much already. She collapsed on her sofa and just leaned her head back and closed her eyes.

***

Pandora stopped at Fairchild's British shoppe on her way home from work, exhausted, and disgusted. No more than most days, she supposed but still, enough to make her stop for a treat for herself. Her Hobart mixer was acting up just the slightest bit, and someone had left her Tupperware of raisins open, and the top layer was dry. Someone had obviously been in her corner of the kitchens and grabbed a snack out of her supplies.

Everyday brought a tiny glitch at work. In her world of almost solitary work she noticed these things, and let them get to her.

"Oh well," Pan sighed, resigned, "The tech promised to look at the mixer tonight, and the raisins, just part of working in a huge corporation." She mumbled this all to herself as she walked through Fairchild's rose and hollyhock garden and pushed open the gift shoppe door. "Hi Jinx," She called out.

Jinx was behind her counter lost in the newspaper. The shoppe keeper simply waved but kept right on reading. Bad business of course, but Jinx recognized Pandora's voice.

Pan headed for the tea section. One of her few indulgences in her budget were fine teas.

Jinx walked over, finally giving the ad a rest. "So, how're you doing Pan?" She asked in a friendly way, not really wanting to know. "I just got some new tea in, Earl Grey with Lavender."

Pan picked up the canister of tea and studied the elegant graphics. "Sold--I'll try it and maybe a roll of Digestives." They both headed back to the counter in casual conversation. As Pandora went to get out her wallet, she saw the open newspaper with the ad for Greater Expectations Dating Agency.

"Jinx--isn't that a scream?" Pointing at the ad, though her own sarcasm didn't ring true. Still she couldn't admit to Jinx she was, well, interested. It would make her sound desperate.

Well, she was desperate.

Pandora had been better off when she didn't think about a social life at all. Now that she and her pals Trish and Maggie were focusing in on the daily newspaper ads for Greater Expectations her conscious, and sub conscious mind, was focusing too. Focusing on her lack of social life, and how sweet it might be to have some, even a little--even mediocre.

Jinx's eyes twinkled but then her face got serious, "It is I guess, but Pan, you and I know it's virtually impossible to meet anyone. My friend Randi's little boy has a teacher--she's just the nicest--a lot like you. Well, you know how many men she'll ever meet in an elementary school! And what about you hid in that kitchen in the sub--basement at Cat?"

Jinx felt she was stating the obvious because it was hard, okay nearly impossible, to meet anyone. Even the usual hangouts didn't work after a certain age, because of course there was a whole young crop doing the same thing, with the same quest--looking fresh, and well, young.

"Yeah--and even if Mr. Right did get lost and wander down there to my sub—basement kitchens, I wear what looks like white scrubs and a hair net!" Pandora knew she would possibly scare someone before she attracted them at work.

Jinx sympathized. Pandora was an elf with huge hazel eyes, auburn hair, and a turned up nose. With her hair tied back, and tucked under the regulation shower cap, her best feature was hidden. Her cooking clothes engulfed her petite frame. She could be hiding anything under there, Jinx thought, the uniform so amerced her. Pandora was a face in a uniform, in an area with no people.

Jinx nodded sagely, "I see what you mean." As she put peach colored tissue around Pan's tea, her gaze fell back to the ad. Pandora's eyes followed. "Well, just a call? I mean to see what it cost?" Jinx asked encouragingly. Of course she was dying to know herself and really wasn't sure why she didn't just pick up the phone and find out.

Just out of curiosity.

"If it cost as much as this canister of tea and the Digestives, I'd be in," Pan compromised, because there was nowhere else to go. She was reduced to a dating agency. Her friends were desperate also so that ruled out the meeting people through your friends. And they were finally all voicing it. She knew work wasn't making it happen. And the bars? There was no way she was going to the bars and looking like a short older elf. No.

Jinx gave a half hearted laugh and handed Pan her little shopping bag. Pan stared off into middle space, came back to reality, took her bag, and said good night. And as Pan left Jinx pondered the ad one last time.

***

Trish was the first through the cafeteria line. She had her black coffee, poached egg on one half piece of toast, and glass of grapefruit juice. Her newspaper tucked under her arm, she headed toward their corner table. She looked at her regulation breakfast and sighed.

She knew it gave her the protein she needed to sustain her energy, the tiny carbohydrate to get her going in the morning, and the black coffee to kick start the whole procedure. The grapefruit juice was her rational for some vitamin C. It was boring, it was sustaining, and it was her routine.

"Just like my life," She muttered more to herself than anyone. Her mind started to drift back to her youth. The days she literally had her pick of the crop, not to mention a higher metabolism. And then she stopped, and forced herself back to the here and now. After all, those days were gone.

Long gone.

Trish opened her paper and flipped through all the world news--depressing. She folded under the front section just to hide the latest crime and saw it: another ad, for Greater Expectations.

'Greater Expectations

Are you caught in a routine where your day
dreams
Are the most exciting part of your day?
Find the compliment to your inner personality
And make those dreams a reality.
Call us today
Greater Expectations
A dating service that taps into your dreams
1--800 — 555--D--A — T — E
We accept all major credit cards'

Trish tossed back her golden mane of hair and laughed out loud, "My dreams! I doubt it--he's not out there!" And yet she had to admit to herself her life was so quiet even her dreams had toned down. She dreamt about her job ... and wondered if maybe she might feel better if her name was on a form, being evaluated for a new position--a new chance.

As she sipped her coffee, Maggie and Pan sat down, "Hi girls." They mumbled a response. "Oatmeal Pan? Are you a glutton for punishment? Don't you work with oatmeal all day?"

Pan just nodded and swirled in the brown sugar, not up for banter. She knew there was another Greater Expectations ad waiting for them in Trish's newspaper. And she rather dreaded it. Somehow it had become her own personal wake up call. Trish sensed it and actually felt the same. Trish toyed with her minimalist breakfast. Finally she spoke, "Look at this!" And slowly pushed the ad over to Maggie and Pan.

They both just stared at it.

Maggie shook her head of short bouncy brown curls. "My day dreams--well, I don't even know if they're fit for day time." And she huffed, almost laughing.

Pan stared off into middle space. "My day dreams--ah, well they're just dreams." The girls discussed the ad, finished breakfast and headed off to work all lost in their own day dreams. "See you," They all called.

The next morning found them at their favorite table. Maggie spoke first, "So, is there another ad today?"

Trish hadn't unfolded the paper yet, fumbled and found the back section. They all read:

'Greater Expectations

Ladies: Mr. Perfect is here
In our files,
But could be in your arms.
Greater Expectations

The dating service with the perfect person for
you.
1 — 800 — 555--D--A — T — E
We accept all major credit cards'

First Maggie spoke, "Mr. Perfect, ah let me see, six foot two
inches, and hair the color of …"

"Not thinning," Trish added with a bit of a frown, "Just
hair."

'I don't mind a receding hair line," Pan muttered, "But I'd
like him to be nice."

"Yeah, nice is nice," The other two agreed.

"He doesn't have to be six foot two. I'm only five foot two,"
Pan added.

"Well, so your perfect build?" Maggie asked.

"I like men lean," Trish put in.

"But not too lean--I don't like it when their jeans are smaller
than mine," Maggie lamented and looked down at her thighs
as she pushed her Danish on her plate.

"Well," Pan started, "Not too thin, I like to bake and I want
a man willing to eat."

"What about a career?" Trish said warming to the game.

Maggie squinted, "Well, he should be employed. I'm
desperate but not that desperate--I already help support Mom
at the nursing home." Maggie let loose, "And not such a fussy
job he's afraid to get dirty, though not too dirty," After all
Maggie was an accountant, and somehow, that translated to
neat little columns and well … neat.

"Yeah, with starchy shirts that I'd have to iron," Pan added.
Then she frowned, not wanting to iron. Did anyone still iron?

"And not so grubby I wouldn't want him on my white
carpet," Trish threw in.

"What about a sense of humor?"

"Yeah, but sensitive, not someone into crank jokes, but not
so sensitive everything upsets him."

"And single."

"That goes without saying!"

"What if he has children?" Pan asked.

Both Maggie and Trish stopped.

"That depends," Trish started, "On ages and how many, and well, how I like them ..."

They all nodded. "Children are almost a given--or at least previous marriage at our ages," Maggie said softly. She knew, they all knew, that first swipe at a child free man was pretty much over.

All three girls were somewhere in their forties--somewhere they'd been for a while--somewhere far from their thirties.

"But how many previous marriages are okay?" Pan asked biting her lower lip.

"Well, I think one allows for mistakes," Maggie nibbled her Danish. "Two tops, if he's really special."

They all agreed over two meant some kind of problem, even if the problem was the man didn't know how to pick a woman. Or commit. Or work at a marriage.

"And compatibility of course," Pan put in, "Astrologically perfect--or close — or ... in the range." Pan studied the stars and felt there was a link up. She just had never found her link, or what to link it to. But she knew it was there. Well, she'd read it was there. And she wondered if anyone still followed that old method, other than Trish, that is.

"Like a Mars Venus connection would be nice," Trish looked dreamily out into middle space. Though no one was ever sure what that actually meant.

"Is that the sexual attraction one?" Maggie asked. Wondering, just wondering.

Trish and Pan merely nodded.

"Ah yeah," Maggie said, "That would be nice. I remember sex--well, sort of. But I'd like to remember sex."

"And commitment," Trish added wanting to get off the sex thing. "I'm too old for flings. I'd like someone committed to me. Mine."

They all agreed.

"So, yours should be six foot two Maggie," Trish started, "With a nice job and thighs bigger than yours. And yours Pan could be heavier than mine, shorter, semi bald but with a sense of humor--oh yes, and a Mars Venus connection." Trish pushed her egg around her plate.

They all laughed and headed for work.

Trish, lost in thought daydreamed; "Well, if he'd be perfect, I do have a thing for blue eyes, and accents. And well, I've never actually seen green eyes on anyone other than Pandora, and hers are more 'muddy' tinged in green—maybe hazel. I've just read about green eyes. Green eyes and an accent ..."

And she settled at her desk and dug into her work. And as she worked she knew, she was a dreamer--a day dreamer. Reality was not going to plop a green eyed man in her lap, or any man.

The next morning Trish sat at their table with her poached egg, one half piece of toast, and black coffee. Her newspaper lay folded. She hesitated to open it, but as she waited for her two friends, she decided to sneak a peek. Trish just couldn't help herself.

'Greater Expectations

How much are you worth?
There are cheaper services
You get what you pay for
Invest in your future
Greater Expectations
A dating service that will make you forget what
it cost.
1—800—555—D—A—T--E
We accept all major credit cards.'

Trish was fuming! She read it and read it again. The ad was almost insulting. She knew it had to be expensive but she had no idea how expensive. Well, today's ad gave her a pretty good idea! Plenty! And her day dream fizzed away.

She slammed her fist down on the table annoyed. Her Chloe purse jumped in response. She went to grab it, to make sure it wouldn't roll off the table, and her fingers lingered on the butter soft leather.

She glanced at the table next to her where a woman in a basic boring suit had a leatherette carryall on the floor. The carryall looked to hold the woman's spare shoes, which were quite horrible though probably comfy, a pile of reports, a newspaper, and a thermos. It was ugly, albeit functional, on the floor where it belonged. If it picked up a little of the floors grime, well there you go.

Trish looked back at her Chloe bag, lovingly and caressed the silver Chloe logo. "Yes", she thought with a sad shake of her head, "You get what you pay for." A cough had her reach inside for a Kleenex. She saw her Kate Spade change purse, her Ralph Lauren sunglass case all next to her practically empty matching Chloe wallet.

"Well, so I like nice things." And she shrugged. Of course she did.

Trish started to envision the bargain men at the bargain agencies. Gone were the Armani shirts replaced by Teflon ones--too short, too pastel, too geeky for words. Styled hair replaced by six dollar walk in buzzes. And Trish knew everything she couldn't see fell in line with what she could. "No, you get what you pay for." Looks wise alone she shuddered at the thought.

Then her mind drifted to her idea of a nice dinner out. There was no question in Trish's mind when she thought nice she thought table cloth, and candles, and fresh flowers all in a lovely atmosphere. Was she a snob because she liked a nice dinner on a table cloth? Well, if that was the definition of a snob then she was going to have to accept it. And, well the simple fact was, Trish was a snob, regardless of a table cloth.

Trish could go basic. She could go to the movies on a date. But she didn't want to go before six o'clock before the prices changed. And if she wanted a snack, and she more than likely did not, she wanted the offer to be made, even at those outrageous movie prices.

And, well, she wanted, well expected, to stop for a little bite somewhere afterwards. And it didn't have to have a table cloth. But it did have to have a table ... That left out some of the drive thru fast food places. And she supposed she didn't want to eat anywhere where the chairs were bolted down to the floor. Okay, maybe she liked life nicer. Well she knew she certainly didn't like it grubby--or cheap.

She was a snob.

Period.

Trish thought of Pandora stuck in the sub basement kitchen mixing her endless oatmeal batter, making barely enough to splurge at TJ Maxx. Even Pandora deserved better than what Trish's mind told her the bargain agencies had to offer. Probably unemployed men and sweet Pan would have to work overtime mixing and spreading oatmeal to support Mr. Bargain. And even if he was unemployed, what kind of man would he be? Trish suspected not great, "Or even good."

Her mind wandered to Maggie, already supporting her aging mother in the nursing home, doing without so Mums could have the extra first cup or cable TV in her cell--er room. Maggie needed a man with a decent income even more than she needed a decent man.

Maggie needed it probably more than any of them. Her mother might live to be one hundred or one hundred and twenty like the holistic people seemed to think possible. With proper vitamins and exercise, the articles implied one hundred and twenty was expected. Poor Maggie could be ninety five still supporting a one hundred and twenty year old mother in the nursing home, being nagged at, and made to feel guilty every Sunday when she visited. No, Maggie needed a man with a decent income more than she and Pan.

"And," Trish thought, "I'm going to help her get one."

By the time Trish had taken a peek at her checking account balance in her Louie Vuitton check book, Maggie and Pan arrived with their trays. Trish slid the ad over to them and watched their faces while she tackled her chilled egg.

Their eyes were wide.

"Well, that settles it, we're out. Not that we were ever in," Pandora said sadly.

Maggie looked off into middle space and nodded, watching her dream man wing away to fulfill someone else's dream--someone with money, scads of money. Or at least more money than she had.

"Now look girls," Trish began, "We need this agency. It's our ticket out of here." She looked around at all the other employees trying to steal one more moment before they headed up to their dreaded jobs. Their eight hours of boredom, dictatorial insults, and endless work.

The others didn't even question Trish's change of heart. They felt it too, even if they couldn't admit it. "Even if we choose to continue with our careers, we would like someone to come home to ... someone to share with on the weekends. We need this agency."

And sadly both Pandora and Maggie nodded. They would probably always work, they were working girls. But they wanted the rest: the kindness, the love, the companionship that was not an unreasonable thing to ask for. They looked around at their co workers who didn't seem to be grumbling as much as they were.

Maybe they had that person to come home to, share a meal with, and talk about their day with. Maybe work was not the only thing in their life. Because they already had what all three of the girls wanted.

"Well, I have two thousand dollars, and a gallon cider bottle full of quarters; I've been saving for a new car," Pan said desolately as she pictured her old Escort rusted and coughing.

"And I have three thousand dollars in the bank for Mom's down payment for next year at the nursing home," Maggie confessed. She had been adding to it slowly whenever she literally had a spare dollar. Even spare change.

"And I could sell something," Trish stated wistfully. "A set of Limoges dishes that I never use because I think I should only drag them out for company, one of my rarer Staffordshire figures I don't even dust anymore, mind notice--something." She wouldn't miss them. Not if it meant happiness ... or a shot at happiness.

"Let's call them!" They all said in unison. Trish whipped her tiny cell phone out of her Chloe bag and dialed.

"Greater Expectations," It was a voice on the other end of the line. It was their link--their link to their future. It was neutral. Trish could read nothing into it--nothing at all.

"Yes, I saw your ad in today's paper, and well, I wondered what it, er cost, to join." There, she got it out and hoped she didn't sound too nervous.

There was a pause as Trish held the phone nervously.

"You mean to become a member of the Greater Expectations family?"

And as Trish heard this she squinted. Not a good answer-- a leading one--leading her to the poor house.

Trish squeaked out a yes, seeing even more dollar signs.

"Ten thousand dollars," Three words—huge--huge and disappointing. Okay, shocking, very shocking, and of course disappointing.

Trish dropped the phone. And in dropping it, disconnected it.

"What?" Maggie asked.

Pandora looked hopeful. She wasn't sure why, she just did. She needed hope. This was her hope, her secret indulgent. Well, no longer a secret as she shared it with her friends.

"It was a silly idea girls--just silly. Now let's just forget it and get to work."

Trish looked at what was left of her meager breakfast with no appetite left. Actually she was numb. And as a big shopper she was not easily shocked.

Pandora saw herself chained to her mixing bowl, dumping out oatmeal for eternity, and going home to her empty flat, killing time until work the next day. "No!"

The other two stopped and looked at her.

"No!" Pan's eyes flared. "I want hope! I want out! I want more than I have now!" She raised her voice and fellow diners started to stare, "How much Trish, h ow much?" Pandora demanded.

Trish sank back in her seat, "Ten thousand dollars," She sank wearily. "Even I think that's a lot of money!" And she did. There was no rationalizing the fee.

It was like a slap on the face, and a bucket of cold water at the same time. Maggie let out a little yelp as her shoulders sagged. She picked up her brief case and started to head to her office to her ledgers and computer.

"No!" Pandora's eyes blazed. Pandora, who bought oatmeal and a cup of tea with a tea bag she parlayed into three cups every day. Pandora whose passenger door on her old Escort was permanently stuck shut. Or as permanent as Duct tape could be. Except in the winter, then it froze nicely in place.

"Wait!" Pandora yelled.

And Maggie and Trish just stopped and stared.

Pandora's eyes flashed, her mind raced, "We can do this together! Between the three of us we have ten thousand dollars. We can become a composite! A computer generated dream woman! We can share our findings!" Pandora was on a roll, not to be stopped.

The other two stood still.

Very still.

They stared in disbelief, not wanting to let the scheme sink in. The thought that just maybe there was still hope for them to join.

"Cheat?" Trish asked quietly, brightening ever so slightly.

"Cheat!" Pandora hollered, "We can combine all our best attributes on one application and share the men. Look at us girls! Maggie is a whiz at numbers, Trish is a people person, and I'm 'Martha Stewart!' Trish has got those long legs, I've got these round eyes, and Maggie has skin like velvet. I could go on and on but I have to get to my kitchen. Now think about my idea, oh please, and come up with a list of your best qualities, and we'll create a woman no man can resist! A dream woman!" And she left, for the sub—basement.

***

Jinx, and her friends, all sat around a picnic table at Dink's Roadside Diner. They nibbled on grapes and celery sticks, and giggled, sipping diet Cokes. Grapes and celery sticks that Jinx brought in her oversized tote, in an effort to stay on their diets. She knew it was rude, and, okay wrong, but she also figured Dink wouldn't mind. In all honesty he simply ignored guests who did this type of thing.

"Have you been following those ads for Greater Expectations?" Randi, from the bed and breakfast, asked, celery stick mid air.

They all talked at once.

"I wonder if they really get results?" Another one of the women asked thinking of her husband's older brother in Scotland and how lonely he was. He was a solicitor like his Uncle Larson and fast approaching what the family considered old maid status.

Dink appeared at their table, "Good evening girls, and how do I get the honor of serving you lovely ladies without your men?" They all chortled and Dink just winked, and wandered back in to the small Cape Cod house he'd converted into a pizza and beer restaurant. But not just pizza, the best burgers in the county, the crispiest Texas fries, chilled pitchers of beer.

The yard was covered in old picnic tables with Chinese lanterns strung between the trees. It was rustic, well actually tacky, but loaded with people, and a great place to hang. Dink owned the diner, ran the restaurant, kept his patrons smiling, and seemed to be there for everyone whether they needed a shoulder or just to pig out on spare ribs.

Dink returned with a tray loaded with huge blossom onions, batter dipped and deep fried, cut like giant chrysanthemums, cream cheese stuffed jalapeño peppers, called poppers, and huge sautéed mushrooms smothered with Mozzarella. He passed out napkins, removed the grape stems and end of the celery.

"Now girls, let's have some real vegetables."

They laughed and plowed in, savoring the crunchy batter and oozing grease, forgetting the low cal tidbits they'd actually brought themselves.

"I'll have to ride my bike to China to burn this off," Jinx lamented.

"I'll join you," Said one of the girls as she popped a mushroom in her mouth.

"Well, when you want grease, there's no place like Dink's!" Added Josie, who owned an everlastings business in the old barn next to Randi's bed and breakfast.

"And he's so nice--always ready to listen, and always says something to make you feel good," Another one added.

"Even if it is 'hi gorgeous'!" Jinx laughed.

"Mrs. Dink is one lucky gal," Stated Randi, who ran a B&B with her husband, well actually the only bed and breakfast in the village.

Josie nodded in agreement.

Jinx stopped mid bit, "Oh Josie, Randi, I don't think there is a Mrs. Dink. I mean, Jefferson and I have been coming here forever and well, I've never seen one."

"Are you sure?"

"Well no, I mean Dink is that much older than me, and well, I've always just thought about him as Dink. I don't even know his real name."

Dink was pushing fifty--maybe. Or maybe he'd pushed over it. His shaggy long hair was tied back in a tail. His robust personality made biker, or businessman, feel at ease. His picnic atmosphere always implied a party--a party you just stumbled on and felt included in.

But, Mrs. Dink? Well, no one had ever seen one, and Dink was so gregarious, and outgoing, no one ever questioned if Dink had a mate.

As if he heard them, Dink re-appeared with an assortment of cold dripping bottles. "Hey girls, are you ready for that Pizza yet?"

"Hey Dink ..." Jinx started carefully trying not to make eye contact.

"Yes Darlin?" And he flashed her that full wattage smile that kept everyone happy.

"Do you have a social life?" Jinx asked tactfully.

"You asking me out Jinx? Do I need to go in there and call Jefferson?" He laughed at her.

She actually colored to the ends of her braids. "Ah no, Dink--just wondered that's all."

Dink's grey eyes changed from twinkling to storming in just a blink, and he answered seriously, "You mean other than my customers?"

She nodded, and in just that second, he reverted back to the jovial teasing man they all loved.

"Why Darlin, I can hardly socialize more than this now can I?" And he gathered a few empty bottles and wandered off.

The girls all shared a meaningful look. All happy and settled with men, they felt the world should be paired off. After they finished their pizza, and counted their money, Jinx slipped the Greater Expectations ad under their tip.

***

For some odd reason Maggie, Trish and Pan all got to breakfast early.

"Do you have the newspaper?" Maggie asked, knowing Trish had it.

Trish nodded and ceremoniously opened it to the back page. There sat the Greater Expectations ad.

'Greater Expectations

A day without companionship
Is like a day the sun forgot to shine.
Greater Expectations
A dating service that will brighten your life.
1 — 800 — 555 — D — A — T — E'

They collectively sighed.

"I was expecting a tough sell today," Maggie mused.

"So was I," Trish agreed.

"Well, I've been working on our composite," Pan added, not to be side tracked, "Because I'm five foot two and Trish is five foot seven I've come up with five foot four as our ideal height."

The others nodded.

"For photographs I thought we'd shoot one in a flowing dress at the park, with a large straw hat--something misty, maybe in the morning. We'll have to use you Maggie, as you are five foot four." Not that Pandora was sure anyone could tell how tall someone was in a picture.

"What about our hair?" Maggie asked as she touched her curly bob.

"The hat will cover it. We won't say long or short." But Pandora looked at Trish's golden mane, Maggie's sable cap of curls, and fingered her own long auburnish brown pony tail, "We'll say highlights from honey to sable with touches of auburn. And we'll all get highlights--just a few," she added, never really dreaming that idea would fly.

Trish looked a gasp. "Highlight my hair brown and auburn. Pan you know that would look strange." Would it? Maybe it could be interesting ...

Maggie contemplated, "I could go for some highlights."

"We could always say we just changed our hair color," Trish added.

"Or cut it," Maggie threw in.

JACQUELINE GILLAM FAIRCHILD

"Okay, we'll think on the hair," Pan agreed.

"We could say 'works at Caterpillar'--since that would be true."

All three agreed.

"We'll need a name," Maggie proposed.

"I was thinking--Des. It may sound like a nickname for Desire or Desiree." Pandora nervously twirled the end of her pony tail. "But it will be our own joke: Des for Desperate. Not that we're desperate."

Maggie and Trish laughed loving it already! "Okay, we'll be Des."

"What about a last name?" Trish asked, "Nothing too unusual or hard to pronounce."

"What about Pickme?" Pan asked with a twinkle in her eye.

"Or Sleasee with two ee's," Maggie countered. "Or Easee with two ee's," Maggie went on. Pan and Maggie were close to tears, as they added 'Harmony', 'Richer' and 'Cashly'.

"Jones," Trish proclaimed. Pan put down her oatmeal spoon. Maggie stopped grinning. "Jones, it's simple, it's dignified, near the front of the alphabet, and one less lie to remember since its Maggie's name."

They tried it out. "Des Jones."

"I like it," Maggie said simply.

Pan nodded.

"Now girls, let's get serious. Let's pool our money and get that application." Trish put order back into their project. As they settled down, Trish admonished them. "Isn't the name of this agency GREATER Expectations? Let's think greater. No sleaze, or fast cash, or whatever. Let's create a classy girl. Let's concentrate on the type of man we want, and we'll clone his interests."

And for just a flash of a second Trish cringed, feeling like a sellout. Wondering what happened to the person she used to be--the one who had real interests, and well, wanted to find a compliment to those interests. But it flashed away on a wave of excitement.

30

Everyone agreed to bring a list to breakfast the next day. A list of not only what they wanted and could work with, but what they thought might be lurking in that agency.

Pandora went through the motions of mixing oatmeal, and raisins. Her mind raced as she tossed in pecans, "Ideal man ... hmmmm, tall--no not too tall; a business man--not too stuffy; a Mr. 'Fixit'--someone handy. Yeah, handy like cuddling, and kissing, and ..." Her mind drifted to cozy situations that were getting pretty steamy. She reached over to her pad of paper, trying not to get it greasy and wrote down 'handy'. That was good.

Good enough.

Pandora started spreading her batter in pans, trying to conjure up an image of Mr. Perfect. She saw a suit, and a tool belt, and a Ralph Lauren looking ad for a man in yachting clothes. That looked pretty good, even though boats made her sea sick. She saw abs--lean and muscular. Then added rippling, whatever that meant. A phrase she'd read in a romance novel, so she added rippling to her list: Works out, lifts weights. Of course if he worked out, would he expect her to work out? Well, she liked to work out hefting cookie sheets and cake pans, in her own kitchen ...

Then Pan saw him quiet, almost reserved, possibly shy. Her experiences with dominant people ... well she didn't really have any, but felt maybe she wouldn't be able to handle one. Yes shy, she'd like to encourage a shy man. So, she wrote shy on her list. She'd like to peel back his layers of shyness to his core and well ... she'd know what to do when she got that far.

Of course, she admired outgoing because she simply was too shy. And if two of them were the same, well, would it be a bit of a stale mate? So she shirked. She didn't know. She really didn't know. But she did know she'd be open minded. So, it could be an outgoing shy fit guy who still ate cookies ...

Humming, she started her next batch of oatmeal bars, picturing her well built hunk puttering around the house after a day at the office, shyly telling her how he was going to fix the door on her Escort, and how she was the only woman for him.

***

Maggie looked at her 'in' stack and shrugged. She took the first file and began booting up her computer. She loved numbers, the very order of them always put her mind at ease, but the endless monotonous stacks of work, well, those stacks were tedious. Too bad she couldn't do what she did with some kind of variety ... but she knew perfectly well that kind of job didn't exist.

Her mind drifted to an open field--a golden field with a golden man walking along, followed by two, maybe three, golden dogs. He wore a skin tight tee shirt and a pair of grubby jeans. No suit, no tie. The dogs were golden retrievers, and they were all frolicking, almost racing, in the sunlight. In her day dream, they were racing to her!

She blinked back to reality and thought, "That's what I want. No more corporate rat race. No more corporate rat race types. No starched shirts and creased trousers. No more designer ties and 'claw your way to the top' attitude. I want an outdoor man--a man confident in a pair of jeans--old jeans; a man not afraid to get dirty, maybe even one who likes animals."

Maggie had never had so much as a gerbil in her life. She'd always wanted one, but never fulfilled that childhood desire for a pet. Ultimately she left childhood far behind, gerbils seemed like too much work, and all other animals, well, intimidated her. Okay, so did the gerbils.

Yet, when she returned home after a day of paper work, a friendly dog to meet her at the door might be nice. As long as it didn't jump, or drool, or shed or ... Or when she did reports on her computer into the wee hours, a cat curled on her lap so she could stroke its fur ... She could possibly conquer her fears.

Possibly.

Maybe.

Who was she kidding? No animals--period. Messy, unpredictable--too much work.

But a rugged man who liked animals. Yes, she'd like that. Maggie slipped her spiral pad over and wrote 'rugged' and went back to her numbers. She worked for a few more minutes and then reached over and wrote 'gentle'. Yes, she wanted someone gentle, maybe even tender. With that decided, though she knew it was still vague, she went back to work.

It was a start. A start in an area she had given up on.

***

Trish sorted the newest stack of applications in Human Resources. She was old enough to know it should be called 'Personnel,' and smart enough to get with the program. Shrugging her shoulders, she went back to her task. There was a rhythm and a science she found in sorting job applications.

She'd make notes of a dominant trait, good or bad. She'd read between the lines, and add a comment. Her evaluations were always appreciated. Although she never actually met, or even saw, any of the applicants, she felt she had a good inner sense for putting the application in the pile it belonged.

This was her gift.

The gift of sorting people.

So many 'would—be' employees had no clue what they could do at Caterpillar International. The applicants just wanted to work there. Trish would study their applications, and if they met the base requirements, she would try to find them an area.

An area that reflected something they'd said on their forms, or something that seemed to compliment their personality. Sort of like astrology--the astrology of placing man and position. Trish laughed out loud.

A devotee to all things under the stars, Trish suppressed a smile. An introverted Sagittarius wasn't going to go in her sales pile--nor was an extroverted Scorpio. Too busy sending out sex signals and all bark--very little bite.

No, she usually sent a Cancer, devoted to a cause and universally liked. It was easier, of course, when they had work experience, and education, in a certain field--easier to add that in to the mix.

And it wasn't that she was so astrology devoted that she relied on the science. It was just a nice coincidence that usually, okay more than usually, worked out that way. It was a tool, no more.

Often Trish saw applicants had background but it had shifted from job to job. In those cases, she turned to the stars, knowing the applicant wasn't unhappy with his or her last employer, so much as unhappy in their chosen field. So, she chose another one, wrote her note, and put them in the appropriate pile.

Long ago Trish had told herself there were no perfect jobs, or perfect people--but there were fits. Like good shoes. Comfy shoes, practical shoes--shoes that would go the distance. With that she slid out of her ivory heels, and wiggled her cramped toes; ivory heels that matched her ivory silk dress--shoes that literally didn't fit.

She sighed, "I don't want a perfect man; I want a perfect pair of shoes. I want … a man that fits me, my personality, my likes, my moods." But for the life of her, Trish had no idea what that man would be like.

"Make a list," She told herself. "I've never actually made a list." She nibbled on the end of her pen, note pad open and finally wrote:

'Tall, long legged, and blond,' "That's me," She thought. Do I want me--in a man? She didn't know and went back to her stack of applications. She worked for another couple of hours, the thought of Mr. Perfect always on the edges of her mind, though she just couldn't quite see him.

Finally she wrote: 'Likes what I like,' and laughed. Well, maybe not shopping or spending. She looked down at her Feragamos--and maybe not expensive shoes. But then added to her list: 'No cheap shoes.'

Trish tried to picture what turned her on and came up short. She had no idea. She always thought she'd know it when she met it, but to date, hadn't met it. Maybe, she needed this agency more than she was willing to admit.

Chapter 2

It was one in the morning. The last beer drinker had left, and so had the waitresses. Dink mopped up, found a stray glass and carried it to his pristine kitchen. Jim Hart played, still on the CD player, a continual loop that Dink never heard when he was busy.

But when it was quiet, Dink heard Jim sing about lonely days and lonelier nights. Jim, his piano, and his guitar often played in one corner of Dink's dining room. Dink's customer's loved him. But when Jim Hart wasn't there in person, he was Dink's favorite on his CD player. Tonight, Jim touched a spot in Dink, and somehow instead of his usual comfort, the music just saddened him.

It had been a full night, for a week day. Business was good. He really had no complaints.

Dink rubbed a hand over his eyes, and pinched the bridge of his nose to relieve the tension. He was happy--he knew he was happy as he looked around his little road house with pride, the restaurant and really more roadside diner he'd created out of an old dilapidated Cape Cod house.

Over the years, he'd built a fine reputation. During warm weather he rarely had an empty seat--inside or out. People loved his oversized burgers, wide cut fries, and his cobbler. Cobbler that had been his mother's recipe--rest her soul. Cobbler he knew he'd have to whip up in the morning--none left, not even a scrap for his supper--supper at one in the morning.

He laughed and popped open a bag of chips. Munching as he sorted the nights receipts. His mother, gone so long now, he couldn't really remember when. But she'd taught him to cook. And make cobbler. She'd given him his key to a future. And she'd saddled him with his name:

Douglas

Ignatius

Nathaniel

Kirtland

She'd wanted him to have a classy name--a name that reflected their ancestors back in Ireland. And he did. But as a boy, he had shortened it to Dink. And Dink it remained. But, now and again he thought of himself as Douglas, when he was tired … and just a little lonely.

Oh, there'd been women, plenty of women over the years, but for some reason never just one--a special one. They'd come and go as casually as his customers. Some had even been his customers. But one? Well, never one. And he'd never thought he'd needed just one. He had his business, and it consumed him day and night. Still …

And there wasn't a pretty young thing out there, willing to work day and night for little money--in basically a roadside diner--a roadside diner with food; which translated to food to make, and clean up. And a menu that seemed to grow in complexity every year. Girl or woman--didn't matter. Because it wasn't like he'd ever found this person, but he knew it was no life to offer someone.

None at all.

There'd be no dinner dates--unless she counted grabbing a bag of chips at one in the morning. He laughed. He was so used to being glib with his customers, he'd probably dole out his three or four standard lines--most starting with 'darlin' or 'gorgeous', and ending with a wink.

His social skills stank. Well that was a lie; he really had no social skills. And his outside interests included a little sports he'd catch on TV at the counter. He had no interest in politics except the politics of his produce man, or his beer distributor. Every time he thought he'd add a new item to his menu, he thought of the hassle of delivery, or if his vendors would keep it in their stock, and he usually gave it up.

And it wasn't a bar per say, the actual bar took up a small section of the restaurant. Heck, he often had kids in to grab a burger and Black Cow, remembering when Angus had brought Bart, now Angus's step son, in for paper cones of hot greasy fries, Black Cows, and man talk.

Angus had shown the seven year old you could eat with your fingers out in public. Dink smiled, envied Angus just a bit, and got back to his receipts.

Dink looked at the ad Jinx had obviously left for him. Why she was curious about his social life, he didn't know. He did know Jinx was nuts. He had a good life. And he didn't have time to get lonely. Not too much.

***

Dev's social life was shallow. Okay, he could say it out loud. Shallow. It was pitiful; casual dates with casual women-- casual conversation that bored him. He never even heard the conversations; they just rolled out of his mouth, though he had perfected his end. He finished a cold beer and sighed. Okay he could say it out loud.

He was shallow.

He looked at his suitcase on the top shelf of his closet. Maybe he needed to get away for awhile--just a short time. Breathe in some fresh air. Maybe meet some new shallow women in a new location. A break, that's what he needed.

A break.

***

It was Saturday morning and Trish was determined to keep her eyes closed and sleep. She wiggled a toe and rotated her ankles. Hmmm--it felt good to indulge and sleep in. She tried to drift back off but sleep eluded her, so she stared at her bedroom ceiling, and thought about her ideal man. Well dream man, though she hadn't dreamt of him.

Still ... dream man.

She pictured him having blond hair, just a little longer than conventional right now, touching his collar. He was tall, of course, and she saw him in a dramatic black trench coat.

"Well this isn't an ad for a fashion magazine," She chastised herself. What else? What did she really want? For years romance had evaded Trish. Her dates had let her down, and after a while she put little, and then no work, in pursuing them. Why should she? The men she attracted did little or nothing for her. The occasional man brave enough to ask her out, was usually discouraged early on.

She didn't try.

She should.

But it seemed like such effort. And she didn't want to open her eyes every morning and face effort! And was that what romance should be? Is that what a relationship should be? Effort? She didn't know. She crawled out of bed and began her routine of stretching out the kinks.

She knew what she wanted, but hadn't ever dared to put in words. She wanted a magnificent man, devilishly handsome, witty, and possibly just a little scheming--with energy. Energy he would lavish on her as if she were the most important aspect of his life.

She wanted the best of all the applications she saw constantly, rolled into one man--a man who radiated excitement. Not afraid to take a chance. A successful man, but a man not bought and paid for by the establishment.

A man with an imagination--imagining her perfect for him; and of course, tall, and blond. "I guess that goes without saying," She admitted that much to herself.

Well she wasn't going to admit all this to Pandora and Maggie--no matter how close they were. It sounded egotistical. Not at all practical, and in a way, just a bit dangerous. But now that she had admitted it to herself, she liked it.

A lot.

Not that she put much stock in finding this composite and yet ...

As her shower sluiced over her, an idea was born. "If I could get my hands on those Greater Expectation files--all of them--I'd know what's really out there." And being the Human Resources pro that she was, she could read between the lines of those files, interpret them just as she interpreted the Caterpillar applications. Maybe her man was hiding--hiding in a file at Greater Expectations.

Waiting for her to find him.

She put on her favorite Ralph linen jeans, padded to her kitchen, and turned on her kettle to make a pot of Yorkshire Gold tea. The newspaper was right outside her door. Her first cup sat cooling, her apple ignored, as she flipped through the paper.

"Little Bobby Fumbleman was named newspaper boy of the month. Good." He was her delivery boy. She'd have to remember to tip him an extra couple dollars. "Edith White was engaged--her cross the hall neighbor, still in the throes of her first bloom. Looks like she found herself a man," She read on, not admitting she was looking for the Greater Expectations ad, taunting herself.

She flipped to the want ads. Maybe there was a job out there, doing what she did, only better, or more interesting.

And to her utter shock her eyes locked on the single spaced ad: "Looking for Human Resources person--must have experience. Call Greater Expectations."

It was after nine o'clock.–granted a Saturday, but she knew the agency was open every day but Sunday. She picked up the phone and dialed.

"Greater Expectations," A voice said--a male voice.

"I'm calling about the help needed in today's paper." Trish was nervous; a good nervous.

The voice on the other end of the phone let out a sigh, "When can you come in?"

"When can you see me?" She retorted.

"How about ten thirty this morning?" Mike let out a breath again.

The appointment was written down, and he hung up smiling to himself. If his cousin wanted to leave him in charge while he was off on a singles cruise, he'd be in charge. And that meant no more paper work. No more files. No more applications to be sorted. Not to mention evaluated.

No more.

It was too much. It was swallowing him up, not to mention hurting his golf game. No, he needed help.

Now.

Devin had been gone only one week but it seemed like a month. And with one more week to go, Mike was going to make some changes.

Drastic changes.

And suddenly Mike remembered back to when they started and Dev wanted to call their agency Kalalou. "Kalalou? Dev, what are you talking about?"

But Dev had just grinned, "It means innovation, determination, courage, and sincerity--perfect for our agency!"

"You're crazy! That might be some obtuse meaning who knows where but Kalalou is a stew—with okra. We want to name our agency after okra? Get a grip there old man! We will call it Greater Expectations!"

And Dev was forced to admit it had a little bit better ring than okra! No, as Mike thought back he knew he had to take things in his own hands—again. And make some changes …

Now.

The agency was a great scheme, Mike told himself, and his cousin Dev, was a genius. The money rolled in, and so did the applicants for dates. Applicants he and Dev cherry picked off. What had started as a scam to meet women, turned into a business--a complicated business, with people wanting to meet other people, or whining to meet other people.

Originally they simply posted a picture and short bio on their internet site. An applicant's fee gave them the access code to browse this inventory. But many of their clients complained.

It was too hard. They didn't know what they wanted. They couldn't tell from the bios.

Couldn't Greater Expectations match them, or suggest matches for them, based on their successful history? After all, if they could do it all by themselves, why were they paying him and his cousin the big bucks?

Mike laughed at himself. Sure, they could, and they did--almost randomly. But they were no better at it than their clients. If they knew how to put two people together, they wouldn't have created an agency to find them dates. And as if that wasn't enough, now Dev was out on a singles cruise to meet more women.

Why Dev toyed with the idea of that ideal woman escaped Mike--couldn't he just be happy to rifle through the candidates of lonely hearts? What was so special about special anyway? Mike shook himself, and decided he better tidy himself, and the office up.

He had an interview at ten thirty--a possible employee, a possible escape from some of his duties. Whistling, he reached in a filing cabinet, pulled out a tie and slipped it on.

Mike's mind wandered to the basis of Greater Expectations. Their only claim to fame was quantity. They bombarded their clients with tons of choices, believing in odds and probability; and let Mother Nature do the rest. And she usually did. He guessed.

Mike and Dev discovered a bell curve with their client's ages. Starting with their thirties it trickled into their late sixties, early seventies. The bulk of their applicants were in their forties and fifties. Love had passed them by, burnt out, or because of busy careers, never even knocked at their doors.

Their tastes changed as they aged. Hardened somewhat by divorces, and the cold reality of life, yet still harboring that glimmer of hope. The hope that Mr., or Ms Right was right around the corner. And with that would come someone who understood them, with compassion, sharing their interests, sparking some excitement--all with a flutter of hope.

Hope to end loneliness--even if it only amounted to a dinner date. For a lot of lonely women, one dinner date meant shopping all week for an outfit, laboring over coordinating shoes that a man would never notice. Sitting for hours at the beauty shoppe; having what ever done where ever in an effort to glaze, coax up, and highlight whatever they had.

Mike rolled his eyes. He hated to imagine the prep work the women went through, and hated it worse when they called, whining for more choices, and detailing all their efforts, which of course was how he knew what effort they made.

He took in a deep gulp of air.

He hated it.

Well who ever this candidate was for the job, Mike was pretty sure he was going to hire her on the spot. They had plenty of cash flow, and it was time they cut someone in, and he cut out some of his drudgery. The golf course beckoned as he sorted through lonely applications. Sometimes, he'd just grab a fistful from the male pile, and one from the female pile, and randomly put them together.

Anything to be done.

Mike started losing his own taste for his own applicants. It always involved a lengthy explanation why he selected them when they found out he worked at the agency. Well, owned the agency. And blonde and gorgeous was never the answer they wanted to hear.

Plus they felt cheated out of the real dates from the Greater Expectation files. So, Mike had actually started cruising the bars again, relieved how a little alcohol made everyone look better.

He looked at his watch. Ten twenty four. The door rattled. He looked up from his computer game and his heart rattled.

Coming in the door was blonde and gorgeous! Wearing a tiny little business suit reminiscent of a nineteen fifties movie. Her long legs ended in high heels! Amazing, he was noticing her shoes. They were ivory, like her suit, and seemed to extend her already long legs another three or four inches.

She smiled at him nervously, looking up at him with round blue eyes--the color of a perfect sky, on a perfect day. Mike was standing, though he didn't remember getting up. He went to shake her hand and introduce himself, and almost passed out when he saw she wasn't wearing a wedding ring.

Perfect.

More than perfect.

Trish looked up into the good natured face of the big sandy haired man--a man who seemed to loom over her. His eyes were friendly, his hand shake firm--she sighed. Maybe this will go okay.

Maybe.

He appeared to be in his late forties, early fifties, possibly an X foot ball player, based on his size. His youthful muscles were already headed in a softer direction. His probably once tight abs now rounded a bit over his belt. But he still looked good. Not nineteen, not twenty six, but good--his age.

And he seemed friendly and enthused about her. She was sitting across from him at a desk before she knew it, his gaze welcoming as if she were an old family member.

"Now Trish--tell me why you would be good for this job," Mike said smiling.

Trish swallowed a bit of confusion. This wasn't a normal job interview, why he hadn't even explained the job! One quick glance at his scattered desk, littered with files, and she guessed he wasn't going to.

He probably didn't know. She looked behind him and saw rows of filing cabinets--some hanging open. A computer had faded to screen saver and was winking at her.

There was a chaotic sense that she just itched to organize. Suddenly she realized she wanted this job. Not just to rifle through the files for Mr. Right, if there was a Mr. Right, but to put some order to things--create a system, as she was sure that if there was one, it wasn't very good.

And to match the perfect applicant with another perfect applicant--this was what she loved to do.

And she wanted to do it here.

She suddenly knew she no longer wanted to place someone in sales or heavy machinery or clerical. "I want to match their personalities, their horoscopes, their likes and dislikes and place them where they'd be happy--with soul mates."

She felt like an old Michael Bolton song--'Soul Provider' and brushed it off. She thought of the newer version Jim Hart sang and sighed. It was still a song that resonated, regardless who sang it. She gave Mike a critical once over, saw his paper weight that said "A Day without Golf is a Day without Sun Shine' and smiled. Reaching deep, she decided to pull up all her ammunition and get this job.

"I like your paper weight," She said sweetly.

"You do?" Mike was shocked and well, surprised she even noticed it.

"Why yes, I play golf and know how you feel," Albeit it was only miniature golf, on a miniature course--with a paddle wheel and a wind mill, and her two nephews. But it counted--it was golf.

She could see Mike swallow that line and confidently she went on, "I live to organize," Which in fact was true, much to the chagrin of her friends. She could see Mike let out a little breath.

She slipped her resume out of her Chanel briefcase and handed it to him. "I have been an integral part of Caterpillar International's Human Resources department for almost twenty years."

That comment hit home and Mike let the breath escape. In this town Caterpillar International meant something--something big.

Trish was warming to the situation, "My primary responsibility is sorting the applications as they come in ..." She paused for effect, "And placing them in the category they'll best be suited." All true, boring, but true.

"I take this evaluation process very seriously, and pride myself in being able to put my finger on someone's best abilities and find a 'home' for them. I am ready to trade job matching for people matching. I want to take my skills to a higher level; a more personal one." More true--oddly, very true.

"The nuances of people's personalities fascinate me. I follow the stars." She slipped that in.

Mike was breathing heavy. "You, er, don't have psychic powers do you?" He asked almost embarrassed, hoping maybe she did.

"Why some people think I do," She added meekly, crossing her fingers. Maybe she was psychic because she had a feeling she was landing this job.

Mike cleared his throat, "I see you make a nice salary."

Trish felt it was now or never. "Of course, I have fabulous benefits. Benefits that I would need matched or compensated for," She paused.

He hadn't cringed.

"And vacation time. Caterpillar is very generous with vacation time," Which was part of the reason people never left. Caterpillar was very generous.

He nodded. What else could he do? This was his answer-- right in front of him. No more looking, or struggling ... He saw himself teeing up.

"And freedom. I'd like a certain amount of freedom to organized things." Then she paused, afraid she'd gone too far, "With your training and guidance of course." Hopefully she hadn't gone too far. She knew she wasn't leaving without this job ...

"Of course," He nodded as professionally as he could. He wasn't even sure what she was asking for.

She beamed.

"And if we were to--uh ..." He glanced down at her salary and winced "Raise that figure ten per cent." She looked crest fallen so he added, "And another five per cent at Christmas. And of course we have Health Care."

She looked wary.

"I could have our lawyer draw up some papers for you." Mike crossed his fingers. He needed her--desperately.

Trish started to feel excited again but got caught in the word 'our'. Suddenly she saw complications. She saw her freedom to organize winging away.

"Our? You have a partner Mike?" She asked it as sweetly as she could.

"Ah yes--my cousin. But, please be assured I'm totally responsible for hiring." Our staff of …? He thought, since we've never hired anyone.

Trish smiled a genuine wide grin. It was getting back on track--her track. "I think we could work beautifully together," She said, and meant it.

"And you could start?" Mike asked. "I could have all the necessary papers in place by dinner time." He hoped.

"When would you like me to start?" She asked sweetly, cautiously.

"Monday," He said daringly.

Trish decided then and there to go for it. She'd take the plunge. No notice--well it may cost her, but she still had her 401K's, or at least she thought she did. And maybe she had some vacation time they would consider using as her notice. So she dared.

"Monday," She said.

***

Pandora couldn't sleep. Her mind reeled. She dreamt of the perfect man, but he didn't have a face. He didn't have a face because she couldn't visualize him. Even when her subconscious was free, she had no idea what she wanted.

She wasn't even sure what she didn't want. "Well, it goes without saying I don't want an ax murderer, or someone ugly, or hygiene deficient. But short, tall, blond, brunette--I don't know." She knew she'd know him though, when she met him.

Pan eyed her digital clock—two thirty in the morning. She willed herself back to sleep starting with deep breaths. Then she

47

visualized oatmeal cookies, plump and round, soft in the center with a bit of crunch on the edges. Not bars. Not pan after pan of bars, but cookies. The real shape cookies were meant to be. She dreamt she added white chocolate chips and raisins.

How radical to mix them up--radical for Caterpillar's kitchens that is. And a handful of coconut, and pecans, a hint of cinnamon and almond extract--crispy, soft, chewy. Perfect. Her mind relaxed, and she slept, baking perfectly round cookies, one little batch at a time.

Pan got up at her usual early hour for work even though it was Saturday. She wanted to sleep in but her brain said get up and so she did. A shower helped, but before she stepped in the shower she got some butter out to soften. As the hot water beat on her, she tried to recapture the cookies of her dreams. Yes, she had mixed raisins and white chocolate chips ... She toweled off, tossed on her favorite jeans and began making cookies.

Pandora decided they should be over-sized, fist size, and loaded with goodies. She experimented with some dried cranberries and white chocolate chips and pecans. The scents were heavenly. They sat cooling on racks as she micro waved a cup of tea.

Hearing her door buzz; looking at her watch, she realizing it was already ten thirty.

"It's Maggie," said a voice. A voice Pan knew.

As Pan unlocked the door, Maggie inhaled! "I could smell whatever that is in the hallway!" "Hi Maggie, what brings you by?" Pan was listening for her timer.

"Oh I thought I'd drop off my thoughts for our application. Did you really mean it when you said you'd work up the composite?"

Pandora nodded and put another cup in the microwave. She got out a dish and slid a White Chocolate Chip and Raisin cookie on it for Maggie. "Time for a snack?" she asked mischievously.

"Just barely, I'm on my way to that new bed and breakfast--'Estate of Mind'. The girl who runs it was referred to me, and needs some help with her books." Maggie nibbled on the cookie Pan had placed in front of her, and then looked at the counters, covered in cooling cookies.

"Looks like you're feedings an army!" Maggie said teasingly yet still a little in awe.

"No, couldn't sleep. I was just experimenting." Pan was eating her own cookie now, still warm from the oven.

"With Oatmeal?" Maggie asked incredulously. "Don't you get enough of that all day, every day?" she shook her head, rather incredulously.

"Oh Maggie …" Pan let the dam break, "You don't understand. All day, every day I make exactly the same thing the same way. Why I suggested adding white chocolate, white chocolate mind you, last week and my Super almost bit my head off! And Maggie--they aren't round like cookies should be! They're economical bars! Sometimes I feel like a machine just a machine!" And then the tears fell, slowly and steadily.

Maggie quickly rushed to her side and patted her head. "Now, now Pan. We're going to join this stupid dating agency, and our lives are going to change. You'll see."

And Pandora started to gulp in air and calm down. "I'll work on our application today," Pan promised. "Would you like a sack of cookies to take with you?"

Maggie nodded eagerly. Of course, she did. Who wouldn't?

As Pandora layered an assortment in a bag, Maggie beamed, "I almost forgot." She dug into her tote and pulled out an envelope of photographs. Spreading them on the table she looked hopefully at Pandora.

Pan stopped bagging cookies and focused, "Why Maggie, they're magnificent!" She picked up one of a woman in a soft billowy dress and oversized straw hat--standing on a cliff, the ocean behind her. The wind had caught the edges of her long dress. The woman's hands were holding her hat in place. A bit of a profile showed but it was impossible to see what she really looked like.

The next one showed the same woman standing at a gazebo. It was twilight and the figure was caught in shadows. She stood at a profile--no hat. Her hair was tied back in a knot. It was hard to tell how long it was. Wispy bits were caught in the breeze. Pan was immediately captivated by the architecture of the gazebo silhouetting the romantic woman, and the last rays of the setting sun.

The pictures were done in sepia, they almost looked old. The romance of the settings, and the vintage style dress created a mood that was both innocent and provocative at once. And the hair could have been sandy blonde or light brown. Or even auburn. Well, maybe not auburn, but still it was hard to say in the sepia.

"Maggie these are great--no spectacular! Where'd they come from? Who are they?" Pan was now cheered up; pumped actually.

Maggie beamed, "They're my cousin Jillian. She lives in California, former model. She had one of her photographer friends help stage and take them."

Pandora kept looking. "They're brilliant--it's hard to tell exactly what she looks like, even how tall she is." Pandora fidgeted her five foot two inch frame.

Maggie smiled pleased, "Well Jillian said she'd take any of our over flow. You know, left over men!" They both giggled at the thought.

"Sure, we'll just ship them off to sunny California."

"Well, actually, she's had it with the coast and all that youth youth youth stuff! If you think we feel old, you should live in Southern California!" Maggie had heard it from Jillian a million times.

Maggie paused to get her breath.

Pandora raised her eyebrows; she didn't feel old at all. As a matter of fact, she felt as though she'd never gotten started!

Maggie continued, "She says she's been thinking about moving to the Midwest. Starting her own little photography business, maybe doing some weddings, graduations--you know."

"Well she certainly knows her stuff!" Pandora faded a bit at the prospect of the gorgeous, and obviously talented, cousin moving to town and wanting now one fourth of their investment. But still, the pictures were impressive. Far better than anything they could have come up with.

The next photo Pandora flipped to showed Jillian, still in the billowy flowered dress, bending over a basket of puppies, one of the little dogs was caught hammock style in her skirt, another one, wiggling under her arm. Four more looked up from the basket, wanting to be picked. It was good, no 'Miss America, save the puppies' darling. It was, Pan decided, irresistible--a beautiful woman and puppies.

"Let's cut her in!" Pan instantly decided.

Maggie beamed. "I thought you'd agree!"

"These pictures are too good! We're in Maggie--I can just see the men lining up!" And Pan saw her day taking a turn for the better.

Maggie proceeded to get a typed list out of her tote. "She also sent this list of advice. I made you and Trish a copy so we could all study it."

Pandora idly picked it up, still awed by the photographs. She started to glance at it and sputtered. "Maggie it says here we should all wear the Wonder Bra! I'm not wearing the Wonder Bra! What is the Wonder Bra? And work out to tone up! I haven't time to work out!! And makeup! Why there's a list--can you believe a list of makeup we should wear! It reads like a prescription! And, if we don't know how to apply it, we're to go to some health club called Fitness Is, and give the makeup artist her list! Maggie--this is too much! Over the top! How could she possibly feel we need make--up?"

"I sent her all our pictures," Maggie confessed.

"You did?" Pandora marveled, and then faded.

"There's more Pan. Keep reading."

"Heels won't be a problem Maggie--I own a pair of heels," Pan kept reading.

Maggie looked at Pandora's Bergenstocked feet, "Yeah, when was the last time you wore them?"

"Without missing a beat Pan said, "Last year at my niece's wedding."

Maggie shook her head, "Not good enough. Jillian says you'll never be able to wear them through a whole date if you don't wear them a little bit every day."

"Every day? Maggie, I stand all day--in case you've forgotten! I bake all day! Heels? With my uniform? Down in the kitchens? You've got to be joking!"

But Maggie wasn't joking, nor did she waver. After all, Pandora could come home from work and put on her heels for a few hours. It was a solution, though Maggie was pretty sure not one Pandora would go for.

Maggie softened her gaze and said tenderly, "Pan--we're alone. And we're tired of it. We have been alone for a long time. We can be alone, we've done it. We're both tired of it. You know all the jokes about girls who wear Birkenstocks. We'll go to the mall tonight and hunt for shoes," And on an afterthought added, "And Wonder Bras!"

Pandora started to sulk, "Well, Miss Trish doesn't need to shop for heels!" Thinking about all the ridiculous shoes Trish wore, making her five foot seven frame even taller. Not to mention her legs.

But Maggie just brushed off Pan's comments. After all Trish was as lonely as they were.

"What else do we need to do for this make--over?"

"Oh, whatever it takes. You know the words 'make--over'," Maggie sounded serious and Pandora didn't doubt it.

"Listen I have to go see about this little accounting job. I'll be by around six thirty to go to the mall?" At least Maggie had the decency to word it like a question.

Pandora nodded glumly.

"It'll be fun--you'll see." And as an afterthought added, "We'll make it fun."

Pan gave a weak smile and held the sack of cookies out in front of her. "Well, don't forget your cookies," And gave Maggie a quick hug. As the door slammed, Pandora stood on her toes trying to envision heels. She tippy toed to the refrigerator for some orange juice, thought better of it, and grabbed water.

***

Maggie pulled up to an old grand Victorian house. The carved sign read 'Estate of Mind Bed and Breakfast'. Another one read 'MacTamara's Apple Orchard' and still a third one said 'Everlastings'.

"Well this must be the place." Maggie looked fascinated at all the signs. She pulled in only to be met by a huge golden dog and a little girl with golden hair.

Maggie sat in her car willing the dog away, but of course the little girl wandered over to the car. Maggie looked straight ahead at her steering wheel, ignoring the little girl. Then she heard a soft tapping. She could see out of the corner of her eye that the small child had wandered right up to her car. Why she was tapping on her window. And still Maggie stared straight ahead.

"Hello Lady," Said a wee voice, "My dog Braeburn is friendly."

Still no answer from Maggie, no eye contact.

Hearing his name Braeburn lumbered over to the car and leaned against the door. Maggie was sure she could hear the beast breathing.

"Honest Lady. It's safe to get out." All the while she continued tapping as if Maggie hadn't heard her. "When we moved here, Mom and I were afraid of the dogs--just like you. But they're sweet, see."

And with that Annie climbed up on Braeburn's back as if he were a small pony. Fascinated, Maggie turned her head slightly, and the child whooped with joy at her progress.

Braeburn still stood with the elfin girl perched on his back as if he were bored. The child hugged him around the neck saying silly things to the dog like, "Braeburn, you're such a good boy. Annie loves you." Then she added, "Braeburn eats dog food, not ladies. See?"

Maggie was facing the window now studying the child and beast. As the words were spoken, the little girl slipped both hands in the drooling dogs mouth and started to pry it open.

Maggie was horrified. Her first instinct was to get out of the car and save the little girl. The big beast let her mess with his mouth, and suddenly swung his head back and forth, sending drool flying. Annie cried with joy over this great feat and Maggie watched slobber slide down her car door.

"Annie! Braeburn!" A voice from the distance hollered out. Maggie watched as the child and dog turned their heads and ran off to the barn. The big door opened a crack, and both girl and canine were swallowed up.

"That was close," Maggie thought. "Too close." She started to collect her nerves when she saw an elegant thin blonde woman come out from the house and start approaching the car. She was intimidatingly beautiful, and of course at least a good ten years younger than Maggie. At least.

But the blonde's face lit into a huge grin and Maggie's fears all melted.

"I'm Miranda—Randi—MacTamara," She said from her side of the car window. "And last year when I married Angus I was scared stiff of the dogs. We're down to just two--sort of-- and well, they honestly are gentle, no wimpy." She looked beseechingly at Maggie and Maggie softened.

Teasingly, Randi went on, "You don't have to get out of the car; I can go get a chair."

Maggie laughed and opened the car door. She looked dead pan at Randi.

"Well, I've never been around dogs ..." Maggie started.

Randi laughed and gave her a quick hug.

"I understand, but they're great company, and so loyal--especially if you're alone."

It hit Maggie like a shot. Was it so obvious she had no one?

Randi picked up on her freaked expression and added, "I didn't mean to imply you were alone."

Maggie let out a breath, "Its okay. I am alone. And I am lonely. But, I never considered a dog." And then Maggie shirked a little.

By this time they'd reached the porch. Randi stopped and turned to Maggie, "I was too up until less than a year ago. I had my two children and my dad. But I was widowed, and well, I guessed I'd had my one chance at happiness with someone."

And then she started to relay her very personal story about leaving Chicago and her high powered job in the advertising world--all to settle her dad in a quiet retirement center--out of the city. And finding this old house, being hired as housekeeper, and transforming it into a Bed and breakfast.

"My husband's brother and his wife live in the barn. It's converted into a great home; they hired me while Angus, my husband, was wandering the country and sulking." With this admission eye contact was made and so was a friendship.

"Angus came home, and my son actually tried to check him into his own house--like a paying guest."

Maggie laughed.

"Mother Nature took care of the rest." She twisted her wedding band, tears quietly filled her eyes. Although Maggie wasn't leggy, blonde, nor in her thirties, somehow she felt hope.

They proceeded inside, and Maggie was awed by the house!

"Would you like a quick tour?" Randi asked. "When I came, I literally used a shovel to dig it out." And Randi knew they didn't have time for the full story.

So, they wandered the elegant rooms and got to know each other. Ending up at the kitchen table, Randi pointed to a pile of papers. "I need a system," Then sighed, "A better system."

Maggie looked at the mess and slowly nodded. Yes she did. This was no way to run a business.

Here Maggie felt confident and in her element. She started to sort through all the riff raff, making tidy little piles. "Why I think it will be quite simple to organize you." And she could see Randi let out a breath in relief. They discussed a plan and Maggie barely noticed another golden dog sleeping on a rag rug.

Randi's eyes followed hers. "See, they are gentle. That's Honey Crisp. Named after an apple we grow." The dog opened one eye, hearing her name and rolled on her side.

"Gee, she's kind of fat," Maggie said before she stopped to think.

Randi just laughed, "Oh you would be too if you were ready to give birth," And then added, "To a litter."

Maggie looked at the mom dog in fascination.

"Would you like a pup when they come?" Randi asked gingerly.

Suddenly Maggie looked longingly at the sweet contented dog's face and sighed.

"She wasn't possibly bred with something smaller? Like a Pomeranian?"

They both laughed.

"No, you met the proud daddy at your car."

With that the French door swung open and Annie appeared with a girl, no small woman, with long curly hair. "I told you Josie--she was scared to death!" Then she looked over at the table, spotted Maggie and her Mom. She ran over to her Mom and jumped on her lap. "Mommy, the scared lady got out of the car."

"Annie, the scared lady is Miss Maggie. Say hello."

Annie smiled a toothy grin. "You aren't afraid of Honey Crisp!" Annie said in amazement, noticing that Honey Crisp was in fact in the same room as them.

"Maggie this is my very precocious daughter Annie," Randi introduced.

"Anastasia," The little girl said solemnly.

"And my friend Josie--married to my husband's brother," Randi went on.

Josie pulled up a chair and the three chatted like old friends.

"Well since you've settled on all your accounting--why don't we drive over to Dinks for sandwiches. The guys said they'd meet us there later?" Randi asked, hoping Maggie would come.

"Dinks?" Maggie asked afraid of what Dinks was.

Josie and Randi laughed! "You'll like it--it's a bit of a hang out." Even Annie nodded.

"With great French Fries," Added Annie, "That come in a paper thing like an ice cream cone."

No one bothered to explain but Maggie pictured hot fries in a paper come similar to the ones she'd had as a child at the state fair.

"Will you join us? Say yes! We'll celebrate your taking over Randi's book keeping!" Josie was sure she'd enjoy it.

"And conquering your fear of dogs," Randi added, because Maggie had completely forgotten about Honey Crisp.

"And being our new friend," Little Annie finished.

How could Maggie say no, so she followed them over to Dinks?

***

Maggie was amazed she'd never been there before. The old Cape Cod cottage turned burger joint was loaded with charm. What had once been a grassy yard was covered in picnic tables; Chinese lanterns strung haphazardly over head. People were laughing, and carrying on, and the scent of good old fried food was in the air. It was a party, and she was suddenly part of it.

Maggie's mouth watered thinking of so many of the forbidden calories she very rarely consumed. Contemplating a small house salad, dressing on the side, or a half a Caesar, dressing on the side, she allowed herself to be led to a picnic table. People hollered out to Randi and Josie and they waved, hollering in return. Suddenly Maggie wanted to be part of it all. Have more friends — have people happy to see her.

"Mommy can I have a Black Cow?" Annie was tugging on Randi's sleeve. Randi and Josie were admiring a football being passed among burly men in the parking lot and absently said, "Of course."

Maggie's eyes followed their gaze. Four guys in jeans worn low and cut off sweat shirts were tossing a football, their muscles flexing, their good natured yelling bounding. Maggie gaped. She lived alone, rarely went anywhere but the supermarket or work. And at work men wore business suits-- all nicely buttoned up and tailored.

It had been a long time since she'd seen rugged men simply horsing around.

She smiled slightly and Josie nodded, "I know. It's fun to come here and we haven't even had our food yet."

As if on cue, a cute very scruffy guy in a butcher apron came over to their table. "Hi gorgeous," He said to Maggie, "You new in town?"

Maggie was so flustered she didn't even answer, just stared into the rugged good looking face and twinkling eyes.

Randi spoke up, "Dink, this is our new accountant and friend Maggie--now be nice to her, she's not used to people like you."

"Is that right Darlin?" He asked jokingly, looking hurt.

Maggie was so flustered she blurted out, "I'm not used to anyone. I rarely go anywhere but work." Then she blushed mortified at herself. She had no social skills at all, and now she was being reminded of it.

Dink's eyes softened and his teasing disappeared, "Now don't you worry Maggie--'ol Dink'll take care of you."

Maggie's face freaked to crimson. No one had ever, and she meant ever, offered to take care of her. Even if it was a waiter, she added to herself, in a burger joint.

Dink turned to Annie who was folding napkins into little hats. "Moo-o-o-o!" He bellowed. She stood up on her seat and clapped her hands. Dink laughed and she threw her arms around his neck! "That's my girl!" He said, returning the hug. Dink wandered off and Annie settled back to her napkin hats. Maggie looked bewildered and Randi caught her eye.

"Dink does that to Annie to see if she wants a Black Cow-- you know, vanilla ice cream, and Root Beer. Anyway he moos, she cheers. It's a ritual!"

Maggie thought little Annie had to be only four, possibly five. Had there been time in her short life for a ritual? Obviously yes.

"So, Maggie--you told Dink you don't go out or date?" Josie asked just curious of course.

"Well actually that about covers it. I've got these two friends. We all work at Caterpillar and meet for breakfast. I guess you'd say that was the extent of our social life." Maggie was embarrassed but well, there it was. Facts were facts. And there was no real point in pretending otherwise.

Maggie's huge canvas tote sat on the picnic table. Her new accounting notes for Randi crammed next to Pan's bag of cookies. The daily newspaper stuck out in a roll. It had been turned to the Greater Expectations add. Josie eyed it and pulled it out of Maggie's tote.

"Hey--have you seen these ads?" and Josie read:

'Greater Expectations

Longing for companionship that's not your dog?
Greater Expectations.
A dating service that really matches your
personality

To someone you'll want to be with!
1 – 800 – 555 – D – A – T--E
We accept all major credit cards'

Maggie laughed, "Yeah that was one of my favorites, especially since I don't even have a dog. As you noticed, I'm afraid of them." She bit her bottom lip.

"No you're not!" Annie yelled and walking on her bench, put an arm around Maggie's neck. "I saw you pet Honey Crisp. You must mean dates. You're afraid of dates!" Humored by this idea, she walked back and slid in her seat laughing at herself.

At that Dink returned with a tray loaded with deep fried cauliflower, stuffed mushrooms, onion rings, poppers, a Black Cow and a pitcher of Dink's punch! Maggie looked for her half salad and realized she hadn't ordered it. She sank her teeth into a cream cheese jalapeño pepper and forgot about her salad. The punch had a taste she couldn't quite pin point as she continued to munch on the array of hot crunchy veggies!

"Dink knows we are all diet junkies. These are our vegetables!" Josie said in way of explanation as she dipped an onion ring big enough to be a bracelet into what looked like Thousand Island dressing. "But back to the Greater Expectations. We've thought of signing up Dink. We know he's lonely."

Maggie looked over at Dink talking to another table full of happy people--joking, passing around a tray of burgers. He didn't look lonely, she thought. Not the lonely she and her friends were.

"We have no idea what it costs, but we thought we'd chip in and, er, sign him up. Oh yeah and Margaret O's brother in law Hale--lonely too of course."

"And my son's second grade teacher," Randi added. "How much could it be? We'd spend a couple hundred we don't have to find these guys someone." And the look in Randi's eyes told Maggie she meant it.

Maggie swallowed a mushroom cap oozing with Mozzarella, topped with bacon bits. "Ten thousand dollars," She said and drank more punch. She was adjusting to the price at this point. Not liking it but adjusting. The shock was over. It was now the price of change. A change she wanted ... or the hope for a change.

Same same.

"Ten thousand--what?" Randi asked, as her eyebrows shot up. Surely Maggie was joking.

Maggie looked up a slight shrill ting to her laugh, "Dollars. We called--my friends and me." And she reached for an onion ring.

"You must be ... desperate," Randi said and then regretted being so brutal. Why did she engage her mouth before her mind?

"We are," Maggie admitted forlornly. The truth just was what it was.

"Oh no you aren't," Josie said patronizingly. "You're cute, very cute--and bright."

"Very bright," Added Randi thinking of the accounting lesson.

"Thanks you guys. But, well Trish, Pandora, and I are just that much older than you. We're all slaves to our jobs and well the bloom. You know. The bloom is off the rose." She looked from face to face; sure the girls knew what that meant. "Even though you're thin Randi--you've had two kids. I'm sure it's left its mark. A mark you might not parade in a bikini."

Randi nodded solemnly.

"And Josie, even though you are awfully cute yourself-- well, don't you feel that crop of twenty something's was always right behind you?"

Josie nodded remembering, "I was always a bridesmaid." And actually she'd had no friends, and wasn't even a bridesmaid, it was just an expression for being lonely.

"Even though you feel more together it's just a fact. Men at twenty three like twenty three year olds. Men at thirty five like twenty three year olds. Men at seventy five ogle the twenty three year old waitress."

They followed her gaze to exactly that.

"They get old, flabby, and balding but their taste level still wants twenty three."

Josie and Randi had to admit she had a point.

"I'm not saying all men mind you, but lots and lots of them," Maggie said generously. She could be generous, even if she was lonely.

"And at twenty three you think you have forever. You think men are like Kleenex." With that Maggie pulled a square box out of her big tote and started pulling them out.

Annie was fascinated as Kleenex fell on the picnic table, fluttered to the ground.

"You think they'll just keep popping up."

Randi and Josie knew she was right.

"But they don't. You're chances of getting married over thirty are one in a thousand."

Both Randi and Josie looked guilty, having conquered the odds.

"And when you hit your forties--well, you'll sooner have an alien air craft land in your yard," She paused as Dink appeared with a gigantic Pizza. Deftly, the empty veggie platter disappeared and so did Dink.

"And girls, it's been a while since my friends and I saw the beginning of our forties."

Sympathy washed over Josie and Randi.

Annie stuffed her face with loaded Pizza.

"So, it doesn't matter how preserved we are--it's very hard to meet men." They all ate in silence and Maggie picked up the thread of the conversation again, "So Trish, Pandora, and I are chipping in. We've come up with a fictitious name 'Des' for Desperate or Desiree depending on your interpretation. We're pooling our money, our best features, and attributes and we're joining." Then she softened; "Now I'm not saying every woman needs a man. Actually my friends and I are all very self sufficient. But we are lonely. We would like a man."

Josie and Randi were both stunned and fascinated.

"What about a picture?"

"Amazingly--I have a cousin Jillian in Southern California." Maggie started fishing in her large tote bag, taking things out, setting them on the picnic table. "Ah yes," She muttered as she pulled out the package of photographs. "She's a former model, turned photographer. She looks like a better version of me. And then added, "One of her pals took these photos--or should I say staged these photos." And she grinned because she knew they were good.

She passed around the romantic girl in the hat looking out to sea. And then the gazebo shot among others, finally the one of Jillian scooping up puppies from a basket. The pictures were sepia, a faded brown tone, disguising the hair color and really softening any features. It was hard to tell exactly how old the model was. It would be impossible to describe her face save the word serene. One was left with an impression of old fashioned romance.

"Wow!" Randi and Josie said together, "These are great!"

Maggie nodded; she'd been beyond pleased when they came in the mail.

"We're cutting Jillian into the action. She's burnt out on Southern California. She wants to open a tiny Mom and Pop photography business here. Of course ..." And then Maggie looked sad, "Gorgeous as she is, there's no Pop."

Randi and Josie reflected her melancholy look, "Can we help?" They asked.

Maggie thought for a minute and then decided maybe fresh eyes would help. For ten thousand dollars they didn't want to miss anything. "Well, I'll bring the application over tomorrow and you can see if we've missed anything."

With that there was a clamoring of voices.

Maggie looked up to see two stunning men coming toward their table. Different yet similar enough they could be brothers.

"Daddy! Uncle Jamie!" Annie yelled.
"Our men!" Josie said.
And Maggie felt lonelier than ever.

Chapter 3

Trish's very organized world, and very organized habits were shattered. It was Sunday, around six in the morning. The only day Trish allowed herself to sleep in--abandon a schedule. Abandon a schedule till about one o'clock, and then she assumed her orderly ways, put her mind back on track, and treated her personal chores like work, and methodically got them done.

She lay in bed, her sheets in a wad, unable to sleep. Not even doze. "The luxury of my Sunday morning sleep-in is gone--shattered." Her mind whirled with anticipation and fear of the unknown. Of the job she had accepted yesterday at Greater Expectations Dating Agency. Of the resignation letter she would be writing Caterpillar.

And then, of course, trying to get into her office on a Sunday to clean out her desk and take home her few personal items. A comfy pair of emergency shoes under her desk--shoes that played havoc with her image, and therefore there never was an emergency, or exhausted moment, she would sneak them on. "I guess I can leave them."

On her desk was a bud vase, not particularly good quality, her boss had given it to her with a single daisy once on employee appreciation day, and Trish felt to discard it would be a breech in Boss Employee relations--so it still sat there. Empty.

Trish racked her brain for other personal items. Her laptop was always with her. Any perfumes or touch up cosmetics were neatly tucked in her Prada bag. She had no photographs of loved ones, plaques with little sayings, or finger paintings from a loving child.

Trish mentally opened her desk drawer, standard Caterpillar issue. She did have a Mont Blanc pen. A long ago date that had never really materialized into much more than a bad memory, had given it to her. She'd come into work after her token weekend and saw a slim gift box on her desk. Knowing it was too soon for jewelry, she foolishly still let her heart speed up. She carefully unwrapped it. Her heart hit a speed bump.

It was a pen, granted a Mont Blanc pen. It was neither personal nor luxurious. But then again, she guessed it was. Just not the luxury she craved or the personal expression of her dreams. She tactfully called him--she'd even now forgotten his name--told him she didn't feel they should see any more of each other and offered to return the pen.

He huffed and said keep it. The image of a life time with him of receiving romantic office supplies stilled her into the reality that if she couldn't have the genuine article, she'd go it alone.

And the pen lay in her desk, actually too chunky for her hand.

Well her replacement would like it--maybe.

When all was said and done, Trish realized there was nothing to go back to her old office for. Even her calendar was regulation Caterpillar ... sad, after all those years--very sad. She got out of bed and decided to let her shower pound into her.

Refreshed, and picking on a bowl of cherries, Trish started mentally composing her resignation letter. Debating whether to mention her many years of boredom, she ultimately decided to keep it short, professional and say she was pursuing other avenues.

Like an avenue full of men.

She noticed her cell phone light winking at her and tapped play. "Trish, this is Maggie. I've got photographs of my cousin Jillian--you'll love them! Let's all meet Sunday afternoon and finish our application. Call me."

Perfect, Trish thought, I can tell them about my new job! And then a wave of sentimentality washed over her as she thought of their breakfasts together--their only real social life.

"Well, someone was bound to leave the group," She said quietly to herself. She just never pictured it being her.

The day stretched before her. She'd call Maggie at a decent hour. Maybe they could all meet for a late lunch. In the mean time there was laundry. And when the mall opened, maybe some new clothes, she mused, for her new job.

***

Dink always got in early--where else did he have to go? And it wasn't like he had far to go, since he lived in his building. Sundays for him were like any other day, only business started later, so he had the morning to really strip down the kitchen. Give the dining room a good scrub.

It had been a good Saturday night. Business had been brisk. He sat at his desk and chuckled thinking of little Anastasia MacTamara--the way she got when he mooed for her, throwing her little arms around his neck. The child had never had a Black Cow before coming to Dink's having spent her tiny life in the big city, possibly going to MacDonald's for a milk shake when she got a treat. But she and her brother seemed to adjust--no thrive at MacTamara's Orchard. Thrive to the point where she now went by Annie and her brother Bartholomew went by Bart.

And Angus, her step dad's gruff exterior had faded, replaced by a kind look in his eyes, and a glow of contentment. And Angus adored his new kids to the point of foolishness--a very sweet foolishness. Angus and Bart often stopped for a Black Cow after buying a new car or building for Bart's train set. It was a ritual. Like Dink mooing for little Annie.

"Man--what's with me?" Dink muttered, "I'm too old for babies!" In the back of his mind a question formed. But am I too old for love? He'd kept the newspaper ad Jinx had left for Greater Expectations, mockingly at first, now curious. It was taped up on the wall by his desk. As a reminder of just how lonely he was.

"Yeah, like anyone would want me. I can just see my profile. Under style of clothing, I'd put 'Butcher Apron!' "

He sat at his desk entertaining himself. "Like I have time anyway ..." He thought. His eyes drifted to a brown paper sack Randi and Josie had left at their table. He scooped it up late last night and left it on his desk, meaning to call one of them this morning.

"What was in it?" He thought. "None of his business," He added, but curiosity being what it was, he unrolled the top.

"Cookies, well they won't be any good by now, they've sat out all night;" he thought. He dipped his hand in, pulled out an oatmeal cookie almost as large as his fist. It was studded with pecans, looked like raisins, and 'other' things.

Since it was in his hand, he decided he may as well eat it. Absently he took a bite and then stopped. The crisp buttery taste of oatmeal mixed with cinnamon and a hint of nutmeg exploded. The crunch of pecans was mixed with shredded coconut and the raisins turned out to be sun dried cranberries. He inhaled it, finding it still crisp after sitting in a sack all night.

Then he reached in to try another. This one was the same cookie yet different. This cookie was walnuts, raisins, and M&Ms! M&Ms? He ate on--heavenly, just the right contrast, and the surprise between raisins and chocolate. "I wonder if the others are the same or if there's another flavor?" He said to no one but himself.

Sure enough, white chocolate chips and macadamia nuts! He very slowly ate them, savored them, and then they were gone. He dipped in for one more and realized there weren't any. Staring at the empty sack he laughed, "Thank you Randi or Josie." He pleated it down and went back to his cleaning.

"I'll call Randi and Josie and thank them," And got back to work.

***

"Girls we have to get serious about this application," Maggie said impatiently. It was the weekend, they had gathered at Trish's apartment with hopes of making some progress. "Now, I've brought the photos of Jillian--let's start with the profile." Jim Hart sang in the back ground. A cut from his newest CD called 'We Need a Plan.'

"Don't you want to hear my good news first?" Trish asked with a twinkle in her eyes.

"You've been shopping. You got a new Kate Spade bag," Maggie retorted as she spread out the photos.

Trish raised her eyebrows. Geez, "Well," Trish looked guiltily from Maggie to Pandora, "As a matter of fact I did!" Wondering how Maggie knew, she then spied the pile of shopping bags she'd left on the sofa. "But …"

But Maggie cut her off.

"Now we'll start with personality. Let's give it three sentences," Maggie continued without missing a beat, "Or maybe four--one for Jillian."

"Well, I'd like mine to say 'loves to bake'," Pan said and Trish's protests were shelved.

"That's your best personality trait Pan? Come on, add to that!" Maggie demanded.

Trish tapped her elegant nails on the dining room table. She picked up the piece of paper and pen Maggie had supplied and started to write, 'Very intuitive.' And stopped; what else would she want a man to know? And she'd want him to know she was intuitive? Of course not! Scratch that!

Maggie looked at her own blank sheet and wrote. 'Good with numbers, very organized.' She stared at it and thought, "Yeah, that'll get them calling." She idly picked up one of the photographs of Jillian and wrote, 'Very romantic'!

There, Jillian certainly looked romantic. Then she tried to interpret what a man would think when he read that and added 'And loves sports'. Because, let's face it, most men loved sports. But did she even tolerate sports enough to have a sports addict man in her life? She certainly didn't even have the sports network on her cable plan.

Pandora looked at her 'loves to bake' blankly. Surely she had another personality trait she could put down like desperately lonely, no longer picky, except maybe no belching.

She leafed through the photos and came to the one of Jillian bending over to the basket of puppies, one peeking out from her scooped up skirt and wrote. 'Loves to bake and loves animals.'

Trish thought 'loves to shop' would scare most men. Loves to order carry out didn't sound too good either. She looked around her spotless beautiful apartment and wrote 'hobby—cleaning,' and didn't know if that was such an attention grabber.

Then she changed the intuitive part to 'loves people'. She looked at a bouquet of Gerber Daisies she'd indulged in at the florist and added 'and nature'.

"Okay, what have we got so far?" Maggie asked, wanting to get on with it.

With a shirk Pandora said, "I've got 'loves to bake and loves animals'."

"What animals?" Maggie asked while squinting at her.

"Uh, the ones in that picture of Jillian," Pandora gave a little shake of her head. Maybe she couldn't meet anyone because she didn't have any of those great traits ... whatever they were.

Then she stopped. No, she couldn't meet anyone because she worked in a sub—basement and then came home and collapsed. She never went anywhere for someone to dismiss her traits. Or even find out if she had any. She needed this agency.

Maggie rolled her eyes and turned to Trish, "I've got: 'hobby--cleaning; loves people'." Maggie stared at the ceiling, not quite believing that was the best her glamorous friend could come up with.

"Well, what about you Maggie?" Trish asked impatiently.

"I've got 'very romantic and loves sports.'"

"Add that to 'loves to bake, irresistible, and loves animals,'" Pandora added.

"What about movies? Should we say loves movies?" Pandora asked.

"Everyone loves movies," Maggie said with a glare, "That's filler."

"What about old movies?" Pandora asked.

"That sounds like you're trying to be a bargain date--stay home and get Netflix ... maybe not, for ten thousand dollars we don't need bargain dates."

"Read that part of the application again Maggie," Pandora wanted to get it right, very right.

"'Your profile: your profile must reflect the inner and outer you, and express your personality clearly to help another member in making their selection.

Name-

Date of Birth-

Weight-

Who am I?

What is your lifestyle?

Are you a morning person?

Are you a night person?

Are you community oriented?

Politically oriented?

Athletic?

Health conscious?

A planner?

A joiner?

Spontaneous?

Serious?

Frivolous?

What qualities would you use to describe yourself?'"

Maggie paused, "I think we need to say a little more than:

'Loves to bake

Loves animals

Loves people

Hobby cleaning

Very romantic

Loves sports' "

"Well, the hobby cleaning part sounds stupid Trish. How about tidy? Or organized?"

Trish was lost in middle space, "Ah--oh, well let's word it better."

Pandora spoke up, "It is her hobby Maggie and you know it!" Trish's need for order was a bit of an obsession. Still was it the hobby you wanted to put on an application to find a companion? Would a messy person call, hoping to date a cleaning service? Or would a messy person by put off by a cleaning fanatic? And worse yet, why was a messy person such a big consideration?

Finally Trish spoke, "But if it reflects all of us, let's just say 'very tidy.'" They agreed and struck 'Hobby--cleaning'.

"Well maybe we ought to fill in some of the basics," Maggie said and she read: 'Name--Des.'

We need a last name."

The girls looked bewildered of course they would need a last name.

"What about our initials?" Pandora suggested. "T P M and J for Jillian. Can't we add a vowel or something?" They tossed around combinations but they all sounded silly. "What about Des P. J. Tem or P. J. Met?" Pandora tossed out.

"I like it," Trish said slowly. "Sort of sounds like Kismet."

Maggie nodded but not wholeheartedly.

Finally Trish reconsidered. "Hey, weren't we going to use Jones. Isn't P. J. Met silly? Don't we want to be taken seriously?" They all agreed. "We need to take this seriously."

"Date of Birth," Maggie read. They all looked uncomfortable.

"Let's make Des forty six," Trish said, "Still under fifty. Forty five sounds actually older, and well, we don't want to say forty two and attract guys in their late thirties or any forty year old men who haven't had their mid life crisis yet!"

They all agreed. And they knew that magic number for men was forty. They all read the same magazines, watched the same talk shows.

"If we want men in their fifties--late forties at the youngest, forty six sounds good. Any older we'll attract men in their sixties, or seventies, or older, and I'm not ready to tippy toe in to that retirement thing!" Trish was pretty adamant. "And I don't want a man younger than me to make me feel old. Some days I feel old enough." And she gingerly touched her neck.

"Or the beginning of bad health where they need a nurse," Pandora added getting back to the senior crowd.

"With a bed pan and Huggie wipes," Maggie said solemnly. Because she spent enough time at her mother's nursing home to know what was coming.

"Men's egos think they can always go younger. Let's not be any older than forty six."

So, forty six was agreed on.

"What about our day and month?" Trish asked tentatively--she was a big horoscope follower. "What if someone follows astrology the way I do, and rejects us because it was the wrong month?"

"And what man would ever follow astrology the way you do Trish!" Maggie scoffed. "Not to worry." Then she added, "Men don't follow astrology at all."

"Well, I say we simply write age forty six right over the date of birth thing and pretend we just read it wrong," Trish insisted.

Maggie gave in just to keep it moving.

"Hair color," Maggie read next. She had a short cap of sable brown curls; Pandora touched her long pony tail brown with natural red highlights. Trish had a mane of golden hair. And Jillian out in Southern California had …

"What's Jillian's hair color?" Pandora asked.

"Oh, it could be anything--depends on her whim," Maggie answered. "More blonde than anything but sometimes it's a proverbial rainbow of streaks and highlights."

Trish perked up, "That's it girls--we'll all have our hair highlighted and streaked. I know at first I said my hair had to remain as is, but now I'm getting excited … I'll add a tad of red and a few sable brown strands. Maggie have yours frosted or tipped or whatever they call it nowadays. Pandora--you'd look good with a few honey streaks blended in. We'll all go together--a group date at the salon. And we'll call it ... hmmm ..." She paused in concentration.

"Honey brown with auburn highlights." Pandora supplied.

"Exactly!" Maggie and Trish agreed. "That should cover everything."

"Okay," Maggie agreed and then turned back to the form and started up again. "Eye color?"

Trish had blue eyes, Maggie's were brown. Pandora's seemed to change, depending on the light or what she wore. "Pandora, what do you call your eyes?"

"Hazel," She said shyly.

"What exactly does that mean?" Maggie asked, not being critical, just wondering.

Pan looked uncomfortable, "No one really knows."

"Then hazel it will be." And Maggie wrote it in.

"Educational background," She read. Maggie and Trish both had MBA's, not that it had ever substantially helped their careers. Pandora had a liberal arts degree. It was anyone's guess if Jillian had even gone to college. For all they knew she could have spent those years as a love child.

"Let's just say College Degree and leave it at that."

Everyone agreed.

"Marital status? Well, that's easy; we're all and have always been single." She circled it. Then she looked around carefully in case there were any deep dark secrets that one of them had hidden. No secrets. She went on.

"Smoke? No!" Maggie knew none of them smoked. Actually hardly anyone in their age bracket seemed to smoke any more.

"Date a smoker? No!"

"Well, maybe--put down maybe," Trish said. She was so tired of being alone.

"Number of children? None--right? Neither of you are hiding any children?"

They all laughed and said no.

Pandora looked a little melancholy.

Trish patted her hand, "I know we're older--maybe we'll find a man with grown children and can have grand babies!"

Pandora smiled sadly realizing time had definitely slipped away.

They agreed 'date someone with children' was fine.

"As long as they're grown," Maggie added.

"Or almost grown," Trish put in.

"At least past eighteen--no child support." That was easy for them all to agree on.

"Spiritual religious affiliation?" Maggie knew this one could be tricky because she had no clue what Jillian's thoughts were on the subject. Or Pandora's, or Trish's for that matter. She was sure they weren't opposed, but were they members? She had no clue. And would the wrong or right church be off putting? Again, no clue.

"Let's just write the word 'yes' and let them figure it out," Trish said.

Maggie read on, "What about occupation? What should we say? What will cover it all?" All three looked concerned.

"Uh," Trish began, "What if we just say 'office'? It's vague and noncommittal."

Pandora started to pout.

"It almost includes you Pan since your kitchens technically are in an office building."

Pandora relented.

"Why don't we say Caterpillar? We all work at Cat--even though Jillian doesn't; it wouldn't be such a stretch," Maggie volunteered, and besides Jillian wasn't here yet to vote …

"I like it," Pan said, being prone to honesty.

"Then we'll write down Caterpillar," Maggie wrote as she spoke.

Trish thought she should speak up, admit she had written that resignation letter to Cat, but somehow just kept quiet. Now wasn't the time, though it certainly felt like maybe it was …

"Okay, under 'who I am', we've got the list with 'Baking and Tidy'. What if we add optimistic, honest, and sincere?"

"Maybe we ought to scratch 'honest'," Pan said quietly knowing the entire application was a bit of a sham.

So, honest was X'd out.

"What I'm looking for," Maggie read next.

"Well, we don't want to say dashing good looks," Pan said.

"We don't?" Maggie asked. She wanted dashing good looks.

"No, we'll be able to check that out on their applications. And besides we may all have different ideas of what handsome is," Pandora added.

"You mean like six foot two and blond?" Trish asked.

"Well, I prefer dark hair," Maggie added with a twinkle.

"And I'm so short, I can honestly say anything over five foot seven works for me," Pan added.

"I like a ruddy tan," Trish mused. It sounded good.

"I have a thing for red heads …" Maggie spoke softly, "The Irish type." Of course, she had also just preferred men with dark hair.

"I like hair on their heads," Trish stated. And she knew the blondes tended to lose their hair. And bald was rather in for men. Lucky for some of them …

"Yeah, but don't forget James Taylor went from any other hippy to very romantic as he got older," Pan said. "And he really doesn't have much hair to speak of."

They all agreed hair shouldn't be on their list.

"Let's get down to the important things," Trish interrupted.

"Like other physical attributes?" Maggie laughed.

Pandora started to get fidgety because she really didn't know what she wanted, "No, like commitment--as in able to make one." That was what she wanted: a committed man--committed to her.

"And loyal," Trish added thinking of her last rotten relationship.

"Employed is nice," Maggie recalled the dead beat she'd supported a few years back.

"Honest. If he isn't honest, well, I don't want to get started," Pan said even though she'd crossed out honest for their description.

They all looked a little sheepish on this one but put it on the list.

"No belching!" Maggie stated.

"Yeah, like we can put that on our request!" Trish rolled her eyes.

"Okay how about table manners?" Maggie wanted something that showed he wasn't a slob.

"Doesn't that go without saying?" They didn't add table manners or belching.

"How about enthusiastic?" Pandora asked. "I hate people with no passion for what they do, not to mention a positive attitude." She would never make it with someone bored with life.

"Okay, let's word that: Someone with a positive attitude who has a passion for his career." They all agreed that sounded good.

"What if he's still deciding what he wants to do?" Trish asked defensively.

"We don't want him!!" Maggie stated. "In our age bracket, we don't want to nurse maid someone through a new career." She paused, "Didn't we all do enough of that when we were younger?" And Maggie also didn't want someone who didn't really have a career. She was past all that.

Everyone nodded.

"Well our older age should have some perks--no career--no chance."

"What about kind to his mother?" Pandora asked.

"Do you want a fifty year old Mama's boy?" Maggie retorted.

"Well, what about kind to children?" Pan added.

"Do you want a man who coddles his grown children and they never leave home?"

Pandora looked lost, "How about kind to animals?"

There was a pause. Kind to animals met with no objections and went on the list. "I know you're afraid of most animals Maggie," Pan said, "But think of it as a metaphor."

Maggie sighed and nodded, "Whatever," And just squinted. So, she was afraid of animals. Was that a deal breaker? "Well what else should we put on our list?" Maggie asked.

They looked at each other.

"To be honest," Pandora started quietly, "I'm so desperate, I could give you a small list of what I don't want and then, well, I'd take whatever."

Trish looked down her lovely nose at Pandora. "Well I for one am picky!" She said defiantly.

"Yeah, so picky Trish, I can't remember the last time you went out!" Maggie laughed--actually laughed at her.

Trish sputtered, "I, I, I've been out!" She was sure she'd been out--sometime.

"When?"

"New Years Eve!" There that ought to shut them up!

"Which one--we all watched old movies and the ball at Rockefeller Center for the past three New Years Eves--maybe four?" Maggie shouted.

"We did?" Trish whaled lamely. And then of course she remembered the sadness they all shared, and the loneliness. Because New Years Eve was just one of those times you really wanted someone with you.

"Maybe longer--I just can't remember back much farther," Maggie knew those New Years Eves were painful ... for all of them.

"Well, I must have had a date ..." Trish got pensive, and realized if she had, she couldn't remember it. And if she couldn't remember it, well, it couldn't have been that good.

For one brief moment she flashed back to her youth. She'd been blonde and leggy. She had all the things she had then, only some a little lower, others a little worn--and tired. Maybe even the teensiest amount wrinkled, despite all the products she troweled on. Despite all those tacky saying about youth, well, she knew most of them were true. Yet she didn't really feel old.

Not even old-ish.

"There was a time I thought men would always pop up like Kleenex!" Trish laughed as she pulled out a Kleenex to dab her eyes. And of course another one did pop up, Kleenex that is.

Maggie agreed, "I know, if one wasn't just so, I figured the next would be better."

"Or cuter."

"Or richer."

Maggie and Trish laughed.

Pandora bit her nails.

"But it slowed down, didn't it? And then when we weren't looking, it sort of ..." Trish couldn't put it in words.

"Dried up!" Maggie finished with the loneliest faraway look in her eyes.

"Yeah," Trish said sadly, openly, and vulnerably. Because that was exactly what had happened and their picky days were gone, over--almost as though they had never been.

"Well you two can go down memory lane all you like, but I don't have those fond memories!" Pandora stood up. She thought they understood. But nobody understood ...

Maggie and Trish looked at each other. They'd known each other a long time, and they knew Pandora was right! They couldn't remember Pandora dating--at all.

"I was fixed up for Home Coming in my junior year ..." Pan said dismally, "With my cousin. And he was shorter than I was--which is pretty hard!" She was pretty small.

"I wanted dates. I wanted to go to a restaurant with a guy. A restaurant with flowers, a candle, maybe a bottle of wine! I wanted to share a pizza with a date! Go to a football game--or-

-or--or--a walk! Even a walk! I was shy and short! I didn't have a mother like you Trish that showed me how to do my hair!"

She grasped her pony tail. "I've worn my hair like this all my life! My mother was too busy with her world, and assumed I was too quiet to want to go out!" A tear slid down Pandora's cheek.

Maggie and Trish rushed to her and hugged her.

"You're lovely Pan--we think so. And kind and talented. Someone would be lucky to have you as a date!" They fawned over her until her tears ended in hiccups. But still all those facts stood out there, just hovering around.

"Thanks--you're the best friends anyone could ever have. But, you know I'm right. There have been no men in our lives! Why even my paper person is a girl!" Pan hated to admit this.

They all agreed, and after a brief lament of the lack of paper boys except for Trish's, and he was getting a little old now, they began again.

"Okay," Maggie took control. "I'll start. No felons."

"Are we ruling out small law breaking back in the seventies or eighties or nineties?" Trish asked.

Pandora laughed nervously. "No murderers, no one in jail. No wife beaters, no psychos, no cult types. No one who can't read! No gays! Get my drift?" Then she paused, "I didn't mean to clump gays in there. But we know it is useless to date gays no matter how sweet they are they never switch teams."

"You didn't mention short wimps!"

"No I didn't."

"Or bikers."

"No."

"Or tubby men, balding tubby men."

"No I didn't--they have a chance," Pandora looked them square in the eyes. She meant it.

"Or multiple divorces?"

Pandora wavered on this one, "How many times, under what circumstances?" She asked meekly, because, she didn't want to be the next in some man's long list of divorces. She wanted to be ... set.

"What circumstances could be okay that take someone to alter three—four—five-- times Pan?" Maggie practically shouted.

"You know I'm just so tired of being alone. Of course I don't want someone who ... who ..." And her voice started to crack.

"Who knows the route to the altar by heart? Who has a rolodex of divorce lawyers?" Maggie asked. And why she was being so tough she wasn't sure. She was as lonely as Pandora-- maybe lonelier. She actually had dated, and she knew what it was like. And she missed it--terribly.

Trish said quietly, "Don't forget our number one request 'able to commit'! Pan, you do not have to be alone or settle for riff raff. There is the other side to your coin out there waiting for you." And Trish gave her the look that said she really did mean it.

Pandora snuffled and Trish went on, "You just aren't going to meet him in the sub-basement kitchens of Caterpillar."

And Pan tilted her head in admission.

"And we're too old for the bars," Maggie added, "Not that that ever did any good. Now we'll finish this application, give them our big bucks, attach our photos of Jillian, and seal it with a kiss, and wait for our lives to change." And on that happier note they knocked it off.

And they group hugged.

As they headed out the door, Pandora turned to Trish, "Thank you. You're right. I've been alone all this time, I should at least have mediocre or or ... average, not riff raff."

Trish smiled, her china blue eyes just touched with the hint of tears. "You deserve, and we'll find you, 'fabulous'! You're worth it and he'll be the lucky one!"

They all laughed, because they were all hopeful. Finally some hope.

"We're meeting at the salon at four o'clock," Maggie said, fingering her curls. Pandora and Trish nodded.

This gave Trish a small window of opportunity to shop--
and Fairchild's was on her list. Maybe she needed some new
scent and luxurious lotion for the new her. Fairchild's had just
started carrying April's Cottage lotions, perfumes, and
powders in crystal and silver containers. The one Trish seemed
partial to was called 'Ambience', and after all, wasn't that what
their application and photos were all about? Yes, she'd stop by
for some 'Ambience' on her way to the salon.

She fingered a long golden strand of her hair trying to
picture streaks and touches of auburn and honey brown mixed
in. She decided it would be wonderful--wonderful because it
would get the ball rolling on her new social life. And later on
when all was said and done, she could color it back the way it
was now if she wanted to. After all it wasn't her real color now.
She didn't even know what her real color was anymore.

Pandora felt she had time for a quick run to Sam's for some
baking ingredients before their date at the salon. Blonde
highlights! She'd always wanted to try that even though it
seemed extravagant and far too glamorous. Well, regardless,
she thought, she was getting highlights.

***

They met at the salon, Pandora's trepidation rising. As she
got out of her car she thought everyone who came in and went
out looked the same: blonde, coiffed, like a soap star. Every hair
in place in some elaborate trying to appear casual 'do'. She
fingered her pony tail, took a quick breath and headed in. Trish
was behind her.

Maggie was already there reading 'Style'. "Hi you two, are
we ready?" Even Maggie's confidence seemed a little shaky. It
was as though they were signing up for three cloning plastic
surgeons not high lights in their hair.

The girls checked in at the desk with Lynn, a young student
working part time. "Now let me get this straight," Lynn the
receptionist said, "You each have appointments with different

hair artists for exactly the same thing, and you want chairs all next to each other?"

They nodded, refusing any explanation. Lynn shook her own great head of blond hair and led them to three stations--all adjacent. "Marco, Pierre, and Ralphy will be with you in just a moment." She still gave them a quizzical look and they still refused to budge with an explanation.

Maggie still held her 'In Style', Pandora a cookbook out of her tote for easy reading, and Trish had a romance paperback, and the daily newspaper. They settled in their chairs and waited while the din of beauty salon gossip absorbed them.

"There must be a science to stylists keeping their patrons, okay clients, waiting," Pandora thought. She saw stylists--or she assumed they were, mulling around, having a cigarette and coffee as if they had all the time in the world ... while she waited for her fate.

Trish settled back in her chair, her newspaper and book on her lap. She closed her eyes, waiting, having been through this routine many times.

Marco was the first to appear. "And you are Maggie?" He said as he ran his fingers through her short curls. Maggie nodded as best she could under his grip. Ralphy and Pierre sauntered out together. Ralphy looked at Trish as if there was some hope; Pierre eyed Pandora as if he'd just lost a bet. He didn't even make an effort to hide it.

Suddenly all three girls began talking at once. They didn't care if their new stylists were rude or condescending. They were here with a mission, and they were lucky to get three people to work on them at the same time.

"And some red highlights!" Maggie started.

"And blonde tipping for them to match me," Trish added.

"And some sable brown added in." Pandora had read that name 'Sable Brown' and thought she liked the sound of it.

"Now ladies let's get this straight--you all want the same hair cut?" Marco asked as if his craft had been humiliated. He raised one eyebrow and looked them over.

"No--oh no!!!" They all chorused, "Just the same colors."

"You all want to be blondes with darker streaks or brunettes with highlights?" Ralphy asked, almost disgusted. He really wondered sometimes--wondered how he ended up with all the nut cases.

Trish sat up and addressed the men, "We want to retain our basic colors, gentlemen- -and styles. We simply want some of each other's colors woven into each other's hair. I need some sable and auburn. Maggie needs some auburn and blonde. Pandora needs some blonde and sable. We want to share each other's colors." She gave it all her dewiest gaze, saying it as basically as she could.

"But I want to create something just for you," Ralphy whined as he pulled back her hair.

With a radiating smile, Trish touched his hand, "Not this time Ralphy." Her look said there would be plenty of other times. And Ralphy bought it.

Pandora looked exceedingly nervous.

"My dear you don't do much to your hair do you?" Pierre asked her accusingly.

"Oh no--I try to keep it natural," Pandora said with pride.

And he rolled his eyes.

Of course, Pan missed it but Trish saw it and sighed.

Pierre muttered to himself, and Pandora settled back into her copy of 'The Best Cookie' feeling maybe she'd best not watch.

In their own competitive way the three men seemed to get along--even be friends. Trish took Ralphy's hand, "We're having a group photograph done for a book we co-authored. The New York photographer suggested we share highlights for the photograph. Of course ..." She paused for effect, tilting her chin up to catch Ralphy's eye, "He suggested we have it done in the city--New York City that is, and I assured him we knew of a sophisticated salon that specialized in color, and we wouldn't need his recommendation."

Ralphy started to soften.

Pierre listened as he un--did Pandora's pony tail.

Trish gave her little girl look where her china blue eyes widened. "Our publisher was willing to pick up the tab in New York--but I said no--we were coming here!" With this she jutted her chin stubbornly to show how serious she was. "Your reputations precede you, and we will want to become regulars for our maintenance." And then very slyly she added, "And we plan to put your names in the 'Thank You' section of our book."

Ralphy blushed, Pierre started to fondle Pandora's hair as if he liked it, and Marco's eyes glazed over--seeing his name in lights.

"So, gentlemen, you need to know you are our first choice, over New York City, and we're counting on you," And Trish figured she had explained it in their language, and felt confident it would all go smoothly from there on.

Ralphy sighed and started consulting a color chart. He handed it to Marco and Pierre pointed to a variety of shades. They debated and finally all agreed, which in itself was a surprise to Trish. So far so good …

The men settled in to mixing their concoctions. Pandora stopped pleating the pages of her cook book, Maggie closed her eyes, and Trish let out a breath as she opened her newspaper.

The men were painting on hues, and foiling strands of hair, chatting to each other as though they were at a bar. Pandora looked up at Pierre hopefully.

"Bebe--we will make you pretty," He said gently, "No--beautiful! Pierre will make you beautiful!"

Pandora gave a weak smile while her insides were a combination fear and anticipation. But she believed him. She wanted to believe him.

Trish finished Dear Abby and folded her newspaper. An ad for Greater Expectations jumped off the page.

"Look at zat!" Ralphy said picking up Pierre's French accent which Trish was sure wasn't real either.

Trish followed his gaze to the ad.

'Love

A real relationship
A change in your life
Just a phone call away.
Greater Expectations
We expect more for you than you do...
I — 800-D — A — T — E
One simple phone call could change your life
We take all major credit cards.
Go from superficial to real.'

"Marco, have you seen today's ad for that bogus dating service?" Ralphy sighed.

Marco was busy separating Maggie's curls into little strands and nodded.

Pierre picked up the slack, "Can you imagine? Meeting someone through a service?" His French accent was forgotten and he was snide and crude.

The hairs on the back of Trish's neck, the ones not plastered in gel, stood on end. "And just how do you meet, ah, dates?" She asked, in her haughtiest voice.

"I have a friend I live with," Pierre simply replied smugly.

"And before that? The bars?" Trish wasn't letting it go. They had too much riding on this and Trish knew if it was difficult for her to find a date so was it for these guys.

Pierre's face twitched ever so slightly, "Well, no I met him through Marco."

Marco beamed with pride because of course that's what everyone wanted, to meet someone through a friend.

Ralphy was silent. Pandora was half listening and when she looked up from her cookie cook book at Ralphy her heart cracked, just a little, because she understood--all too well.

"But you have to admit--it is difficult," Trish went on, "The bars have the exact same crowd they always have and friends of friends--well, that dwindles too."

Hesitantly Pandora spoke up, "There is a nice gentleman I work with ..." She looked over at Ralphy who hadn't spoken.

Ralphy continued to paint long strands of Trish's hair.

"He's an artist to his craft," Pandora went on, "Very devoted to his career. Tall, well built. Brownish hair he tried to high light but of course messed up."

Ralphy slowed down, listening. He could see the attempted high lights. Still it spoke volumes that this person wanted highlighted hair. It was the home made part that made him wince.

Pan went on, "He's very quiet--likes the symphony, fine wine, fine food. His name is Jorge--with a J." She added for emphasis. "Maybe I could recommend you try and high light his hair Ralphy?"

"Accent, the word is accent, we no longer high light." But as much as Ralphy wanted to sound his usual rude self he was just a tad nicer, softer.

"Or accent," Pandora added, "Or you could comp him a consultation or an accent." She snuck in, boldly.

Ralphy considered as he stared at Trish's hair, "Yes--yes I could. Maybe I could." He stared into middle space, that place of possibilities. "But do you think he would understand me?" Ralphy let out in a sad very audible murmur.

"Well," Pandora said, "You are both artists. Yes, I think he would."

"And his specialty?" Ralphy pictured canvases.

"He is a pastry artist," Pandora said with pride. "Trish, do you have your cell phone? I'll call him."

And as the phone slipped to her, she dialed Jorge.

"It's Pandora. I'm at that trendy salon on the east side." She paused, "That's the one. The kindest gentlemen are doing mine, and Maggie's, and Trish's hair. Yes, all at once. And well, Ralph. Yes as in Ralph Lauren," Pandora rolled her eyes, "Would like to give you a comp color."

She looked over at Ralphy who stared, fascinated. "Well, we should be another hour I think, and if you come you could see our new look, meet Ralph, and he could squeeze you right in."

Ralphy rolled his eyes and Pandora added her best plea look.

He finally shrugged.

"He's doing this as a favor to us." Pause. "Of course you'll like it. You'll love it. I'm having my hair accented." She listened, "Yes I am. Yes it was a big step. Well all three of them are fabulous. I uh, just really think what he's doing to Trish would be great on you. Yes. Yes. No. Okay. I'll see you in about one hour."

She listened intently, "Yes, you can bring Hunter, your neighbor. Yes I think Marco would comp him. Oh, no color, just a style?" She looked questioningly at Marco and Ralphy sent him daggers--his mind made up to meet Hunter also. "Perfect--we'll all wait and see you guys in an hour."

She turned to Marco, "You'll like Hunter. He works with us at Caterpillar."

"Is he an artist also?" Marco asked as he twisted a curl in his hand.

"No--he's in construction. His hair is too long and it needs help," Maggie threw in, and then re-closed her eyes.

Marco colored.

Maggie added, "Come on Marco--do it for our little group. Don't make Pandora look bad. She already promised."

Trish spoke quietly, "It's very difficult to meet new people Marco. Cut his hair and take a chance." And then she closed her eyes and let Ralphy work his magic.

The girl's final stages were taking effect, and as their anticipation quaked so did Ralphy's, Pierre's and Marco's.

Ralphy had to take a cologne break, Marco snuck in back to put on a fresh shirt. Pierre sat in an empty chair and trimmed his bangs, and inspected his teeth. The girls cooled their heels with the drip drip of color solution running down their necks.

The door opened and Jorge rushed in--tall, blonde, and gorgeous; Hunter, tall dark, and gorgeous right behind him.

They ran over to Pandora--each grabbing a hand. "Kissy kissy Darling--we came right over!" Hunter let out.

Jorge took one look at Ralphy--a combination gratitude and lust in his eyes! "You are transforming our little Pandora--I am ever grateful to you." And a relationship was started. Just as simple as that--two people at the right time under the right circumstances.

Marco fingered Hunter's long hair, "Tsk tsk," Was all he said and Hunter wore the look of one about to be saved.

"Boys," Trish began, eyeing Jorge and Hunter, "We're almost done. Be darlings and run get us a latte, and we'll be able to give you our chairs." She glared as she sent them next door, fearful their almost finished treatments would be forgotten.

"Now men, let's finish up here so you can play." And as the stylists added those little touches one can never master at home all three girls looked in their mirrors and smiled.

It went without saying Trish looked even better. Maggie had a glow that was almost a halo as she shook her curls, as just a bit of blonde peaked through. But Pandora was the most transformed. Her blonde and sable streaks brought her long auburn hair to life. Her face glowed, "I love it Pierre."

Pierre softened, "Yes, even Pierre is pleased. The little Pandora, she is transformed, nes't pas?"

The colors added dimension to all the girls. Marco stood back critically, hand on his hip, "You look--you look like--not sisters, but parts of the whole," He said this philosophically.

The three girls caught each other's eyes in the mirrors, seeing bits of each other reflected in their new hair. "Exactly!" They each said.

"Let's celebrate Monday at breakfast!" Pandora said bubbling with enthusiasm. "I'll order something other than oatmeal!"

Trish stood perfectly still--gazing at their reflections.

"No, let's celebrate now! Besides, I have something to tell you." And they linked arms and headed out just as Jorge and Hunter headed back in.

***

Monday found Trish heading to Greater Expectations. Her heart tugged a bit as she thought of her friends meeting for breakfast. She grabbed a power bar from her counter and recalled the shocked look on Maggie and Pan's faces when she told them she'd quit Caterpillar.

They sputtered out benefits, and job security, and so many practical things, which made Trish cringe. Cringe but hold firm. Maggie had informed her that nobody quit Caterpillar. Of course, it only made it worse. And Pandora was so shocked she was literally speechless.

"Girls, this is step one in our new lives. This is a chance." She fingered her newly accented hair. "A chance--well, not that we need to take, but if we don't, we'll never know. It's beyond need. And our time is running out. Another five or six years we won't be meeting to group streak our hair; we'll be meeting to group Botox, chemical peel, or worse yet, the knife. No--it's time." And Trish looked them both seriously in the eyes.

She took in a much needed gulp of air and went on, "Besides--in a few more years we may not want to. We're semi beat now. We semi believe all those statistics, and our mother's years of insults, and pitiful looks. Let's face it--we're long overdue to take a chance. Now I need your support. Look at the hair and application as stage one. This job is stage two. It's too late to go back."

Pan twirled the end of her pony tail with a look of glum depression, her eyes on the verge of tears. "We'll miss you at breakfast," She started. Well, that went without saying.

Trish held up her hand in protest, "Think of it as escaping--breaking out." Her eyes glistened with renewed excitement. "And I'm not leaving you two behind! So, look at your power breakfasts as the end of an era! And so help me--the men of Greater Expectations better look out--we're coming!"

Trish straightened her pale pink suit as she recalled their tears and her promises. She parked the car, took in a deep breath, and told herself it was time to make good those promises.

Mike stood by the door peering through a slatted blind. Would she really come? Had he really hired a tall blonde bomb shell; a bomb shell that had experience--Human Resource experience? Or had it all just been a fantasy?

He watched her walk from her car--determined and confident. A tickle of sweat rolled down his neck, and he shifted his eyes up ward as if in prayer. "We're a scam--a scam of sorts." And for the first time in his life he wanted it to be a real business. And he felt bad. Well, a little bad.

She opened the door and smiled, "Well, I'm here," Trish said a tad nervously, and that human quality made Mike relax. Her eyes were questioning, and Mike realized he hadn't even cleared a spot for her. What had he done to get ready for her other than plan his own free time? What kind of business person was he? But of course he knew. He was a terrible one.

The foyer area of Greater Expectations was bare except for a few folding chairs--tacky folding chairs, Trish thought. How had she over looked them on her interview? A large desk and series of filing cabinets were centered on the far wall. Several doors led off this, one to a viewing room with a computer, two others to offices.

The doors hung open and Trish immediately summed up the situation. Why the place was no better than a dump! And for ten thousand dollars a person! An old TV table held a cloudy coffee maker, fake cream, sugar packets, and paper cups. A waste basket over flowed with crumpled papers.

The air was stale, the overall feeling was gray. The total effect was depressing.

In a heartbeat, Trish decided she was going to take charge. In her heart she knew that's what she really did best. "I'll be out here at the front desk," She said it quietly and authoritatively.

Mike looked relieved. He could hide in the other office, slipping out to the golf course unnoticed. And then he started to explain the files.

Primitive was Trish's only thought. A computer was buried under a weeks' worth of newspapers, maybe more. This seemed to indicate no one had turned on that computer.

"I want you to not only make yourself at home but to take any initiative you feel necessary. My cousin and I are hiring you as a professional. And as such, we expect you to jump in with both hands." Mike thought that sounded good--real good, and somehow let him off the hook.

"Remember we didn't want a clerical--we wanted a Human Resources person to not only organize us but take the rough edges off our little operation." Mike couldn't believe himself. He saw himself teeing up. He made this stuff up as he went along, and he was even impressing himself. And he even liked what he heard, so he knew it was good.

He left her to get settled.

As Trish put her handbag in a drawer, a drawer full of Doritos, she heard a door close. Mike had slipped out the back. She stared straight ahead contemplating Greater Expectations.

Very slowly she picked up the phone and dialed. "Merry Maids? Yes I'd like you to come out for an office cleaning. No, I don't need an estimate first. Yes, bring the works. In an hour? Fine."

She let out a breath and looked at the files. There seemed to be no rhyme or reason. She started to pull them out and knew she'd found her perfect job. Albeit a filthy one for the time being, but then again the Merry Maids were on their way.

By the time she had files in stacks by sex, age group, and alphabetized, the Merry Maids were polishing the wood floor. Trish was actually quite surprised there was a wood floor.

Everything smelled of lemon wax. The windows sparkled. Trash cans were spotless.

The 'Maids' had groaned when they saw the bathroom, but persevered. And of course Trish knew that was why they made the big bucks. Bathrooms like the one at Greater Expectations.

A delivery truck from Office Max was pulling up. "Lady, we're here with filing cabinets. Where do you want them?"

Trish realized the old metal files were inadequate and one phone call had new ones on their way. She also realized with her new system, she would need many more. No sense filing the thirty year olds with the sixties. "Uh--let's put those empty metal ones in that office," She pointed with her pen.

"And line the new walnut ones up on this wall. No, better yet, let's put the new ones in that office." And she indicated the other door. An office that looked virtually un--used, a plastic drop cloth over a desk and computer.

That would be her office. When she got the place under control, she'd hire a receptionist to sit out front with the folding chairs. The public didn't need to walk into a wall of filing cabinets. No, that wasn't the first impression she wanted them to have at all.

So the kind burly Office Max delivery man set up the filing cabinets in her new office and hauled the old ones out of the foyer, to the other office.

Trish was pleased to discover the files were also down loaded in the computer. Actually a little shocked, but pleased. She tapped in a question on the computer keys: six foot two age forty nine male.

The screen started to fill. Mesmerized, she typed in an occupation: male, Doctor. Again the screen filled, then another, and another. By the time Trish looked up from the computer screen she realized the light had started to fade. Merry Maids, and Office Max, long gone, along with the day.

"Really--I can't believe I lost the day," Chuckling to herself, she got her Prada bag out of the now Doritos free drawer. She stuck her head in Mike's vacant office and saw a wad of keys on his desk. Surely one worked the front door. Helping herself, she left.

As Trish drove home her mind whirled. Before she knew it her car had headed to the Hallie Great Furniture Store.

"There is no way Greater Expectations can charge ten thousand dollar an applicant in that ugly setting--I can't believe they have any applicants, unless they're really desperate, like me. But on the other hand, if I'd gone there with my check book, I'm afraid I would have bolted." These thoughts whirled through her head.

"Cheap setting--I'm sure my first reaction would be cheap dates."

Trish laughed as she pushed open the door and waved at Hallie--the owner, and name sake of a fabulous furniture store and more.

"Trish! Long time no see!" Hallie said in way of greeting, "What brings you by tonight?"

After a quick hug, Trish relayed her story.

Hallie's eyes twinkled. "Come on--let's shop!"

The first thing they found was an English leather chesterfield sofa--deeply tufted in oxblood leather. "Something the men could relate to," Hallie said, "Very old boys club." It was a stunner.

"And an oriental?" Trish asked. Because now with the wood floors done to a sheen they really could use a feature.

"Absolutely!" They headed to the rug department where one lush Tabriz in wine colors was tagged.

"Some chairs to make a seating grouping?" Hallie suggested while pointing to a pair of Ralph Lauren forest green club chairs. Trish liked them so much she wanted them for herself.

"Perfect! Ralph can't be beat!" She grinned.

"Let's update it all with a brass and glass coffee table." Hallie explained it could hold that nervous cup of coffee and show off the rug. And the glass would keep the room from getting heavy. "And a small side board for the coffee maker and whatever else goes with that."

Trish nodded in agreement. She saw it coming together, and couldn't help but know she had made the right decision by coming.

"You may as well go for a couple of end tables to carry out that deep mahogany," Hallie pointed. Of course, they would need end tables to pull their seating group together.

"And lamps Hallie--maybe brass to co-ordinate with the coffee table?" Trish now knew she wanted it to have that look of an old English home, classy yet inviting.

"Exactly!" Hallie headed them in the right direction with her packet of tags.

"Now we just have one long wall. What would you suggest?" Trish was thinking about the endless space that seemed to just dominate the room.

"How about that imported breakfront?" It looked like an English combination bookshelf/china cabinet. "You could put framed pictures of some of your clients in there with some tasteful artifacts." Hallie couldn't wait to come out and help Trish arrange it all.

"Brilliant!" Trish let a breath out. "Gee Hallie that didn't take us long at all to spend how much money?"

Her old friend laughed. "Well, at ten thousand dollars a client, I think there must be a few dollars to spare. You did say you had the company Visa for necessities didn't you?"

Trish nodded.

"Well then, let's go to my office and see what the limit is." They walked to an exquisite English office; it looked like an ad for Ralph Lauren's home store--or his home.

Hallie looked like the model. She sat behind her desk and started punching in numbers. "Yes to the sofa," Hallie said as she fiddled, starting with the main grouping, "And chairs, rug, lamps."

Trish grinned wickedly.

Then Hallie paused and crossed her fingers, "And the breakfront, the big expensive one. Your company is the proud owner of ..." Hallie paused mid sentence, looking at Trish she said, "A new image! I think I can get it out on a truck tomorrow early. What time can you be there? I'll meet you and we can direct the boys where to place everything!"

Trish drove home smiling. Well, Mike had said they needed to class up the place... And she was quite sure she was not enough class to compensate for the interiors, or lack thereof.

Chapter 4

Jillian looked in awe at her mound of luggage, and an even bigger mound of packing boxes.

The movers were due any minute. It was sad how one's life could be reduced to brown corrugated boxes. Hopes, dreams, memories, material possessions--when all was said and done they either fit in a brown corrugated box or went to Good Will. It was that simple.

Jillian knew it was a daring, and gutsy move, but she also knew it was one she must make. Southern California, land of dreams, fantasy, and perpetual youth was no longer going to be her playground. Well, by any ones standards, Jillian was stunning yet she found herself mentoring her co-workers. Her modeling days were long over, replaced by fourteen year olds.

Even though Jillian felt young and glamorous, the girls she worked with periodically asked her for motherly advice. They tried to hide from her their occasional drug or drinking bouts as if she had no clue, and excluded her from boy friend conversations as if sex were a taboo subject to her age group.

Well it almost was since she'd almost forgotten what it was like. Usually she'd just squint and get back to work.

When they discussed their acne, and Jillian found herself reading magazine articles on pre-menopause--well, she knew it was time. The president of the bank she banked at had those sleepy eyes of a high school-er. Everywhere she looked youth reigned. People her age were lined up for Botox and tucks. Where the older than her women were she hadn't a clue. Perhaps they were all dead as her young counter parts suggested.

Along with suggesting that she was next.

When one of the 'children' at work asked her if she had a will, she knew. Knew it was time. After over--hearing a conversation in the hallway about how sad it was that she was going to die never having married--well, she started to pack. Marriage wasn't the answer--the only answer. Still it stung. And it hurt even more because they all still had so much opportunity ahead of them.

Maggie had found her an apartment in her building and sight--un--seen, Jillian had wired a down payment. It almost didn't matter what it looked like, what the square footage was, or where the windows looked out. It was her chance, and she took it. As she gave her worldly possessions one last look she realized there was a knock at her door.

The movers, the beginning of her new life in Illinois. Her excitement washed over the very oddness of how it sounded.

***

Maggie and Pan sat at breakfast, their former power breakfast. "I miss her," Pandora fiddled with her tea bag wondering how it was going for Trish. How the world of real excitement was ... the world outside of her sub-basement kitchen.

"I know," Maggie sighed, "But it's for the best." Maggie knew in her heart if they were going to change they needed to start. Still ... did they have to just jump in?

She missed Trish, couldn't remember a breakfast without her. And just a little bit was jealous. Trish always had ... well everything. Then Maggie stopped--actually not everything. She didn't have a man in her life—just like the rest of them.

"What have you heard?" Pan asked as she absently swirled her brown sugar in her oatmeal. Pandora was a little annoyed, okay a lot annoyed, that Trish hadn't called them all immediately to report what those files were like, to report all the treasures, er, men that were lurking in those files, and to give them the low down on her boss, and the building itself.

She didn't even know what Trish's office looked like--nothing. No word. No hint. Nothing. Just gone. And now they were two. She almost felt as though Trish had moved far away or … died.

"I haven't heard anything except she's exhausted." Maggie stared off into middle space, "Oh yes she did say the place was filthy, and she had a cleaning crew in." Maggie wanted details. She lived for them.

And her report from Trish was hardly enough. She was a numbers girl. She wanted to know how many files there were. How many men were in these files? How many had potential for them? She wanted details--details that could help her, because now she was more miserable than ever. Trish was gone.

The girls played with their food, going through the motions of breakfast."I may as well go down to the kitchens," Pan said gloomily. It was probably a first that Pandora was actually wasting food. Her meager budget just didn't allow for her to throw out groceries even if they were bad. She ate them.

It went without saying if she purchased food at a restaurant, even the Caterpillar employee dining room, she certainly would never throw it out. No. Her income was far too meager to waste. And yet here she was leaving a perfectly good bowl of oatmeal and a tea bag she had only used in one cup of hot water. Pandora really was depressed.

"Yeah--I'm off too." Maggie left her untouched eggs, gathered her handbag and left.

Neither girl had a newspaper--that having been Trish's contribution. As they walked past a table, a discarded paper lay open next to someone's half eaten Danish. The ad was bold and hit them like a lightning bolt!

'Depending on your friends?

When what you need is a companion of your
own?
And not a dog or cat
Call Greater Expectations
Where you can become a 'couple'

1 – 800 – 555 – D – A – T – E
All major credit cards accepted'

***

Trish got to Greater Expectations extra early; hit the lights only to be delighted anew by the assault of lemon pledge that filled the air and the glisten of the shiny wood floors.

Her first investment was actually the basis for the rest, and she knew she'd done the right thing and gotten on with it. And she knew it hadn't taken guts at all. The changes she made were survival. For her, Maggie, and Pandora ... and now it seemed for the agency.

Trish went to her own office and slipped off her Burberry trench coat. Her new filing cabinets sat like soldiers along the back wall, waiting for her attempt to fill them.

Beautiful.

They were really lovely if filing cabinets could be considered pretty. And to an organizer like Trish, well they were exactly that. They were beautiful. The files were in assorted piles on her desk, and floor, waiting for their new homes, and any final tweaking she would give them.

It felt good--no great. Better than great. Trish was a girl of action and she felt every day, and actually every hour, on this new job was important if she was going to whip it into shape. The shaping had to begin right away.

Things had been neglected far too long. This was an agency she wanted to survive, which meant the agency had to change, or at least grow. It all felt exhilarating--this beginning.

The beginning of order.

Forgotten was the desire to find Mr. Fabulous, Trish was consumed by the challenge of organizing the Greater Expectations office. After all, she'd lived without Mr. Right all this time ...

Organizing? She stopped and laughed. Maybe creating a system based on an idea. An idea that was successful despite the sloppy haphazard way it was run. This was one of the biggest shocks she'd had. Not that the office was a dump, which of course it had been, or that Mike was ready to sneak out, which she was sure he had done, but despite all of that, the business was a success.

Certainly the cleverly written ads did not reflect the interior appearance of the Greater Expectations headquarters, or Mike. Well someone was writing those very effective ads. Maybe they paid an agency, or someone, to write up a year's worth of copy, and had a standing order with the newspaper to just run a new one every day.

It nagged at Trish that there was a disconnect between the ads and the actual business. And Trish had a feeling Mike was no better at matching his clients to each other than he was to keeping the building clean. Or semi clean. Or not infested.

What if clients started wanting their hard earned money back, because there was no magic. Because they were not meeting their dream person, they simply weren't connecting at all. Then where would Greater Expectations be?

And for that matter, now that she'd quit Caterpillar International, where would she be? How long could a company go on if their clients were unhappy?

And Trish knew the answer ... not very long.

Trish was brought out of her day dream by a tapping on the front door. Whirling around out of her office, she scurried to the front door. Hallie smiled and waved, and Trish saw the Hallie Great Furniture truck parked out front.

And grinning like the Cheshire cat, she opened the door.

"We're here and ready to transform the place!" Hallie called out with excitement. The girls shared a quick, somewhat conspiratorial hug, and the delivery men started to lug in the purchases.

Hallie was quick to get her bearings and survey the situation. True to Trish's word, it was radiantly clean and for this Hallie was grateful. She hated to see all her beautiful furnishings go into a musty dusty setting. Suggesting a cleaning service was one of the first things Hallie recommended with most of her clients, whether it needed it or not. No, a clean palate to begin with was crucial.

The magnificent Oriental rug was brought in along with a pad. Both were unrolled. Both Hallie and Trish said "Oo!" It was even more magnificent here, away from all the other rugs.

Next the men hauled in the leather sofa. Hallie pointed. The men placed. On it went. When the grand breakfront was settled on one wall, Trish was beside herself. Finally lamps were lit, and the truck gone.

It had been a blur of unloading and arranging. Hallie and Trish stood in their new room. Even the old coffee pot looked good on its new credenza. Well not good, exactly, but the credenza looked fantastic.

Hallie had two oversized shopping bags left by her feet. "From me," She said in way of explanation, "A thank you for all the business." And she just gave Trish a little shirk and tiny grin.

Trish greedily ripped into the first one. A Krupps coffee maker, and six bone china cups and saucers in the Ralph Lauren plaid and rose pattern. Trish squealed. The old coffee maker and Styrofoam cups went in the shopping bag. Several boxes of Ghirardelli coffee and a beautiful canister to match the Krupps machine completed the gift.

Trish almost cried.

As Hallie placed the new coffee pieces on the credenza, Trish ripped into the second bag. Twelve heavy brass picture frames were unwrapped.

Hallie wandered back to Trish, "For some of your client's photos--for the breakfront."

Trish started to tear up. It was a touch--a classy one. One she was sure the Greater Expectations clients would appreciate. And for those who didn't notice, the overall effect was so stunning even if they couldn't pick out one item. And Mike, well she had no clue if he would notice, appreciate or scream … Trish let a tear leak out, just at the transformation.

The instant transformation.

"Now, don't do that. You know I have ulterior motives." Hallie took Trish's hand and looked her in the eye, "Find me someone in those files of yours. I work around the clock, I'm successful, I have plenty money, a career I love--but I'm lonely," She said it softly because of course it was true. All true. And Hallie was not that different than any number of other career women.

"I know Hallie--so am I," Trish said it out in the open. Not just to Pandora or Maggie but to her friend Hallie, fellow business woman. And once said out loud well, she knew there was no turning back. Hallie nodded because she understood. Lonely was a universal feeling.

"And possibly when some of your clients get matched up and decide to furnish a home they'll think of Hallie Great's Interior Design service," Hallie added just to lighten it all up. Because when all was said and done, Hallie was a business woman. Hallie gave it a sincere laugh--one of hope.

And Trish was grateful for that, because they both wanted to finish the room setting on a happier note.

The girls said their goodbyes as Hallie headed back to her furniture store/design studio and Trish, with one last look at the stunning reception area, headed to her office to really get down to work. The real work she'd been hired for: the sorting, the placing, and the ultimate matching up of Greater Expectation's clients to turn them into happy clients.

Trish started sorting the files in earnest, only to be interrupted by the phone. It was her new boss.

"Mike--I thought you'd be here," She said hesitantly into the phone. Of course, she was glad he wasn't but still. "Golf? You're on the golf course? No of course not--I'm just cleaning," She crossed her fingers as she said this

And did she mind him not being there? Well, not really. She certainly didn't need, or want, him earlier this morning when the Hallie Great furniture truck pulled up, or when she and Hallie were setting the new decor all up. And now, well she needed to get a grip on the files.

But then she felt just a little guilty taking over even if she was a takeover kind of girl. "I thought you'd want to show me what you wanted done," Trish paused, "Anything?" She looked nervously out at the stunning English reception area. It was not to be believed ... "Oh, I can do anything! I'm tidying up er the office and the files. Is there anything special you need help with?"

Mike started a long tirade on some stubborn files that were on his desk. It seemed the owners of said files were tired of browsing the internet site Greater Expectations had by themselves. They couldn't match themselves to anyone, or anyone that they liked, or that liked them.

There was a little clause in the Greater Expectations contract that assured clients that they would be matched by the Greater Expectations professional if they so wanted. Well these clients so wanted, and could Trish take care of it? Because Mike hated to see them suggest, okay, demand a refund ...

"Well, what do I do? How do you match them?" Trish really had her own ideas, serious ideas, but she thought she would make Mike feel as important as she could.

Mike was ashamed to admit he and his cousin did it at random. Unfortunately they had put a fifty five year old woman with a twenty nine year old man once and it turned out she was friends with her date's parents. And that was just the tip of the ice berg.

"We, uh, don't have much of a system for that Trish," Mike confessed. "We always expected the clients to just find their own match on the computer." Expected it, they prayed for it.

Silence from Trish. This was not good at all. This was not ten thousand dollars good. This was not bargain good. This was bad.

"Trish--are you still there?"

Trish saw the word 'rip--off' in neon over her head and her career, or should she say former career, at Caterpillar International down the drain. Bye bye benefits, bye bye sweet vacations, bye bye ever shopping again, bye bye power breakfasts with her pals all for a scam! A scam! An expensive scam!

Oh no! I'm not going to be this age and un-employed! Or employed by a scam! And she shot up a little promise that she was going to turn this agency into the kind of place she had hoped it would be. One she could be proud of--if it killed her.

"Yes Mike, I'm still here. You know putting people together is my specialty--leave it to me. I'm getting the files organized, I'll find them matches. Oh Mike, there's a stack of bills on your desk, a mile high. Should I tackle those too?" When she'd seen the unpaid bills she almost freaked out. Some of them went way back. There was no order. Even the stack was messy.

Now Mike was silent.

"Let me guess--accounting is not your forte. I have a friend at Cat in accounting. She's a genius with numbers--literally. She has some vacation days coming. Would you like her to come in and get those cleaned up and, maybe get you a system?" She asked it gently though she knew he had to get them sorted or she might never be paid. Mind the lights might be turned off. Still she went with gentle.

She could hear Mike let his breath out. They agreed on an hourly rate, after Trish clued him in what a good accountant made, and Mike got over the shock. Trish promised to call Maggie as soon as she hung up.

"Mike--I have a feeling I know the important role you play here at Greater Expectations, but tell me, just what does your cousin do?" Because she really had no clue, and if this cousin was anything like Mike, well when he came back from wherever he was, she couldn't imagine the havoc she'd have to undo.

Mike let loose with a hearty laugh, "Old Cuz is the idea man Trish--why he writes all our ads, and he more or less created Greater Expectations. Yeah, he's the idea man," And he said it with pride.

Trish just shook her head. "I have an idea that your cousin is going to be in for some surprises," She said this silently to herself. "Well Mike--no need to rush back--honestly, I think I have an idea of what all I should be doing. Oh, just one more question. Can I have a cell phone number in case something comes up?"

Because she really thought she just might need to reach him, and she had a feeling she couldn't count on him coming in to work.

Mike let out another breath and rattled off his number.

"I'll take care of everything, and I'll call Maggie. If you need another day or two, Maggie could use your desk. She could do the preliminary and not waste your time until she devises your system."

She could hear the wheels turning in Mike's head. "And I can guarantee you I will have a good start on those files, and that those clients will be happy--very happy." Because she knew this was the least of her problems. Actually, this was her specialty.

"Why don't we give this Maggie friend of yours until Friday to familiarize herself with my system?" Mike was already booking his tee time.

Trish raised her eyebrows. Really, this was how he ran his business? Or should she say didn't run his business! "Right then, Friday it will be. I'll see you Friday. You won't know the place!" She gently put the phone back on its cradle and smiled. No, he won't know the place!

Maggie--I better call Maggie; Trish thought and picked back up the telephone.

"Of course I can take the rest of the week off," Maggie said with glee. "I have more vacation time coming, and earn days, and sick time that I'll never live to use. It sounds challenging and I could use a challenge right about now. Pan and I miss you terribly, and it's only been one day! I'll be there at nine in the morning with fresh spread sheets." And for the first time in years, Maggie felt exhilarated.

"Better bring a shovel Maggie--I think this is going to need some serious digging out!" Trish hoped Maggie sounded half as cheerful when she saw the mess. The mess that was part of the glue that held the Greater Expectations Empire together.

"Don't worry about a thing! That's what I do best. By Friday I'll have it so organized Mike won't even know it. Depending on what we're working with between the cousin and Mike, they can either do basics or I'll be by weekly, or monthly, and keep them going."

Trish laughed.

"And I could use the free lance cash," Maggie added, "And my own peek into the files! Hey, who knows, maybe they'll need me full time."

The girls shared a little giggle and signed off. Reassured that nothing could shock Maggie, Trish crossed one thing off her list and wandered into Mike's office for the files of the unhappy clients.

As Trish thumbed through the first file, she got a glimpse as to the unhappiness. Marge was forty six, and a third grade teacher, never married. Her hobbies were reading, baby sitting, and old movies.

"Poor Marge," Trish thought, "She probably cashed in her retirement money to pay the ten thousand dollar entrance fee. By the looks of her file, no one ever had selected Marge." Marge had selected a construction worker, a doctor, and someone who appeared to just be a play boy.

Trish turned on the computer and brought up the construction worker. Thirty nine years old--well, that was Marge's number one mistake. Loved to hike, play tackle football, and drink. Well, that was Marge's number two mistake. Not a chance there.

She pulled up the Doctor. The age was better, fifty four-- married three times. Well, he certainly wouldn't understand a forty six year old spinster. It appeared the doctor worked around the clock, and also belonged to the country club.

Now what would make poor Marge think he would understand her? Or her career with a work day that ended at three in the afternoon? Marge's hobby was reading. The Doctor belonged to the Club.

Poor Marge.

All wrong.

All hopeless.

Trish wasn't even sure why she wasted her time pulling up the play boy--bad news all the way around. If Marge knew how to pick a man, would she be so desperate? Of course, not but the truth was Marge had no clue ... none what so ever.

But, Trish thought, "I do."

Trish booted the computer back up and typed in Bradley University educators, and then male applicants. A list of Bradley professors appeared before her eyes like magic. Next she picked the age range of ... she took another look at Marge--not bad looking but not kidding anyone with that age forty six thing. She definitely looked forty six, maybe even a little older.

"Okay," Trish thought and typed in ages fifty to sixty. Another list magically appeared. She scanned the teaching professions until something caught her eye. Child development--there were three in Marge's age range. "Amazing!" Greater Expectations really did have a good base of applicants.

Next Trish went back to Marge's file. Birth date: November 12, a Scorpio. Of course, Marge was a Scorpio--a dreamer yet happy with her teaching career. Compassionate of course, romantic--it went without saying. Ambitious--no, not at all, not that this was a good or bad thing—just who Marge was.

Happier, as Marge stated, with a book, or old movies. But Marge's choices? They seemed to reflect a love starved Marge hidden under her school marm set up.

Trish ran her finger down the birth dates of the three potentials. A Gemini--very wrong, too complex, and self--centered. A Sagittarius--not the faithful type and wrong besides. Ah yes, a Cancer. The Cancer man--naturally shy of rushing in yet very romantic. Sentimental, a gentleman, fond of security, and a great compliment to a Scorpio!

Bingo! She read his likes--literature (sounded like Marge's hobby of reading) quiet dinners, the Theater. This man had Marge written all over him. She pulled up his picture: receding hair line, yes, but kind eyes. Tweedy best summed it up; age fifty seven, nice spread, and definitely past the mid life crisis stage, and had never been married.

Now why didn't that surprise Trish? She chuckled. Cancer men couldn't decide and came to marriage late. Well, Marge certainly appeared to have a lot of love stored up. And they could both relate to having never been married. It would be an easy ice breaker.

Trish picked up the phone, "Marge--this is Trish from Greater Expectations. I have given your file serious consideration, and feel confident you would enjoy the company of member 808, a Mr. George Hedges. Yes 808. I'd like you to look him up on your internet sight. I'll be calling him next to suggest he look you up and contact you for a quiet dinner, possibly after a night at the theatre."

Trish was pleased already. She could hear a hitch in Marge's voice. Someone had finally decided to help her. And Trish could also hear the confidence poor Marge had in Greater Expectations. A confidence that Trish was going to single handedly restore or live up to.

Marge sounded so excited, Trish couldn't resist, "Now, I'll get back to you but I suggest you book your facial and hair appointment, and start shopping for a dinner date dress." And she could practically see Marge bouncing off the walls. Shopping and the beauty salon!

Marge assured her she would look at number 808, and that she was already excited to just go shopping and have her hair done.

Well, of course she was.

Trish hung up feeling like, not really God, but well, Mother Nature. She dialed George's number and began her conversation fueled by her talk with Marge.

"George, this is Trish at Greater Expectations. After much serious thought, I've found an ideal date for you. #1112 Marge Wilson. Please look her up on your Internet sight. I've spoken with her, and she is very pleased with our choice of you. Now don't second guess us Mr. Hedges, after all, we are the authority. I suggest you take her to the theatre and dinner. She's expecting your call today. I practically guarantee a match Mr. Hedges."

And with that Trish hung up, and wondered if she should have suggested George take his suit to the cleaners. Well, she didn't want to get too personal, and she didn't suspect that would hold half the fun that Marge would have shopping. No she was right not to mention it. Hopefully he would do it on his own.

The next one was easier. An un--employed female chef with a doctor--someone to cook for. Someone exhausted after long surgeries to be the recipient of complicated fabulous meals. The stars lined up in a 3--11 sun sign pattern that Trish always felt had a strong tie of friendship, mutual trust, and respect for each other's differences. The chef was a Libra; the doctor, as Trish mused so many were, was a Leo. It was a combination she liked. But even better were the careers of these two.

Because she saw a fit.

The calls were made. Trish suggested a homemade meal. Both parties agreed and promised to call her with their thoughts.

Trish polished off the problem files and thanked her lucky stars that Astrology was part of her life. It just made it all go that much easier, though the reasoning was pretty basic with or without the stars. Still ... she liked referring to her books and lining things up.

Things? Okay, people.

The rest of the day was happily lost organizing the files. Occasionally she would take a break and just sit in the new reception area. And sigh. Then it was back to the files. As Trish drove to her empty apartment, part of her was tickled--no proud--of the romances she was sure she'd nudged together. She slipped off her heels and looked in her empty fridge. "I know I can make this work," And she didn't mean creating food from an empty fridge.

***

Maggie came home to her empty apartment. No dog, cat, fish, or man. She flipped on the TV "Ah yes, the company of the national news." She switched it off. She opened her barren refrigerator and found an old yogurt when the phone rang.

"Hi Maggie, it's Trish--I'll see you tomorrow at nine in the morning? I can't wait." Trish wanted to just make sure Maggie had really meant it. And then again, she knew Maggie would be thrilled for any extra income so Trish guessed she just wanted reassurance. And of course when Maggie got there Trish could show off the new reception area.

Maggie assured her she was anxious, and ready, and would see her in the morning.

Maggie perked back up. She was going to work four days at Greater Expectations and sort the books. Organize the books? Create the books? Regardless, it would be fun and challenging. She would be on the inside of the coveted dating agency, doing what she did best--her accounting magic. As her mood brightened she heard a tap on her door.

"Maggie, its Pandora."

Opening the door, Maggie saw another dismal face. Guilt rushed over Maggie. She was going to call Pan and tell her she wouldn't be at breakfast; she'd be at Greater Expectations.

She just hadn't.

Pandora plopped down on the sofa, eyed the yogurt, and wrinkled her nose, "Let's order a pizza! I've brought the finished application, and I want you to go over it before we call Trish." Pan ceremoniously pulled the forms out of her bag. The photos of Jillian were glued on and did look impressive.

Maggie glanced at all the qualities they'd assigned 'Des' and smiled. "Pan this does look good!" Even Maggie was impressed.

"Let's call Trish!" Pandora whispered jubilantly.

"Trish?" Maggie remembered, "Oh Pan--we need to talk. I won't be at breakfast tomorrow. I'm taking some vacation days, and free lancing to do some ones books." There it was out. She'd said it.

"Oh." Pan sank back into the sofa. Breakfasts already were depressing without Trish.

"Whose?" Pan asked idly, more to be polite.

"Greater Expectations," Maggie said apologetically, and grimaced, waiting for the comment or the look or ... but she didn't expect what she got.

Pandora burst into tears.

"Now Pan--it's only this week. I'll be back. Heaven knows I can't quit Cat, what with Mother in the nursing home. I'd have to marry a Doctor for that to happen." She patted Pan's head. And maybe still win the lotto. "Now what was that about pizza? I'll call."

"Oh Maggie, for years I only had you and Trish at work, now with Trish gone, well, I feel such a loss. I was always relatively happy with so little, but now, you gone ..." And Pandora looked like she was sinking--sinking alone.

Maggie did her best, "It's only this week. Honest, why don't you take some time off this week too. Trish said her boss is going to play golf all week. Take some of those vacation days, and just go through the files. Who would know? Just us! And this weekend Jillian comes. She's taking an apartment in my building. We can show her around. I went to a great Pizza place with my new clients from the Bed and breakfast--maybe we could all go and take Jillian--you know a little party--with Pizza? Say yes." Maggie gave it her lopsided grin, with a plea in her eyes.

Pan sighed, "Okay," And dried her eyes.

"Now let's look at that application."

The girls poured over the application for one Ms. Des Jones age forty six. The hazel eyed lover of puppies, who adored people, and sports, and baking, and nature. It sounded like a cross between a Miss America contestant and a Hallmark card. And they were just too desperate to find that could be bad. The photos of Jillian pushed it over the edge.

Was it too sweet? Was there such a thing?

"Who could resist? I ask you?" Maggie stated. "Let's face it, we are the perfect woman!"

Pandora grinned--her mood turned around, "Really Maggie, we have it all! Not to mention a career at Cat with all those benefits. Beauty and income! I feel better already. Maybe I will call in tomorrow, and come check out the files, and meet your friends from the bed and breakfast when Jillian comes." And Pandora let out a deep breath knowing she had a plan that included a few days off work.

***

The next morning found Maggie just a bit nervous. Now this was an adventure, a good one, she reminded herself. Still her nerves persisted. Her tote bag, combination brief case, was loaded with spread sheets and blank books ready to tackle Greater Expectations. Arriving at nine o'clock, Maggie closed her car door and looked at the Greater Expectations building.

"Is this where you're hiding, Mr. Wonderful? In a pile of files just waiting for me to un-earth you?" Her anticipation geared up. Letting out a breath Maggie said, "I don't know why, I'm so nervous."

Trish met her at the door, actually afraid Maggie might have changed her mind.

They were both nervous and happy to see each other. The two girls hugged like long lost friends--friends that shared a common goal, a goal that loomed inside the Greater Expectations building.

The new improved reception area was just the image Maggie had had in her mind all along. "It's hard to believe

Trish that this wasn't here before," She said spreading her arms. "It's just what I pictured an expensive snooty agency to look like." And she loved every little detail. "Why I could live here!"

Trish laughed, "Yeah, me too! I could live here, and this was what I thought it should all look like. You can't begin to imagine my shock when I first came. I actually took a few before photos just to, well, remember. You can thank Hallie next time we see her!"

She led Maggie to Mike's office. "Now this is somewhat untouched by our decorator Hallie; but at least I let the cleaning crew at it."

Maggie blinked back to earth.

Trish hardly noticed because she was just so happy to have Maggie on board. And of course Trish was getting used to Mike's office so there no longer was any shock hitting her. It wasn't quite military, just stark and un--inviting. No art work or Oriental rug. Just one cluttered desk with a credenza behind it buried in mountains of papers.

The old metal filing cabinets from the reception area were lined up on one wall, empty and ready for action. A half a dozen corrugated boxes were also lined up--over spilling with papers. A lot of them looked like envelopes. Envelopes with bills in them that Trish was afraid hadn't been opened.

Trish began hesitantly, "I was rather afraid to call you, but, well, I figured this was really bad, or maybe neglected is the word. Anyway, I knew it couldn't go on."

Maggie just stared. Then she threw back her head and laughed! "Oh Trish, I thrive on this kind of stuff! And this Mike isn't here to interfere?"

Trish smiled.

"Well, then, let me at it!"

And Trish let out a breath she didn't even know she'd been holding.

The hours flew by; all thoughts of hunting for Mr. Right were forgotten as the girls worked. About one o'clock Trish knocked lightly on Maggie's door jam. "I brought big salads and protein bars. Could you use a break?"

Trish had stopped at the deli on the way in to work hoping they might be so involved working they didn't really take time to go out.

"My goodness, I can't believe it's one o'clock! Why I forgot to be hungry!" Maggie marveled at this as she set down a folder.

The two girls moved to the beautiful reception area, like privileged guests. As they sipped their coffee Maggie began, "You know it's not that bad for terribly unorganized. They have their utilities all directly deducted from their checking account. And, they own the building." Both very good things as far as Maggie was concerned.

Trish nodded, "Really?" She said stunned for no particular reason except she just assumed they rented. Maybe it was part of the careless thing.

"They just don't throw anything away. I've filled two trash bags with junk mail!" Maggie sighed at this. "I've had several correspondences that look like complaints, severe complaints for not finding them matches. I've set those aside for you to work your magic on."

Trish nodded absently. She actually found she loved the tough ones--the tougher the better.

Maggie went on, "A few threatened law suits--I put those on top."

This got Trish's attention and she looked alarmed.

Maggie continued, "And they hadn't even been opened." Maggie shook her organized head.

"It also seems they run every expense, personal, and business, through the company, including the liquor store, and the golf course. I've sorted all those into what I call the 'no-no' pile. Those all need to be handled separately, and redirected to the boy's home addresses. I'm sure they won't like that, but if they were ever audited, well, they'd never talk themselves out of most of it. Like charges to Victoria's Secret!"

Trish rolled her eyes. Maggie hadn't met Mike yet but when she did she'd get the picture.

"Can you stand it? Now we know what our ten thousand dollars is paying for!"

Trish sighed a bit of relief for the money she'd spent--their money--decorating. It seemed far more important than a Victoria's Secret account!

"Speaking of our ten thousand dollars, I brought our application, and our bank check." Maggie was so pleased, and she wanted Trish to just give it one last look before they really gave it to the company. Then Maggie laughed. Trish was the company.

Trish perked up.

"Want to go over it, start us a file, and put us in the computer?" Maggie asked shyly. "And let the men start to line up."

The application traded hands like a secret United Nations document. "Lunch is over for me." Trish raised an eyebrow, "You're right; I want to get this right into the computer, and assign Des a number, and give her the access code to our internet rolodex." Trish gathered up their lunch remnants.

Maggie got up, coffee cup in hand, "Well, it's back to the trenches for me. I'm going to sort the rest of the day and just see what's what. Tomorrow I'm going to set up the books. Oh, by the way, I forgot to mention Pandora. She's feeling left out and thought she'd take some time off to go through the files, since Mike's gone. I'm surprised she hasn't popped in." Maggie was sure Trish wouldn't mind.

"I'll call her," Trish said and the girls headed to their offices.

"Oh yeah," Maggie called out, "Jillian gets here this weekend. I thought we could all go to that road house I told you about for Pizza--maybe include Randi and Josie from the Bed and breakfast."

"Great," Trish hollered back already lost in her files.

***

Pandora looked in her mirror at her red nose. "I can't believe I called in sick, and I am sick!" She coughed, blew her already red nose, and held her stomach. "This better just be a cold and not the flu too," She muttered.

Wandering into her kitchenette, she pulled open the refrigerator. The blast of cold air felt good. So good she forgot what she was looking for. Idly she picked up a carton of yogurt, and the very idea turned her stomach upside down. "Yeah, I might have the flu."

Carefully closing the refrigerator, Pandora padded back to her bed. She snuggled under her down comforter and promptly fell back to sleep. The ringing of the telephone slowly brought her back to the surface. Pandora realized she was chilled and thirsty.

And the ringing, what was the ringing? And why wouldn't it stop?

The telephone! How long had that telephone been ringing? Pandora reached for it, sending her Kleenex box to the floor, "Yeah? I mean hello." The phone was heavy.

"Pandora? Pandora are you okay? It's Trish."

"Flu--Trish, I think I have the flu," Pan said humbly. "Everything hurts, and I'm cold, or hot, or both and my nose is running and ..." She really wasn't sure how else to describe it. Pandora just felt awful.

"Dear you have the flu. Now stay in bed. And take some aspirin, and drink plenty of water."

Pandora listened dumbly. How could water and aspirin be the only cures for as bad as she felt?

"Maggie and I got worried when you didn't show up this morning."

"Am I missing all the files?" Pandora moaned.

"No, you're not missing a thing. Actually we're both hard at it, trying to get this place straightened around. Maggie brought the, ah, application, and bank check. Now I have your access code so you can run through all the files on your computer." Trish gave her the access but was sure Pan was too sick to remember. "But sleep now Pan--if you feel up to it later, turn on your computer."

Pandora drifted back to sleep repeating the access number like a mantra, a number that was the key to her future.

It was dusk by the time Pandora re--surfaced. Her throat felt like she'd swallowed cotton, and she was warm--terribly warm. She grabbed a cold ginger ale from the fridge and padded around realizing she'd lost the day. As her head cleared she remembered Trish and Maggie were having fun at Greater Expectations while she fought off the flu.

Trish.

The access code.

Pandora booted up her computer, and put her mind to remembering the access code. It was in there; all she had to do was dig around her stuffy head and pull it out. Typing gingerly she waited.

"Welcome to Greater Expectations exclusive confidential files." The corners of Pan's mouth turned up in a small smile. She sipped her ginger ale, forgetting she was sick and read on, "Your future lies before you. Please type in an age bracket, sex, occupation, or activity that appeals to you. Or type in the word 'index' for all availability."

Pandora stared transfixed. She typed in Des Jones. There appeared her file, well their file, listing their entire make believe qualities: loves to bake, loves nature, and on and on. Next appeared Jillian's pictures. Irresistible, was all Pan could think, especially the one with the puppies.

She could almost hear the phone ringing off the hook. Oh yeah, she thought, we're using Trish's cell phone number. Lucky Trish gets to scan all our men first.

But then she remembered that they would also be assigned an E mail code. She quickly scanned back through Des' file to find 'her' or their new Email code. If Pan remembered the system correctly, prospective dates were to Email their interest before the actual telephoning began. So actually, all three, no four counting Jillian, of them would be able to respond.

Well, they'd have to make sure they didn't all respond to the same Email. But then she was sure there would be so many men unable to resist their file that there would be enough to go around. Plenty.

"We'll need a system," Pandora said to the computer. "When we get mail on our file, we'll all check it out and decide who is best suited. And if we're all suited, we'll rotate. And I'll go first; as I am the shortest, and the sickest." And that alone made her feel better.

Pandora began going through the endless male files at Greater Expectations. She was intrigued, no, mesmerized by what she saw. Even if half of what these men said wasn't true- -well, the other half was quite fascinating. And besides, she knew men didn't lie. Or at least not like women.

Or at least she thought they didn't. Well, actually, she admitted to herself, her dating experience was so minimal, she had no clue. But it sounded right. Pandora didn't want to think men lied.

Pandora fell asleep on the computer keys, the screen long reverted to screen saver.

Chapter 5

The movers huffed with the white washed armoire. "Lady, you're lucky you're on the main floor."

Jillian just smiled, batted her eyelashes, and kept directing the men. Maggie had sent her the floor plan for her apartment but it was still a shock to find her new digs in the quiet brown stone--such a contrast to her contemporary world in Southern California--and oddly bigger. More space for her money. That was a plus right there.

The building was elegant in an old forgotten kind of way. Generous hallways, brass doors on the elevators, parquet wooden floors throughout. Although it was only a one bedroom, with an unbelievably small bathroom, it had a tiny 'den' which was the deciding factor. Ideal for a miniature dark room, because Jillian still loved the old way of printing photographs: the slow way, where she had control.

The magical way.

Besides, Jillian's spirits were so low, she trusted in Maggie and plunged ahead. It would be fun to be right there in her cousin's apartment building. And without Maggie's help, where exactly was she going to start looking on her own anyway? No this was perfect.

As Jillian looked around at the eclectic collection of furniture, and the endless sea of brown boxes, she couldn't quite believe she'd ever acquired so much. "Well once it's all unpacked and snuggled away, it won't seem like much at all," She rationalized to the haphazard piles.

There was a tapping on the open door and Jillian looked up to see Maggie, "Oh Maggie," Her eyes brimming. "I made it."

Maggie gave her the much needed hug. "We've all been waiting for you. Welcome Jillian."

Jillian felt better just hearing the endearments. And Jillian knew she was exactly where she should be.

Pushing back a tear with the back of her hand Jillian managed, "Thanks Maggie, I needed that. I guess I didn't realize how traumatic this move would be. Part of me feels like I'm giving up on Southern California; part of me is excited--like I'm starting over." And of course it was all true, just hard to face.

"Jillian it may sound corny, but you are starting over. This is your new beginning. Let's face it--you just out grew Southern California," Maggie said it gently because it was time Jillian faced it.

"Because everyone is so young!" Jillian whined remorsefully sucking n her stomach.

Maggie looked at Jillian tenderly. "Partly, but I think you're ready for a quieter life, and to be near what little family you have left--namely me. Don't think of it as giving up, think of it as graduating. Besides, what a marvelous place to go back, the museums, the restaurants, and of course the shopping! You may have felt left behind in Los Angeles, but here you are years, no light years ahead of everyone."

Jillian looked encouraged, her huge eyes blinking back tears. She wanted to believe her cousin.

"You aren't giving up Southern California, you're adding to your life. California will always be there." Maggie patted her hand and added, "And a part of whom you are."

Jillian's wobbly smile improved.

"So, are you ready for pizza and to meet Trish, the other corner stone of our joint application, and Randi from the bed and breakfast? Pandora is laid up with the flu."

Jillian grabbed her cardigan and they started out.

Maggie said, "It's Friday night--let's have some fun and get caught up. All this will be waiting for you tomorrow and besides tomorrow is Saturday and I can help."

***

"You must be Jillian," Trish came up the hall; tall and striking with long honey blonde hair streaked a million colors. "I'm Trish." She extended her arms for an embrace. "I feel as though I know you already!"

Jillian felt an instant rapport with Trish. "You know, I've been here just a few hours, and I already have more friends than I did in California." And Jillian just let out a deep sigh.

Maggie smiled, pleased that she could see the beginnings of a friendship just that instantly with her best friend and her cousin.

"Well, you're going to find this is a very friendly little town." Trish's eyes drifted to Jillian's computer. "And once I give you girls our pass word for Greater Expectations --I think it will get even friendlier."

Jillian looked confused.

Maggie countered, "We're cutting you in for one fourth of our composite. After all, your photos are our key." Maggie had a wicked grin. "We'll just divvy up the men!" All three laughed, the strain of the move left behind.

"Trish, you, and Jillian head over to Dinks and go ahead and order our pizza. I'm going to drop off some spread sheets for Randi at the bed and breakfast. I think she and Josie are joining us but I want to make sure she gets these sheets."

Maggie went on to explain to Jillian about the B&B and the sister — in--laws Randi and Josie. "Although they're a tad, okay a bunch younger than us and have husbands, I really like them and think you will too."

The girls parted, regretting Pandora was still sick. Following the GPS, Trish and Jillian talked nonstop all the way to Dinks, almost like a reunion. "You're so glamorous!" Jillian finally sputtered out.

Trish gave a hearty laugh, "You mean for the Midwest--no gingham or braids? We even have outrageous shoes here you know," But, as an afterthought added, "And they're always marked down since hardly anyone gets them."

They both laughed. "Besides, I almost expected you to be anorexic with multiple plastic surgeries under your belt; wearing heaven knows what with rainbow hair!"

Jillian fingered her long honey sable hair and smiled, "So we were both wrong! Good. Because I like you just the way you are, and I think we'll become good friends."

Trish smiled, pleased by Jillian's admission. "But, about the rainbow hair," And she twisted a strand of her streaked, highlighted blond hair and said a bit apologetically, "We all have our own version of rain bow hair--the mingling of all our colors." Trish hesitated. "Because of the application, see?"

Of course Jillian didn't see.

Trish went on, "So; you'll need to get them also. It well, it describes our hair as being all these colors--the application that is." She looked up at Jillian who laughed.

"No problem. I'd love to add some colors--for our cause." And Jillian gave her the smile that had made her tons of money in her youth.

"Great, I'll call the boys at the salon!" Trish knew Ralphy, and Marco, and Pierre would fall instantly for Jillian.

By this time Trish's Tom Tom directed them to Dinks. "Now isn't this charming---a throw back," Jillian started as they pulled up to the Cape Cod cottage turned pizza road house. The yard was filled with picnic tables. Corny Chinese lanterns swung from the trees. People were laughing, and the smells of deep fried food permeated.

"This does look like fun," Trish agreed. "Let's grab a table and we'll get settled until Maggie gets here."

No sooner had they sat down, designer bags plopped on the picnic table next to mustard and ketchup squeezey bottles, than Dink strolled over.

"Hi Darlins--what do we owe the honor of two bee — u--tiful women--I mean Goddesses to?" He was so straight faced they almost just fell under his spell.

Both Trish and Jillian stopped their dialog, unused to even the slightest bit of flirtation, and blushed to their colored roots.

Jillian boldly spoke up, "We're waiting for my cousin. We had reservations under Jones--Maggie Jones."

"Reservations? You girls are new in town, or at least new to Dinks!" He flashed them a big grin. "Why Darlins--you don't need reservations at Dinks. Y'all just sit your selves down and Dink'll take care of you." He almost shook his head but thought better of it--didn't want to scare them off.

"Well, what do you have?" Trish asked hesitantly, not seeing a menu.

"You name it sweetheart--I've got it!" and Dink flashed that big smile again assuring them he had it all.

"I'll have a vanilla mineral water, and maybe some sushi, make that a small order, until my cousin arrives," Jillian started. "And you Trish?" She turned to her new friend. "If you get some organic spring rolls, I'll nibble on one, or maybe a crudités plate."

Dink almost dropped his tray, "Now you ladies have to trust old Dink, I'll go get your order."

"Isn't he sweet?" Trish said absently.

Jillian nodded her agreement.

Dink returned lugging a heavy tray with a deep fried onion blossom, zucchini wedges dredged in hot spices, also deep fried, and stuffed mushroom caps oozing with melted mozzarella cheese. He plopped this down along with a frosty pitcher of what almost looked like flat beer, a couple of plastic tumblers and a fistful of napkins.

"What's this?" Jillian started to protest but Dink was gone.

Trish stared in disbelief, more grease than she'd seen in a life time. A life time of counting calories, measuring portions, and rationing out even healthy foods.

Jillian got up. "I'll tell him there's been a misunderstanding." She rose to leave as Dink came back in view depositing someone else's order.

"Mr. Dink--I believe there's been a mistake," She spoke carefully, in case he didn't understand.

"Nope Darlin--everything's just right."

Jillian looked at him as if he were from another planet. She stared and Dink countered with "Didn't understand me? Should I say it louder or slower?" He winked and moved on. Jillian just let her mouth fall open.

By this time Trish was picking gingerly at the onion blossom with her beautiful manicured nails. "I can't help it Jillian--I've never seen anything like this, why it covers that whole plate, which I also notice is paper. It smells so good, let's just keep the onion." At least she thought it was an onion.

The scent of fried food was not only more than either girl could bear, it was a scent long forgotten, possibly from the carefree days of childhood--before every mouthful directly related to every outfit in their closet; and in Jillian's case, her livelihood as a model.

Jillian looked at the zucchini strips longingly, "I think that's zucchini because it's green, or at least greenish. Or maybe it's a green pepper cut in strips." She didn't know, but since it was green, well she decided there was some merit in it.

Jillian went to pick up a strip and put her hand down, "That Dink fellow forgot our silver ware--I'll go get it." And she quickly disappeared toward the Cape Cod cottage.

"Now little Darlin--what do you need?" The big man seemed to appear out of nowhere. Jillian jumped back almost into a pizza the size of a wagon wheel.

"You forgot our silverware Mr. Dink," She said authoritatively. He reached across a counter and grabbed a fistful of napkins and handed them to her. Before she could repeat her request, Dink was gone.

A little girl sat at a nearby table with the gigantic pizza, watching her. Finally the child spoke, "Excuse me lady, there is no silverware. That's part of the fun of Dinks." And the child gave her a big grin just to emphasis the fun part.

But Jillian just stared at her in shock. Of course, the child couldn't be right ...

Jillian wandered back to their picnic table speechless.

Trish was balancing a gooey mushroom cap over a couple of napkins, heading it toward her mouth. The plate was half gone. "Jillian, I'm sure these are sinful but they are so good! Did you get the silverware?"

"There is no silverware, Trish. They don't use, or maybe don't even have, silverware here!" Jillian could barely get it out. She was beyond speechless!

"Are you sure?" Trish was trying to slide a zucchini stick off the plate, using a napkin like a tiny pot holder. It was sort of working.

"Yes, very sure, a child told me quite clearly, almost laughing at me. Mr. Dink did laugh at me."

"Well Jillian, we are here. And so is all this food. And we are killing time waiting for Maggie." Implying it was probably best while it was hot and sizzling. Trish slid another zucchini stick off the tray. "I think I've got a system."

So, both girls very carefully devoured the veggies and finally got thirsty.

"I wonder what's in the pitcher," Jillian asked. Cautiously they poured out glasses, which of course were plastic, and sipped. "Why it's wine!" Jillian said quite surprised, "White wine!" And then she took another sip. "In a pitcher, like beer!" She looked a little unbelieving. "And it's quite good!"

***

Maggie knocked on the door only to have four year old Annie answer it. The door was opened just a tiny bit. "Hi--Mom said you were coming by." The child grinned up at her.

Maggie looked down at the little elfin child with golden curls. "Oh she did, did she; well could you tell her I'm here." Maggie had no experience with children unless you could count the last time she was here and had met little Annie, the child not afraid of dogs--probably not afraid of anything.

"You're Maggie aren't you?" The child persisted. Then Annie stopped. Maybe she should have called her Miss Maggie. "Well, too late."

"Yes, I'm Maggie." Maggie had no idea how to carry on a conversation with someone Annie's age.

"Good because Mommy asked me to give you this." And Annie slid an envelope marked 'Maggie' through a crack in the door.

Maggie slit it open and read: "Dear Maggie, we had an emergency. I'm leaving the children with you. Can you baby sit? They are both very self sufficient. Please make yourself at home. Jamie and Josie are out of town. We'll be home as soon as we can. Hope this doesn't ruin your evening. And thank you. Randi (and Angus)"

What? Baby sit? She'd never baby sat, ever.

Maggie stared, dumb founded at the letter. Finally she looked up at the crack of open door and the small child watching her. "Annie this says your Mom and Dad want me to baby sit you and Bart."

Annie still stared deciding maybe not to talk at this point.

"Can you open the door and let me in?" Maggie was losing patience--patience with a pint size person.

"What about that I'm not supposed to open the door to strangers?" Annie finally found her voice. She said it in a challenging way, because of course she had met Maggie once before. She was just being clever.

Maggie took it as ornery.

Well, it was both, after all Annie was only four.

Maggie couldn't believe she was having this debate with a child. "Annie, I'm Maggie, your mom and dad's accountant. Now open the door."

Maggie heard a clumping sound and looked through the crack to see Bart. "Hi Maggie, Mom said you were coming by to watch us. Why don't you come in?"

Maggie blinked twice. Children, I know nothing about children! Then Braeburn stuck his nose through the crack. And less about animals.

"Braeburn stay." She could hear Bart command the big golden dog. "Okay," He said with assurance and opened the door. "A lot of ladies are afraid of dogs," He said in way of explanation.

"Thank you," Maggie said, looking around, appreciating his concern. She noticed Annie was gone. Maggie walked in, clutching her canvas tote in case Braeburn decided to get up. The dog was by the fireplace, asleep oblivious to her.

"Come on in Maggie," Bart motioned and closed the door behind her. "I'll show you around, and you can decide what we're having for dinner."

"Dinner--I have to feed these children?"

He led her to the kitchen where she plopped her tote on the table next to a stack of new decorating magazines. "Well, Bart, what did you have in mind?" Honestly, she didn't cook for herself.

"Rice Krispie bars." And he pulled a huge tin off the counter and popped the lid. "And milk," He added as an afterthought thinking there should be something healthy going on.

Well, it was a bit like cereal, and cereal was a meal, albeit breakfast. But hadn't she read breakfast was good all day.

"Okay."

"Okay?"

"Yes, Okay."

Bart couldn't believe it. "Can I eat them by the TV in the living room?"

Now Maggie knew this probably wasn't allowed. Something just told her. "Ah, no--why don't you just sit here at the table." She reached down for some mom authority but found she had none.

It didn't matter; seven year old Bart agreeably sat down, started to take one out of the tin, looked at Maggie and stopped. He climbed on a small stool, opened a cupboard and got out a small dish, hesitated, and got out two more.

She marveled that he thought to get out dishes.

He carefully placed a small amount of Rice Krispie bars on each plate and closed the lid on the tin. Then he got the gallon of milk out of the refrigerator and set it in front of Maggie.

"I can't pour, it's too heavy," He said as if Maggie should have realized this. His eyes darted back to the cupboard and Maggie got down two glasses and poured.

"Annie supper!" Bart yelled and raced off to find his sister.

Absently, Maggie nibbled on a Rice Krispie bar on her plate and opened a copy of Midwest Living. Bart and Annie returned with coloring books, and a gigantic box of Crayolas. They spread out on the kitchen table, eating, and coloring.

Time passed quietly and Maggie thought, "Why there's nothing to this baby sitting." And she was quite pleased. She might even volunteer to help Randi out again--maybe.

Bart was carefully working on a page from Great Trains of the World--a gigantic coloring book.

Annie was scribbling in a 'faerie' coloring book--drawing outside the lines! Imagine! Maggie was horrified. "Annie, you need to color inside the lines," Maggie couldn't help herself, she had to say something.

"No I don't. I'm allowed to express myself, and I'm adding wings to the little girl."

On closer inspection, Maggie saw, sure enough, the scribbles were lacy wings.

"Uh, okay Annie--very pretty." Maggie returned to her magazine realizing she had been a color in the lines, no questions asked kind of child. And she certainly never gave anyone blue hair--she noticed, 'faerie' or not.

The time slipped away peaceably with the coloring.

Finally Bart spoke. "What else can we eat? I'm hungry again."

Maggie looked around the pristine kitchen clueless. "We'll, uh, order pizza," She said. "Pizza, Oh no, I forgot about Trish and Jillian at Dinks!" She whipped out her cell phone to explain to Trish and Jillian and then ordered a pizza.

***

"Trish I think your purse is ringing," Jillian said slowly. Both girls were half way through a huge pepperoni pizza. Several empty pitchers of wine later found them ravenously eating pizza. Had they ordered pizza? Well, they couldn't remember but it had been their plan all along. And it was without a doubt the best pizza they had ever had.

They both stared and finally Trish got it in gear and found the phone.

"It's Maggie--she's not coming. She's, I think she said babysitting." Trish gave it a puzzled look. It didn't sound right at all. Maybe it was code, but for what Trish had no clue.

"Babysitting?" Jillian couldn't picture her cousin babysitting.

"I think that's what she said," Trish slipped the phone back in her Kate Spade bag, and reached for another piece of pizza. Jillian was half way through her modeling career story. And of course Trish was eating it up along with the pizza.

Dink walked by and casually removed an empty pitcher, replacing it with a full one. He could hear Jillian say as he walked away, "It's magic the way that pitcher's never empty. And it's quite lovely. I'll have to ask Mr. Dink the vintage."

Maggie, Bart, and Annie were devouring their pizza in front of the television, in the living room. Maggie had brought a roll of paper towels with her and felt, well, it was a special occasion and there was an old Disney movie on neither child had ever seen.

Annie had her favorite afghan and was wrapped up like a papoose, able to sneak a little pizza in her mouth. Maggie had draped her in paper towels just to play it safe.

Bart was fascinated with the animation and ate aimlessly. But both children were quiet and contained, so Maggie felt she was doing her baby sitting job. Maggie dozed off and on catching herself, her magazine slipping on the floor. Annie had protested going up to bed, and Maggie didn't see any harm in letting her drift off in front of the TV.

The cartoon was over and the old Haley Mills Parent Trap was running. Bart was intrigued by the idea of twins. "Are those twins?" He asked. So far, he had never met any.

"Well, yes and no." Maggie really wasn't used to having conversations with children. "It's actually one person playing twins. She's playing two parts."

"Are twins really two people who look alike?" Bart asked.

"Uh huh," Maggie said looking at an article on relationships in Better Housekeeping.

"Then why didn't they use twins?" Bart asked stubbornly.

"Bart, I don't know. I think Haley Mills was very popular back then and they wanted to use her."

Unsatisfied, Bart resumed watching.

Without warning, Braeburn started to bark. "Quiet Braeburn," Bart called out, glued to the TV. The dog continued.

Maggie cautiously pulled her feet up on the sofa. Finally Braeburn marched up to Bart and barked for all he was worth. Bart threw an arm around him. "Braeburn old buddy, calm down."

Maggie looked nervously at Bart and the big dog, and finally stood on the sofa in fear. "Bart, something's wrong." Braeburn continued to bark. "Where's the other one Bart?" Quickly thinking of the old Lassie movies where Lassie came to get Timmy to save the day. At that point Braeburn started tugging on Bart's pajamas, Lassie style.

Annie watched fascinated, now fully awake. "Go with him Bart. Follow him."

The young boy put a hand on Braeburn's collar. "What's wrong buddy?" And the two of them rushed to the kitchen, Annie right behind.

The barking had stopped and Maggie debated whether or not to get off the sofa. "Maybe I'll just stand up here a little longer," She thought. It was safe up on the sofa.

But she couldn't because Bart started screaming, "Maggie! Maggie! Maggie! Honey Crisp is dying!"

Maggie jumped off the sofa, all fear forgotten, and ran to the kitchen. Honey Crisp lay on her side on her old blanket moaning quietly--little dog yelps. Maggie rushed over to the big canine. The other dog stood next to her on guard.

"Maggie! Don't let Honey Crisp die!" Bart wailed.

Annie was crying hysterically.

Maggie and Honey Crisp locked eyes. The big dog looked in pain, and turned to Maggie with a look of pleading for help. "The vet! Bart, who's your vet?" The vet had to be the answer, whatever the question was.

Bart stopped crying. "I don't know." Then he tried to collect himself and squeezed his eyes shut.

"Dr. Bob--it's Dr. Bob!"

Great, Maggie thought "What's his last name?" Bart didn't know. "I'll call any vet;" Maggie thought and spied a list of phone numbers magneted to the fridge. Running over she saw "Dr. Bob emergency number." Well this was certainly an emergency. Honey Crisp was not about to die on her watch. As a matter of fact Honey Crisp was not about to die period.

Maggie grabbed her phone, "Dr. Bob--Dr. Bob, this is Maggie Jones. No, no, of course you don't know me. No. I'm babysitting for Randi and Angus MacTamara, and it's one of the dogs--we're afraid she's hurt or dying! Could you please come out?" Her heart was racing.

What would happen if Randi and Angus came home and found she'd let Honey Crisp die? How would these children ever get over it? And what about the other one, the bigger dog, weren't they a couple?

Dr. Bob assured them he'd be there in five minutes.

Maggie froze. This dog cannot die in front of these children — or on her watch for that matter. Finally she snapped out of it. "Annie, I want you to go to the door and wait for Dr. Bob, and holler when you see the car. Bart, I want you to sit down and pat Honey Crisp's head real gentle and talk to her."

Hadn't she heard him talking to the dogs last time she was here?

Annie flew for the front door. Bart crouched down until he was sitting next to Honey Crisp, tears rolling down his face. He patted her head and cried. Maggie watched, fear gripping her heart. Unconsciously, she sat down with him and raised Honey Crisp's head onto her lap. The dog looked at her with trust and love. And her heart split.

Bart started talking to her quietly in his little boy voice, "Honey Crisp this is Maggie, she's afraid of dogs." Maggie patted the dog's silky head and kept eye contact with her. "But, I think she's not afraid of you Honey Crisp. We're going to save you. Dr. Bob's coming. He's on his way."

The gravel crunched under Bob's tires. He jumped out of his van, doctor bag under his arm, and ran up the steps. Annie swung the door open and yelled, "They're in the kitchen."

Dressed in worn jeans, and a sweat shirt, his dark hair tousled as if he'd been asleep, Bob raced down the hall. There he saw her. A crown of sable curls, bending down over the big yellow dog.

She raised her tear stained face to him. "Thank God you're here," She said in a small voice. "Please save Honey Crisp."

Bob dropped to his knees, "Honey Crisp old girl," And patted her back. Honey Crisp continued to tremble, panting, heavily. He looked at Annie. "Can you get a stack of clean towels?"

And the little girl ran off.

Bob opened his bag and started getting out instruments, the whole while talking to Honey Crisp in a soft gentle tone.

Bart's chin quivered, "Is Honey Crisp going to die?" He asked Dr. Bob, fear in his voice.

"No Bart, Honey Crisp is going to be a mom," Dr. Bob said it softly but with confidence.

Maggie started to sway--Bob reached over and took her hands in his and looked in her eyes, "And you're going to help."

Fear rose in Maggie's eyes.

"Maggie's afraid of all animals," Bart said to Bob, and then turned to Maggie. "But you have to help." Then he paused, "Please."

Bob squeezed Maggie's hands. "We can't move her--it's too late. I need your help Maggie," He said her name with such tenderness Maggie simply nodded.

"Good." Bob looked relieved. Honey Crisp started to strain, doing her part, and in a blur the head and paws of the first puppy started to appear. The complete delivery took about fifteen minutes.

Maggie held the new tiny life in the palm of her hands while Bob broke the amnionic sac with his fingers. Bob held the puppy in his hands, supporting the head and moved it in a wide arc. Maggie froze. "To clear the fluid," He said. He then rubbed the pups chest and body with a towel. And the young pup gave a little breath of life and tiny yelp.

They no sooner got the first new life tidied up and settled with Honey Crisp when the process began again. Honey Crisp helped now, freeing Bob from the job of breaking the amnionic sac. Tears of joy streamed down Maggie's face as she and Bob helped Honey Crisp give birth to four tiny little pups. None of the other three needed Dr. Bob to 'jump start' them as Maggie put it, as he had with the first, the weakest.

They were exhausted. Fear had been replaced with wonder and all of it had drained Maggie.

Even Dr. Bob looked tired.

The kitchen was a wreck. Towels were mounded around them, and still they sat next to Honey Crisp, and watched all the new life, and the extremely tired mom dog. But on closer inspection it appeared Honey Crisp had a little smile going on. The babies were so tiny and adorable Maggie couldn't help but grin and cry at the same time.

The pups were settled with their mom and automatically Maggie and Bob started the endless clean up, all fears set aside. They had done it. Not only had Maggie helped save Honey

Crisp, she had brought new life into this world. It was an exhilarating feeling. One she was sure she would never forget.

Annie was asleep; Bart could barely hold his head up. "Come on big boy, let's go up to bed." Bob picked up Annie in his arms and held out a hand for Bart. "Lead the way Maggie. It's been a big night for all of us."

Maggie's heart was in her throat as Bob tucked Annie in her bed. The room was all softly lit pinks and fluff--Annie's safe haven. The child's stuffed animals were all lined up on her window seat. Bob selected a well loved bear, and tucked it in with Annie, and then gave her a little feather kiss on the top of her blonde curls.

"How about a ride Bart?" Dr. Bob asked the sleepy boy. Bart climbed on Annie's bed and clung to Bob's back, piggy back style. He carried Bart up to the attic and settled him in his bunk. As Bob turned the light out a little voice called out, "Thanks Dr. Bob."

Bart knew Dr. Bob had not only saved Honey Crisp but that he had literally performed a miracle. One he was never going to forget. And Maggie had helped, despite all her fears. He owed them both. He sighed, exhausted.

Maggie met Bob in the hallway. Together they walked down the stairs to the kitchen. Silently they continued to clean up their make shift hospital. What had been panic and chaos was now contentment.

Braeburn slept next to Honey Crisp and their brand new pups. Maggie looked over at them tenderly. "We did that," She said shyly.

Bob came and stood behind her, gently placing his hands on her arms. "Yes we did--thank you. Let's keep an eye on the happy family for a little bit longer. Can you make us some coffee?"

Maggie rummaged around until she found coffee and the coffee maker. They sat with their coffee steaming in mugs, exhausted. She tore her gaze from the pups to Bob. "How do you think the little first one is? The one you had to jump start breathing?" Maggie had shot up a little arrow prayer for its life.

Bob gave a hearty laugh, "Maggie, you say the funniest things. I think she'll be okay." They both looked over at the four little miracles, and then he shifted his gaze to her. "Is Bart right? Are you afraid of all animals?" He asked tenderly looking over the rim of his mug at her pixie face framed in tousled curls.

Maggie felt the color rise up her cheeks, "I guess I am. I've never been around any." She looked into his almost black eyes not sure what was more startling, the fact that she helped a dog give birth, or that a startlingly drop dead man was having a coffee with her in the wee hours ... It was a tossup.

He reached for her hand across the table. "I guess you can't say that anymore."

And that's how Randi and Angus found them, holding hands gazing into each other's eyes. They broke apart quickly as Randi and Angus stepped into the kitchen. "Bob?" Randi started hesitantly, "We saw your van ..." And then her eyes fell on the new mom and her babies, the proud dad asleep next to them.

Randi dropped to her knees, "Oh Honey Crisp--you had your babies!" Tears of joy filled her eyes. "Angus--we're grandparents!"

Angus gave a short laugh. "And this from the woman who was deathly afraid of animals not so very long ago!" But of course he was right there with her, looking tenderly at the new family.

Maggie felt embarrassed, as if she were invading a very private moment. "Well, I better be going," She started to get up. "The children are asleep." What a stupid thing to say--it was dawn; of course the children were asleep. "And I'm glad you and Angus are back. Everything okay?"

"Water line broke at Bix and O. T.'s farm," Angus said, he looked exhausted. "But it's finally under control."

Maggie gathered up her tote and purse, and fled to the door, no longer sure of her role in this intimate setting. Bob rose to follow but Randi and Angus started in their thanks for delivering Honey Crisp's puppies.

And Maggie was gone.

Chapter 6

Trish stretched her arms above her head, weary from studying the computer. File after file. Endless files. She'd taken it upon herself to start matching people up not just leaving them to their own devices. Not waiting for them to call or write unhappy.

Of course she would still encourage any, and all, of them to look for themselves, but she had a feeling that once the initial excitement of getting their hands on those files wore off, they were stuck. Of course they were stuck. If they were so good at figuring it all out they would never have come to Greater Expectations to begin with.

Then Trish stopped, because if she was so good at it, what was she doing here? Why had she plunked down her hard earned cash? And then it sank in, oh yeah, it was hard to find these people. Dates were hard to find. Men were hard to find, mind work out the personality quirks.

Trish had looked everywhere she could think of, and then some, exhausting a lot of places. No luck. How could Trish apply all her methods if she couldn't even find any? Men weren't lined up on the grocery store shelves like groceries. Except, actually they were, only the shelves were files--files at Greater Expectations.

Trish started with some of the companies earliest clients, figuring they probably were discouraged trying to make their own matches. After all, they'd had a chance now, and somehow hadn't found their heart's desire in the files. And did they even know what their hearts desire was? Deep down? New applicants were few and far between and with the initial outlay of money, who could blame anyone for not signing up.

So, her rational was it was just possibly that some of the earlier applicants occasionally looked at the files for new faces, and when they didn't see any they gave up. They figured they had looked over all the old ones. But by Trish's way of thinking, maybe they hadn't looked close enough.

Maggie was stopping by on her lunch hour to review the books with Mike, who was due in at nine o'clock. It was seven. Trish had come to work early for a bit of quiet time since she knew Mike was due back. She wanted to feel calm and confident when he walked in the front door ... to the new office. The new look, the clean look, the updated quality look.

Trish knew the furniture was the right decision; there really hadn't been any choice as far as she could see. Not to mention the cleaning. That was a given. Time would tell what Mike thought. It could cost her the job that she was just starting to sink her teeth into.

"Of course he'll love it. Still ..." For just one second Trish second guessed her use of his credit cards. After all, maybe he never noticed how dumpy and dirty the place was. "Well he had said take over ..." Still she bit her bottom lip, and told herself she better keep busy. She couldn't hold her breath until he came in.

"Maybe I'll try to match up Des," Trish said as a hopeful distraction. "After all, we did plunk down our ten thousand dollars." But, like probably everyone else she wasn't sure where exactly to start. So, she thought about her birthday.

"Let's see, as a Pisces, I'd be thrilled with a Cancer or Scorpio, happy with a Taurus. Probably not mind an Aries, only because I like them, but he'd probably run rough shot over me. I guess I'll rule that out."

"Maggie is a Leo and I think she'd be very compatible with an Aries or a Sag--even though Sag's never seem to settle. Although Sag does eventually settle and I guess we're at the settling age." She talked to herself almost as though she was trying to solve a puzzle, a complex one with four parts. And in a way she was--a human puzzle.

"Pandora is a Capricorn, and I've always thought she needed a Taurus, outgoing and gregarious. Even though Virgo is compatible for her, they're so precise, and critical, and poor Pan doesn't need the criticism. No, I'll just look for a Taurus for Pan." That was a good place to start, and she'd see what the computer coughed up.

"Jillian is so strong. Well, that's Aries--a leader. She needs strong back at her, maybe a Leo. It's too bad Sag just doesn't like to settle down." She thought about Jillian with all her glamour and all her strength. Jillian needed just the right man.

"Okay, I'll surf for a Leo for Jillian, a Taurus for Pan, an Aries for Maggie and maybe a Scorpio for myself. I guess I might pass on a Cancer. They traditionally always want what they don't have. And I don't need that. So, I'll stick with Scorpio." And then she realized she was back to her old method and laughed. "Well I'll see what I can do." At least now her old method had a computer file full of other lonely people ...

Looking at her list she realized it was rather limited. Well limited or not, it was a starting point. She booted up her computer and typed in male, age forty six to--fifty nine Aries. A small list appeared. She hit their files and print. She repeated this for Taurus, Leo, and Scorpio. Her stack grew and she set it aside by her purse for evening reading. And hoped after some serious reading she would have some good suggestions for her friends.

"Well, before I really get back to work, I'll check Des's file and see if anyone has noticed our girl." She typed in the password and saw there were five responses. She hit print file for all five and let her printer work. And wondered just exactly who Des had attracted.

As the printer whirled, she heard screaming--her name to be exact--coming from the reception area.

"Mike! Rats! I meant to be by the door! Well, time flies when you're looking for Mr. Right!" She raced out of her office to the reception area despite her tall heels.

"Hi Mike--welcome to Greater Expectations!" She said rushing over and linking her arm through his. "Now don't freak!"

Mike looked like he was on the verge of a heart attack!

"Sit down; I'll make you a cup of coffee." She guided him to the leather sofa. Or maybe she shouldn't give him a stimulant?

"Trish ..." He barely got it out. He was pasty looking. And angry, of course that went without saying, but more just shocked.

"Mike--you said I could do what I want!" She said with determination mustering up her confidence. "And you have to admit, it desperately needed an over haul!" Which she felt was the kindest understatement she could make. And then she held her breath.

Mike took a deep breath and started to growl.

Trish patted his hand and looked him right in the eye and added, "We couldn't have people come in here to find their life mate (she tried to emphasize the life mate part) the way it was, could we?" Before he could speak, she went on.

But actually up until she came along he thought they could.

"At the prices we charge, we have to look the part! Besides, I got a new client while you were golfing last week! And I took care of all those problem files of yours, and they are all beaming," She paused, "And say they'll be referring." She hoped this part would get to him because she had a feeling he had no intentions of dealing with the problem files and complainers.

Mike softened. Trish was so darn pretty, and seemed to have everything under control, and well, he had to admit, it did look impressive--very impressive. Like the place he would want to come to looking for his life mate. Or come to work at.

"And how much did all this cost?" He tried to sound authoritative again, knowing he'd already lost the upper hand. Still he felt obligated to say something.

"Your accountant Maggie seems to think you can afford it. Also, she's come up with a million ways to save you money!" There, that sounded good, Trish smiled triumphantly. Before he could react, she took his hand. "Come on Mike, I'll show you what I've been up to." And she took him into her office. Her CD player softly played Jim Hart's newest CD about finding love.

They reviewed the new filing system and Trish proudly showed the results of the difficult files, including notes she'd made on happy telephone conversations.

Mike couldn't quite believe what she'd done in such a short time. His mind was still reeling from the front reception area. But as he read a few of the happy comments from their clients he had to be impressed.

"I've started going through the older files Mike, and hand picking dates for people. I seem to have a knack for it." Trish beamed because as far as she was concerned this was the fun part of her day.

"I'll say you do." Mike was impressed with the glowing compliments he read.

"I have a little system of matching their common interests and uh, other things." She just wasn't ready to admit astrology played a big part in her choices. And was it really astrology or just personality compatibility? Okay, it was astrology.

And with that Maggie appeared. With her elfin smile and crown of curls, she looked up into Mike's eyes, "I'm Maggie, your accountant. I know you're going to love your new system." She led him to his office. Before the door closed she could hear Maggie saying. "I've saved you thirty percent already with just the smallest changes."

Trish laughed as she booted up her computer. Maggie was so good she knew she didn't have to worry about a thing. So, she let her mind drift back to work.

"But I want to run everything through the business," Mike whined sounding like he was twelve or maybe thirteen.

Maggie was ready for this because basically everyone wanted to run everything through their business. They thought it was one of the perks of opening and running a business-- didn't matter what kind. "Michael, you'll be audited. Yours is a very visible company. You need to follow a few basic rules. If you are audited, you'll be red flagged, and you'll never have peace--ever. That red flag never goes away. Listen to me. That's what you're paying me the big bucks for." And she stood firm, even though she was tiny and sweet looking.

"I'm paying you big bucks?" He asked cynically. Why hadn't he been paying more attention when Trish arranged it all?

"Yes Mike, very big bucks. So listen to your professional. You wouldn't fill your own teeth would you?"

Mike raised one eyebrow.

"Of course not, you'd go to your dentist. Well, you know you need a professional for these books. There's a lot of money just sitting, not working for you, a lot of deductions you're not taking, and several foolish things you're doing."

Mike squinted at the foolish things comment but Maggie ignored it and plunged on.

They continued to work well past Maggie's lunch hour. As it got even later Trish turned her own desk light out and heard them still closeted. She overheard Maggie practically shouting; "Now I know you'll be thanking me when this is all set in place."

And she knew Maggie was probably starving and exhausted. And Mike was probably wishing he hadn't come in off the golf course, even though it was his business. Well, his and the absent cousin ...

Trish decided not to interrupt. She was tired--tired of putting people together, and going home to an empty apartment. This was Maggie's war to win with Mike. And by the sound of things, Maggie seemed to be winning.

As Trish headed to her car, the idea of a deep soak in her tub, maybe in Lavender bubble bath, appealed to her. Just enough time left in the day to stop at Fairchild's for some April's Cottage and Nancy's Garden Lavender bath gel, and maybe some lotion ... and maybe a snack, just a little one.

Her car headed to the tiny English shoppe. The same Jim Hart CD she had been playing at work played quietly as she let herself in. It was comforting. Bone tired, she waved absently to

Jinx who was deep in conversation with a man by the counter. A man with dark almost black hair in a short pony tail was describing something to Jinx in great detail. A pile of packaged cookies sat on the counter between them.

"No, these were thick, chewy, and crunchy at the same time Jinx. And there were unusual combinations; white chocolate and dry cranberries with macadamia nuts, raisin and chocolate chip with pecans." He looked exasperated. He looked back down at the pile of packaged cookies Jinx had pulled out for him, and just shook his head no.

Trish over heard this conversation as she headed to the bath section looking for her lavender. And that voice--oddly familiar. She found her lavender bath gel, added a couple fat bars of French milled soap, and got in line behind him.

"Jinx who ever made those cookies--I'd make my queen!" He was practically swearing an oath.

"Dink, you are so silly. They sound good though." Realizing Jinx wasn't going to sell anything she had, and of course, enjoying just seeing Dink away from the restaurant.

"Good? Good? Jinx! These cookies keep me up at night!" Then he composed himself. "Let me make a little room for one of your buying customers." And embarrassed by his outbursts and ranting he stepped aside.

Trish laughed as he moved over. As he turned he recognized her from her evening with Jillian. "Well Darlin!" He began and Trish blushed to the tips of her blond streaked hair.

"Oh, you know each other?" Jinx piped in happy to have the cookie quest over.

"Well, not exactly," Trish began. "Jillian and I ate, or should I say drank at Dink's Saturday evening." What she could remember of it.

"Trish this is Dink. Dink--Trish." Jinx offered in way of keeping in the conversation. She really hated to ever miss a thing.

Trish discreetly raised a hand to Dink which he immediately clasped in his big bear paws, and instead of shaking it, just held on, "Nice to formally meet you Darlin. And your friend, did she survive a night at Dinks?" His eyes sparkled now; all quest for cookies put aside. But of course Trish had that effect on men.

Jinx watched it all, impressed.

Trish blushed and nodded.

Jinx interjected, "Trish works at Caterpillar in Human Resources Dink, in case you ever want to give up the food business and get a real job." Jinx's eyes twinkled as she knew Dink worked around the clock--beyond around the clock.

"Well," Trish began nervously, "I've actually quit Caterpillar." There it was out. It was time, because she was never going back to Caterpillar no matter how great the benefits. No, she was having far too exciting a time rebuilding a business. It was almost as though it was her own business.

As a matter of fact, that was how she thought of it. Mike was just an adorable guy who showed up now and again and had to be dealt with. Like a puppy or a child. No, it was starting to feel exactly like her own business. And since she had redecorated and now was turning around the files, well it was her business ... almost.

"Quit Cat with all those benefits?" Dink and Jinx spit out in unison--both being self employed, both knowing what a job at Caterpillar meant. Benefits, sick time, vacation time, wonderful conditions. Not just a starting time but a quitting time at the end of each day, as opposed to the endless hours a self employed person put in. And Caterpillar, well it was an institution. People clamored to work there. They didn't leave there ...

"Well yes, I er took another job. Another Human Resources job," She paused, slightly embarrassed but plunged on, "At Greater Expectations." Again, out there. And this time it felt a little easier--just a little.

Jinx and Dink's chins both dropped. They were basically speechless; first of all the quitting, and then the Greater Expectations part.

"No!" Jinx could barely mouth it. Her mind reeled with the possibilities--all that insider information. She forgot about Caterpillar's health plan and focused on those files, and all her lonely friends … and friends of friends.

"Well, yes, it seemed like opportunity knocking and …" Trish tried to explain, knowing she was never going to get it right. How could she explain how exciting it was to clean up a mess and then rebuild it?

"The files--you have unlimited access to the files!" Jinx's mind was stuck on those files--those files that cost ten thousand dollars each. She thought of little Bart's second grade teacher and how lonely she was, and Royal's twin brother, the shy one, Hale, and then Jinx just couldn't take it in any more. It was too much. It was Christmas. It was the lottery. It was the lottery on Christmas.

Trish cringed because of course that was exactly why she took the job--to get her monies worth and more. To get her hands on all those files--all of them. "Well, now Jinx you know that wouldn't be the most ethical thing in the world to do …" And she tried to look ethical but of course that wasn't working either.

"Nor the worse," Jinx added and Trish relaxed and laughed. Because of course Jinx was right.

"Well, okay--you're right!" She hated to admit any of this in front of Dink but the conversation was like a snow ball--out of control, gathering momentum. Trish looked at Dink from under her lowered eye lashes, giving it her best 'I'm not desperate' coquettish look.

And he picked right up on it, picked up on the fake-ness of her look. "You Darlin--You can't find a man, a glamorous dish like you? What about your gorgeous friend, how about her over flow?" Dink teased, because as stunning as Trish was, Jillian out did her by a long shot. Together they were show stoppers. Even old Dink had been impressed when they had sauntered into his restaurant. He really thought a couple of men were right behind them.

Trish blushed again and her eyes started to cloud. She fought it but it was just too hard.

"You mean to tell me that knock out friend of yours is desperate too?" Dink was struck by the unfairness of the world. How could that happen? If a gorgeous girl like that couldn't find men, a rugged bar keep like him would never find anyone.

"Dink!" Jinx started, "We don't like the word desperate." She hesitated, "It's so desperate." And she glared at him.

And he had the decency to look a tiny bit reprimanded. Because of course Jinx was right. No one liked the word desperate.

Trish pulled herself together, looked Dink in the eyes and said, "And your social life Dink? At least you're at that great ..." She groped, not wanting to call Dink's a bar, "Uh, establishment where people flock. You have tons of opportunity to meet people." And she gave him her wide eyed look that said he was literally in the land of opportunity.

Every day.

Every night.

Dink actually looked a little ashamed of himself, because he was in the land of opportunity. But for whatever reason it didn't seem to come his way. Or he go its way, or whatever. It just didn't seem to work that way at all.

"Ah ha--the pot calling the kettle black!" Trish said with gusto realizing she had struck a nerve. But when she saw the look in his eyes she knew she'd gone too far. Then she clasped his hand in hers. "Truce, let's be friends, and if I find any one-- er illegally in those files, I'll send them out for pizza," And she finished this up with her sincere smile.

Dink's face broke into a huge grin, "Now you're talking Darlin. And ol' Dink'll keep you in pizza for life!"

Trish groaned, grabbed her miniscule waistline, and they both laughed.

And a friendship was born.

***

At home Trish laid out the five files that had shown interest in Des.

"File number one 'Gus' code #18341.
Birth date--August 28--Virgo
Hair color--Brown
Eye color--Brown
Height--5'11"
Weight--170 pounds
Marital status--Divorced
Number of children--0
Children living at home--0
Date someone with kids--Maybe
Occupation--Investor, Developer
Smoke--No
Date a smoker--No
Drink--Socially
What I like to do--

I'm one of those lucky people who get to do exactly what I've always wanted to do. I buy parcels of land, engineer subdivisions, build the homes and create neighborhoods. I've been into nutrition and fitness most of my adult life and take pride in my appearance.

Dining at fine restaurants is a passion. An excellent dinner on a Saturday night is a reward for getting through the week. Golfing is my favorite sport. Teeing off at seven o'clock on Sunday morning is my favorite thing.

Who I am-

I'm a conservative man who enjoys an active, healthy life style. I'm a morning person who likes to get up and see the sun rise.

What I'm looking for-

I'm looking for an attractive confident woman who carries herself well. I'd like to meet a woman who is successful in her work. I'm interested in meeting someone who is optimistic, upbeat, outgoing, honest, sincere, caring, and affectionate; someone who knows who she is, and where she's going. She should be an independent woman yet know how to share. Finally, I'm looking for a woman who is wholesome."

Trish read the file twice. Her initial thought was wow this guy sounds too good to be true. Then she read it slower, more carefully. "Well, if he's a nutrition junky, he wouldn't work for her sweet little baker Pandora. And if he likes to tee off at seven in the morning on Sunday--well, long term, one of her friends would be a golf widow. And let's face it, this whole project is to eliminate being alone."

"He could go for Jillian but she just gave up her photography career to move here. But that doesn't mean she isn't going to start another. How successful at a career does he imply? We're all out going, sort of; optimistic, sort of; upbeat, sort of; honest, semi-sort of; sincere, sort of; caring--well yes, we're all caring. Affectionate, who knows, it's been so long since we've even dated. But we could be. Yes, we could all be affectionate."

"Wholesome--are any of us really wholesome?" She thought of her own high maintenance and addiction to designer clothes, and her perfectly polished nails--"No, I guess, I'm not wholesome. Ditto for Jillian. But Maggie, she's semi wholesome, and Pandora--very wholesome, but not physically active, or into nutrition."

She glanced off into middle space, "This Gus sounds like he wants a Hallmark card--not a woman! But, he's better than anything we've found pre Greater Expectations. Okay-- he goes to Jillian."

"I'm banking on his Leo attraction to her Aries, even though he's a Virgo--which works with none of us. It's close to Leo. But close doesn't mean Virgo has a Leo personality ... poor logic. What am I thinking? I'm not thinking. We're desperate."

But she had to decide. And knew she was breaking all her own rules by not just calling him what he was, a Virgo. And a sign that was not a Leo.

Picking up the phone, she called Jillian. "I think I've got a date for you. Turn on your computer and pull up #18341. Call him. And don't forget your name is Des." She didn't wait for Jillian to give her an answer or even a comment.

No, Jillian was a big girl; she could figure this one out on her own. And if she didn't like him, fine. This was what dating was, the going out and seeing, the trying it out. It wasn't all going to work, and certainly not the first time. So, she hung up without another thought, and went back to her stack.

Trish went through the other four files, deciding two sounded fair for Maggie and two for Pandora. She had no interest in any of them. "Oh well, next batch, and that's not to say I can't find someone's file and contact him," Because at least she would be screening it for every little detail that made sense to her. And she liked being proactive. It felt better than waiting for someone to show an interest in her.

***

Nervously Jillian picked up the phone. Now was as good of a time as any to plunge in. After all, wasn't that the whole purpose of this dating agency Greater Expectations? Well Trish, had given her the home telephone number of Gus, file #18341.

"Hi Gus, this is Jillian, er Des." She paused and listened, "Well, it's actually Des Jillian. I go by Jillian, though." She let out a breath, not starting out too good. "Yes, I'd like to meet ... for coffee at Barnes and Noble." And we can decided on dinner from there she thought. It could be a really long evening; at least coffee at Barnes and Noble could end with any number of excuses. Like her cat needed her at home, or she'd left the water running, or some other stupid excuse.

No dinner. If she was half way through the fish course and she felt stuck, or couldn't stand him which meant she would feel stuck--well, there'd be no escape. Not until dessert ...

Tomorrow? He wanted to meet tomorrow. Was he desperate? Well, she was, so Jillian agreed on tomorrow. And after she hung up the phone she decided that wasn't so hard. Not good. No great vibe from Gus, but not bad. And at least she had something to look forward to, a date for coffee.

Tomorrow.

***

Pandora looked at her two choices for dates. A computer geek and an agricultural engineer read farmer. "Hmm," She thought, "I kind of like both options. I'm addicted to my computer and I love gardening--even though I live in an apartment. I love reading about gardening. Okay, I love looking at the pictures of gardens. Gardening, farming--isn't a farm just a bigger garden?"

Of course it was.

There was a time Pandora would have turned her tiny turned up nose up at both of these options. Sadly, that was a long time ago. Not that she'd ever really had that opportunity, if she was being honest with herself. Today it looked good. It looked go — out — and — splurge — on — a--new--outfit good. And out she went.

***

Jillian decided to wear the floral skirt from the photo--minus the puppies. The skirt said romance. She paired it with a soft pale blue cashmere sweater. The sweater said lust. One look in the mirror had her add a blazer--for the career part of her request list. And maybe to cover up the cashmere sweater just a little bit, just in case. High heels were always on her list so she just slipped into a pair that matched and thought she had it covered.

"Well, it would have to do." She gave her glorious long honey blonde (and now accented) hair a quick toss and headed for Barnes and Noble.

Early.

How could she be early? Why when she'd been a model a million years ago she'd always been late--dramatically late. Well now she was older and desperately early. "Maybe I'll just shop for a book and kill a few minutes." Because she knew if she left there was no way she would be coming back.

The romance novels all reminded Jillian of what she didn't have, histories were too war like. The cook books looked too much like work, ditto for the gardening books.

She found herself deep in the self help books lingering over 'How to Find Your Soul Mate in Six Months or Less' by Heather Rockingham. Taking it to the checkout counter, she discreetly slipped the bag in her purse and headed for the Café. And figured if it was an early date she would have something entertaining to read later.

Thank goodness the file had a picture. Jillian spotted Gus lingering over a black coffee. As she approached, he got up. Knowing their picture was vague, even though it was her, she boldly made the first move.

"Excuse me, are you Gus?" She asked it sweetly with a bit of forced confidence. She knew she looked good, better than good. Still this was a whole new world for her. And a world she wasn't even sure she wanted to venture into. Okay, she did.

His face went from pensive, to relief, to a big smile.

His picture hadn't lied; five feet eleven inches, nice looking in a conservative kind of way, short brown hair; pleasant, no outstanding glitches. Big brown eyes--the kind you could lose yourself in. She could do this. "I'm Des Jones."

They both breathed a sigh of relief and began talking.

"Aren't we silly to act so nervous?" She said in way of an ice breaker because of course she meant it.

Gus laughed, "Well, I'm new at this." And as good as he looked he looked even a little better humble.

"Really? You're my first date since I joined Greater Expectations," She admitted, and they settled in to their lattes. Conversation was lively but surface. Still it was nice. Jillian wasn't sure if it was cautious, but then she almost laughed out loud at herself. Of course it was cautious. It was all cautious. That was part of the game.

"Would you like to go to dinner?" Gus asked in way of extending their time.

"I'd like that," Jillian answered trying not to sound too eager. They settled on a nice little French restaurant. True to his file, Gus liked good food.

He told Jillian about his dreams to be a builder starting with his Lego's as a young boy, and how his fascination grew over the years from summer jobs apprenticing with carpenters, to business classes at Yale. Ultimately his fascination for building extended into becoming a developer, and then an investor. His story ended as Jillian pushed a Crème Brulee around with her spoon--full to overflowing with food and information about Gus.

At one point while Gus took a break from talking to chewing, Jillian let her mind drift to the calories she was absently packing in. Calories she knew she hadn't wanted, and would have to really work to get rid of. At that point she listened and just fiddled with her food. And Gus's life story continued to roll out in front of her like an endless buffet. He hadn't seemed to skip any of it.

As they parted to their respective cars, Jillian sadly pictured a hot bathtub waiting for her and maybe a few Ibuprofens.

"I'll call," Gus said with gusto. He flashed her that great smile that early in the evening had been so inviting.

Jillian merely flashed her smile and was gone, safe in her car.

She drove aimlessly trying to let the evening soak in. "Pleasant--yes it was pleasant. Almost like a refresher class in construction. Yes, that's what it was like." Cliff notes. Cliff notes on a subject she really had no interest in--details that meant nothing--too many details. "I hope I didn't say the wrong thing," Jillian mumbled as she pulled into her space at her apartment.

By the time she was neck deep in her bubbles in her tub it dawned on her, "No, I didn't say the wrong thing, I didn't say anything."

Well, old as she felt, she obviously wasn't too old to be a decorative sounding board for Gus' ego. "Why hadn't he asked me what I like to do? I never had to tell him I was starting over, or that I'd just moved here, or why. I hadn't made it sound like I was giving up on California because I didn't even have the chance to talk about it. Why he even ordered my meal for me, which I hated."

It wasn't the meal itself; it was the taking charge of her meal that she didn't care for. Part of the fun of eating out was picking and choosing. Her picking and choosing part of the night had been taken away from her, along with her opinions and thoughts.

And as she thought this over a sadness washed over her because she wanted more than that--a lot more. And the longer she dwelled on it the sadness turned into just a little bit of anger for her not forcing herself to jump in and talk about herself.

And then back to sadness because Gus hadn't wanted to hear about her. Or if he did, why didn't he ask? Or even give her a chance to catch his breath and let her slip in? And what were the common grounds? She couldn't come up with any. "Other than his nice eyes ... And how long would they look nice? If we were to get together our common ground would be Gus." And Jillian knew in her heart, she wanted more, just a little more.

Okay a lot more.

Jillian's new book 'How to Find Your Soul Mate in Six Months or Less' lay on a hand towel on the edge of the tub. She sank deeper in the warm water, and after drying her hands carefully on a wash cloth, picked up the book.

Gently she cracked the cover trying not to get water droplets on the pages. Flipping around as was her nature, she settled on a chapter called: 'The First Date' and read:

"It is imperative to treat the first date like a job interview. Remember at all times, you are investing your time. You may be lonely, but your time is precious even if you don't think so. You are older; your job consumes large chunks of your time, and energy. There is less of it—energy and time." Rude, but true, Jillian read on thinking this Heather person made sense.

Then she stopped. Does this book imply I'm dropping dead in a few years? And as she soaked she knew, of course not, it meant she just didn't have the endless time she'd had in her teens … or twenties. Or even in her thirties. That's what it meant. So, she read on.

"Conversation should be like ping pong--back and forth, back and forth. If you do all the talking this is a sure sign you will end up with a sounding board and no conversation. Conversation is one of the elements we crave in a relationship (See Chapter 6)." Jillian thought she'd have to see Chapter 6 because this book was right; she wanted someone to talk to.

"If he does all the talking, ask yourself, why am I here?"

"Why was I there? Oh yes, I am desperate!"

"Are you so desperate you are willing to be talked at, talked to, but never talked with? Do you want to team up with such a big ego there is no room for your opinion, your inner thoughts. Or worse yet--he doesn't care!"

And Jillian thought she had just spent an evening with someone from Chapter 6. And the book was right, she didn't like it. If she could have been asleep with her eyes open would he have noticed? And she thought maybe not.

"Conversation, pay attention to its flow: back and forth, happy subjects, important subjects; not depressing ones. You are not his shrink. This is not his chance to vent his life of misery, or an opportunity to solve his problems. You are his potential life partner. This is supposed to be fun, stimulating, invigorating."

Jillian sighed and read on, "You want to hold on to his every word, anxiously waiting for the next one. Remember our motto--'The first date is the best date'. Well this is his best effort. You are new. He wants to impress you. Don't feel impressed? Well, that was his best effort! It will only slide downhill from here."

Jillian set the book down and with her toe lifted the plug to the tub. Her first date was pitiful, she sighed, and fattening. Not to mention boring — very boring. That possibly won out over fattening.

Chapter 7

Devin, Mike's absent cousin, couldn't believe how great a cruise could be--endless ports, endless chicks. Blue sky, bluer waters, and nothing to do but mingle.

And mingle is what Devin did best, "A blonde for breakfast, a red head for lunch, a lovely brunette at dinner. A blonde for the floor show, a red head in the bar; a brunette to walk the deck with under the moon light ..."

So, why did he feel so disconnected? This is exactly what he wanted. And everyday he'd start it all over again. The faces blurred. The conversations were all the same, short and shallow. The only thing that deepened was his tan.

It had been one and a half weeks of repetitious pickups, and his tan was a glorious bronze. His overly long blond hair streaked by the sun, his body baked by it, and his mind fried.

It couldn't be Dev was losing his touch. Women were practically magnetized to him. But he wasn't magnetized back. Oh, attracted yes, and flattered. Of course he was flattered. That went without saying.

But in the past ten days not one of the women he'd met asked him anything past his name. And usually just his first name at that. Devin had planned to try out different careers on the women he met, not being comfortable with the truth. He'd practiced lawyer garb, and doctor phrases. He could toss around architect jargon.

No one asked. No one to toss his planned lies to. No one cared.

They liked that he was tall, blonde, and bronze. The same types of things he actually liked about them. He had spent years mastering the small conversation. Conversations that said nothing, gave nothing away--let no one in. No ties. No bonds. No entrance.

"Look but don't touch. Well touch yes, but don't feel anything."

So, what was the problem? Why wasn't it working for him? Well, it was working but it wasn't satisfying. It was like eating handfuls of cheap chocolate when his mouth wanted to savor one fine piece of Belgian chocolate. Or drinking cheap Scotch when he knew there was a bottle of Glenlivet stashed somewhere.

It shocked him to realize he wanted someone to know him, and then like him, because they knew him. Look past his exterior. Take a peek inside. Like what they saw. And talk about it. And banter it around.

Question.

Tease.

Encourage.

He wanted someone to stimulate his mind, his body would follow.

And listen. He wanted to listen, and be listened to. He wanted conversation, real conversation.

Where had this all come from when he'd spent years perfecting superficial? Avoiding traps? He'd been so smug not to get snagged as he called it. What about all those things people asked for on his Greater Expectations applications?

The things past appearance like does she like opera, or rock and roll, or both? Or walks in the snow, or follows politics, or indulges in hot dogs from street vendors? He'd never asked. He'd never cared. He never thought he needed those questions, let alone those answers.

Yet his clients paid ten thousand dollars each to find someone who could answer those questions for them. His clients, from his business, which had started as a scam to make money, and find chicks. Faster money than if he'd ever started that psychology practice he'd thought as a child he wanted.

He referred back to that innocent boy who wanted to understand people, study how they ticked, and help them. Back when life was as innocent as he was, before he knew heart ache, hatred, or the living hell that existed for some people. And then there was the fear that he'd fail them, and their ever so big needs--a fear big enough to make him think twice about his chosen field.

Well, he'd been right. A psychology practice wasn't for him. But years of drifting weren't either. It was too bad his dating agency was just a scam, randomly sticking people together. The only calculated thing he did was depositing their checks.

And now that he and his cousin were making money, how could he give that up to do what? He flipped over on his lounge chair. He didn't know what. Didn't know what he really might like to do, or if he had the nerve to go after it. And if he had what it took to make it work ...

Dev did know he'd been trapped on this floating singles bar long enough. He was ready to go home.

Chapter 8

Maggie didn't want to get 'the' book, but Jillian made it sound like a 'must read' so she headed over to Barnes and Noble. While there she snapped up copies for Pandora and Trish too-- might as well have them all on the same wave length. "There was a time I would have been embarrassed buying a self help book," She told herself. "Mind three copies!" But that was a long time ago, a very long time ago.

The clerk had snickered a little as she put them in the bag but Maggie didn't care. Maggie looked at the all of eighteen year old clerk with pity and thought make the most of it while you can honey, your days are numbered. You'll be my age in the blink of an eye. And your attitude just won't work anymore.

Maggie headed back to her apartment and started debating what to wear for her big date with Stan. His application was a little vague and his picture a little fuzzy, but then again, it was a night out. She couldn't blame him for not having a great, or even good, photograph. Well she could, but it might be harder for a guy to come up with one--a good one. She laid out her black dress--safe, and then thought she'd just curl up with her new book for a few hours before she got ready.

And read: "If you want to meet your soul mate in six months or less you need to get serious. You need to treat the first date like a job interview."

"Hmmm," Maggie fussed. "That's an odd approach." Job interview--she basically forgot what a job interview was like, she'd been at Caterpillar so long … But she read on.

"You don't have time to waste if your goal is a six month period. So, on your first date ask some simple questions-- questions that might take weeks, or even months, to find out. And if the answers don't measure up, neither does your man.

We're talking finding your soul mate, here, not just a warm body."

Maggie sighed, even a warm body sounded nice. But in her heart she wanted a warm body on a permanent basis. A temporary one would only make her all the lonelier. No, the book was right. She wanted a soul mate. Now Maggie's attention was alerted because the book hit it on the mark. "That's right!" She said out loud.

"Question number one (that you would boldly ask him)-- Have you been married before? (We are assuming he is single now). A reasonable question anyone might ask. But; you need to add the follow 'up' question. How many times? Don't be shy; remember you are interviewing your potential soul mate. If his answer is more than once, put him mentally in the question mark column. If it is more than twice, read that as trouble. You could be number four or number five, and probably not the last."

"Put a little x in your mental file." Maggie sighed, was that really a bad thing? Maybe he was a victim or or or … well she didn't know 'or' what. And then she shirked. Of course, the book was right. She didn't want to be number four, and then possibly discarded for number five. No.

So, she read on. "Now that wasn't so hard, was it?" Maggie rolled her eyes. "Next it would be a natural to ask if Mr. Potential has children. Such a common question, he may ask you also. But let's add our soul mate spin. Remember you don't want to waste your time. Ask how many children he has, if any of them still live with him (we are assuming if you are reading this book your age bracket and his would reflect a man with grown children). If you fit into this category continue on, and ask him what his children do i.e. employment? Are they employed? This is important to find out early."

Gee, Maggie thought it was getting a little personal. Of course, wasn't the idea of this whole dating thing to get personal?

Still, the book had a point about children living at home. Maggie didn't want to finally have that dream man, and have to share those intimate dinners she had always dreamt of with grown children. And what about their dates? If they were old enough to still live at home but 'grown' would they be bringing their dates home? For over nights?

Would she be doing laundry for a house full, cooking for a gang, grocery shopping for a group? What about those cozy Sunday mornings sitting around in their bath robes, nibbling on breakfast or each other ...

If there were grown children living with them she knew she would be far too intimidated to do that. She'd stay in her room, like a teenager herself. And suddenly Maggie was sure she didn't want a man with children living at home. Not grown ones.

"How wonderful could Mr. Wonderful be if he has two adult unemployed children living with him--more than likely he's supporting. Translate that you will be living with and supporting. If this is the case, no matter how sweet the reason, you know where to put the x."

Maggie saw her meager pay check getting even smaller. Not only was she supporting her mother in the nursing home, if she married a man with unemployed children, she would be supporting them too. And even if she knew better, she would probably like them and want to. No, she was not ready for that complication.

"Now's the time to ask about his employment ... It goes without saying there are degrees of acceptable jobs for your soul mate. 'Unemployed' does not have a column."

Maggie just nodded her head yes to this because she knew how many hours she put in day in and day out. How tired she was at night. How strung out she was by Friday night, and how precious her Saturday and Sunday days off were. How could she relate to an unemployed man?

And if he was retired at an early age, wouldn't his mind need more stimulation? And if he was the right age to retire, were they the right age for each other? Or even on the right page? No, she needed a man who worked. She didn't need to start a relationship out with resentment.

Maggie was engrossed. She skimmed on to a section called 'ordering dinner.' "Maybe I'll skip that; I know how to order dinner."

The subtitle was 'Ordering Dinner. Do not skip this part!'

"Okay, I'll read it!" And she just glared at her book but read on.

"The ideal first date is a dinner date. A dinner date gives you weeks, even months of insight into your potential soul mate if you know how to order dinner correctly."

Here Maggie laughed. Of course she knew how to order dinner. Skip the bread, dressing on the side.

"Rule number one--Order a drink. If your date does not order a drink boldly, but sweetly, ask: Are you a recovering alcoholic? If the answer is yes, and you find yourself in an age bracket where time is slipping away, ask yourself: Do I have the time and the energy to help a recovering alcoholic? Place your mental x accordingly. It is possible he may answer he is an alcoholic--no recovery word mentioned. Remember the AA creed--once an alcoholic--always an alcoholic. Possibly he will say he refrains for religious reasons. Weigh this. Or that it affects his medication. All reasons you need to pay attention to."

Maggie's eyebrows shot up. Okay, she'd keep reading.

"Rule number two--Order an appetizer, even if you are on a diet. This is simply to see if he is cheap. If he winces, well there you go.

Rule number three--Order beef. If he doesn't follow suit, ask him if he objects to eating red meat, or has health issues. He could be a well dressed cardiac patient with more bypasses than a highway. Do you want an unhealthy soul mate after all your work? Possibly he is all patched up and healthy. Still you would like to know. Did he order greasy fries or the broccoli?

Ask if he likes vegetables. You may team up with him and have to buy a Fry Daddy to feed him."

Maggie held the book tight and read on.

"Rule number four--On to dessert. Order it even if you push it around your plate. If he doesn't order dessert, ask if he's diabetic. If he says yes, just weigh the baggage that goes along with that. Will you ever get to eat a chocolate chip cookie again if he's the one? Will this condition shorten his life, and your time together or worse yet, his ability to perform in the bedroom? All questions you need to consider. There is also the possibility he is cheap (refer back to the wincing when you ordered an appetizer).

Now that your dinner is almost over check for a few more things. Did he rush? Can he relax? Did he share the conversation? Did he steal peeks at the big screen sports game? These things can tell you a lot. After all, when you find your soul mate, dining out is a nice part of your new life together. A part you have been missing as a single."

She nodded sagely.

Then Maggie looked at the clock in horror--just enough time to pop in the shower, get ready, and meet Stan at a restaurant called 'The Berquest.' How had she gotten so lost in her new book?

***

Stan was already at their table. When Maggie told the hostess the name on the reservation, she was led right to him. He got up and a look of pure pleasure spread on his face. Maggie's first reaction was that he looked better than his picture. Brown hair, conservative yet not buzzed, and blue blue eyes--great eyes.

"I'm Maggie--er Des Jones. Des Maggie Jones. Everyone calls me Maggie."

He grasped her hand and their eyes locked--so far, very good.

And she let out a pent up breath.

She noticed he had been drinking a mineral water. And after she sat down, he proceeded to hold it, moving the little plastic swizzle stick around and around. The waiter came up for her drink. Maggie was prepared to order her usual no calorie diet soda but something clicked. "Thank you, I'll have a Manhattan." She wasn't even sure what a Manhattan was. It just rolled out of her mouth as if she drank them for breakfast.

The waiter turner to Stan, "And you sir?"

"Another mineral water."

When the waiter left, Maggie looked over at Stan. He smiled at her and she started to melt. Then her new book clicked in. She couldn't do it, could she? And with her new found resolution she got brave.

"Are you a recovering alcoholic?" She asked meekly. Then shot up a prayer he wasn't.

He looked so relieved she thought he was going to hug her, "Yes Des, er Maggie, I am. I've been sober nine months, twenty two days and five hours. I'm so glad you understand."

And she saw him sigh.

Maggie was shocked. She didn't want to know this at all, especially the hour part. That implied he thought about it every hour. Gingerly she said, "I hope it won't bother you that I ordered a drink?" A drink she really didn't want. Calorie wise, and not to mention trying to keep her head clear, so she could follow along her new book.

"Oh, of course not."

So gracious Maggie almost believed him.

But at that point their drinks arrived and he looked at hers like a starving man.

Slowly Maggie sipped, "To us," She said feebly and let the alcohol seep into her. Fortified she went on, picking up the menu, and then she smiled up at him. "Stan, tell me a little bit about you." She read the menu as Stan started to talk.

"I'm a free lance artist--I work out of my home, so my hours are my own, and you?" He said it with pride.

But Maggie heard something entirely different. Something she never would have thought about had she not read her new dating manual. He's home all day, every day waiting for work, not a good sign. Maggie sighed, "Oh, I'm an accountant at Caterpillar--you know, little office in that big building."

Now she was trying to make jokes. His smile came, and she noticed his teeth were very straight and white--possibly bleached. It added to his overall good looks. "Have you ever been married?" She heard herself ask.

He nodded a yes.

In for a penny, in for a pound, Maggie sipped her Manhattan, which was really quite good, "How many times?" There, she did it.

Stan looked shocked but Maggie tried to throw in her little girl look that in her youth had been charming. He shrugged, "Three or four times."

He didn't know how many times he'd been to the altar? Maggie gave a little choky sound on her drink. She couldn't help it.

"I married my first wife twice, so I'm never sure how to count it," He said in way of explanation.

And Maggie tried to hide her question mark. Obviously marrying his first wife twice was still not quite getting it right, because he was single. Again. Or at least she assumed he was.

At this point the waiter returned and Maggie ordered the first appetizer on the menu. Stan declined and she coquettishly said, "Then we'll share mine." As they started on the Brie baked in puff pastry, Stan ate with a voracious appetite. Cheap, too cheap to order his own.

Poor Stan--yet so sexy. And she saw a future with a cheap man that she would have to support, unless he decided to marry his first wife again, just for old time's sake.

Lost in his deep blue eyes as Stan gave some kind of recount of his unhappy days as a married man, Maggie actually felt sorry for him. His stories were sad, and in all honesty, they were starting to depress her. He had problems. He seemed to take them with him from marriage to marriage. And she wondered if she spent more time with him if it would all be depressing.

The waiter came for dinner and of course Maggie ordered the petite fillet of beef. Stan ordered the chicken. "Don't you eat beef?" She asked already afraid she knew the answer. The answer had to do with five bypasses, and a something else she didn't understand. She understood his heart was shot. Or at least shot like.

"Well, I do, for very special occasions." What else could she say? She actually didn't eat a lot of beef because keeping her weight down was easier with chicken. They seemed to eye each other's meats with true envy.

"Do you have any children Maggie?"

Now Maggie was pleased, one of her next questions brought out into the open, and happy that he was making an attempt to get to know her.

"Sadly no--but I do love them," Then as an afterthought added, "All ages. Do you?"

"Why yes I have two boys--chips off the old block." And she could see the look of pride in his eyes. It actually endeared him to her.

"And are you lucky enough to have them at home with you?" Bold, something she never ever would have asked--ever. She was never bold. She was becoming bold, because she wanted to know, even though he already had quite a few, well too many, strikes against him. Still it was good practice, and she had to be able to get it out.

"As a matter of fact I am." He seemed like, if not a good dad, at least a proud one.

"And what do they do?" There, she got it out.

"Well, Bruce is in graduate school. He just thirsts for knowledge. And Billy, well, he's just finding himself. I feel so close to you Maggie, I can tell you ..."

Please don't, she prayed.

"Billy had a tiny problem but now that rehab is over, he seems to be coming around." Stan looked relieved to be able to spill his guts--even if it was ever so subtly.

Maggie looked at his chiseled face with regret. She immediately thought of her favorite Freddy Mercury song 'Barcelona'. When she walked into the restaurant it started. 'I had this velvet dream. This dream was me and you.' As dinner progressed so did the song in her mind. Slowly Stan let his stories unfold. 'Wind as a gentle breeze. The bells are ringing out.' Maggie pushed back a tear of regret. The bells were all warnings.

She duly ordered her dessert and wasn't surprised to find out Stan was a diabetic--actually the least of his problems.

As the waiter discreetly brought the check, Maggie reached for her lipstick in her purse and quickly pulled out some bills. She clasped Stan's hand in hers, and looked into those melty blue eyes. "Stan," She began, "I had a wonderful time."

She hesitated and then went on, crossing her fingers, "We both took a chance tonight, and as much as I enjoyed your company, I'm sorry to say there was no real chemistry between us."

"No chemistry?" Stan looked bewildered. He was positive he was going to get lucky.

She shook her head. "But please, let me pay for my dinner." She pulled the crumpled bills off her lap. "I insist," And then fled. Her last sight was of Stan unfolding her money.

***

Pandora looked at the book Maggie had dropped off for her: 'How to Meet Your Soul Mate in Six Months or Less.' There wasn't time to crack the cover. She flipped it onto her bed and it fell face down. The back cover blared out at her.

"Looking for Mr. Wonderful? Appearances may not be important but initially they're all you have to go by. They are telling. What are they telling you?"

Pandora opted for black--a simple dress that she thought made her look taller and glided over her thighs. Black is safe she told herself. She added pearls, also safe.

She was meeting Harry at the Italian Bistro. Heaven knows her thighs didn't need pasta but he hadn't asked about her thigh diet.

All phases of dating intimidated Pandora, and the idea of walking into a restaurant alone was daunting. As she gave her hair one last brush she decided just a nip of the brandy she used in her baking, just a nip, might get her out the door. No sense in spending all this money, and then being too chicken to down two fingers of Napoleon.

Pandora just knew as the maitre d' showed her to Harry's table that this was a bad idea. Granted she was no movie star, she wasn't even Jillian, or Trish, but she thought she had a sweet almost pretty look. The man she was walking toward was geeky. Was that a problem? Hadn't she implied, okay said, she was desperate?

And he wore a pullover sweater that zipped about six inches down the front--an acrylic zip sweater.

An acrylic zip sweater--that didn't look too clean. She was sure there were some un-coordinated poly pants hiding under the table. Sure enough, the only thing that matched was the pilling on his trousers.

Oh, this is going to be a long night, she sighed to herself. "Hi, I'm Des," She was afraid to use her real name--afraid she could be traced.

Harry smiled, introduced himself and Pandora sank in her chair.

Maybe I can just order antipasto and skip the pasta she thought.

"I've taken the liberty of ordering for us," Harry began.

What? Was she three years old and couldn't read a menu? Don't make waves, she told herself, eat, and escape.

She had antipasto as a starter, and some kind of exotic pasta for dinner. But as dinner progressed, Pandora discovered

Harry was interesting and sincere. Her stomach groaned but she ignored the discomfort while listening to Harry. His life had been one fascinating phase of construction after another, and Pandora found herself thinking he's really a nice guy.

She pleaded off dessert.

"Can I see you again Des?" Harry asked.

Pan hated anything that sounded confrontational but knew she had no future with Harry. "Harry, I honestly had a great evening, but I don't think we have any chemistry." Pan had to be honest with herself.

"Are you sure? Maybe it's too soon to tell." Harry began rather desperately. Pan's heart broke just a bit.

She reached over and took his hand. "No, I don't think so, but I think we could be friends," She paused and then added, "How's the agency going for you?"

Harry shook his head, "Horrible. You're the closest thing I've had to a real date since I started."

Pandora's sympathy went out to him—she knew what it was like to be lonely, very lonely. "Harry, at least your construction career seems to be going very well. It's only 8:15. Let's go to the mall--as friends. And window shop."

He brightened to her idea. He got up to leave with a glimmer of hope and followed Pandora to the mall.

As they walked in together Harry said, "You know I've been here all my life and I've never been to the mall."

Pandora just raised an eyebrow. They headed over to Macy's, past the endless cosmetics, to the men's department. Harry just went along. They stopped at the Ralph Lauren area and Pandora started pulling shirts, and sweaters, and trousers off the racks. She had an armful and finally asked Harry to help her carry some.

"Where are we going?" He asked, looking confused.

"You are going to the fitting room. Come out in the first outfit," She said it with authority she didn't even know she had.

'Outfit', Harry hated the word, and the word 'fashion'! He was, after all, in construction. But fortified by his wine, and the cute date he was on, he dutifully headed into the fitting room.

He emerged in khaki trousers and an olive drab Faire Isle sweater over a brown check shirt. He came out very reluctantly.

"Amazing!" Pandora said almost in glee. She aimed him toward a threefold mirror. "See how great that color is with your hair? And how good quality clothes look on you! Go try on another outfit." And she knew there was hope for Harry. Not with her, but hope for him.

He came back out in faded denim jeans and a pale grayish blue pullover. Underneath was a pin stripe blue and white shirt. "Fantastic!" Pandora exclaimed almost dancing around.

Next was a rusty brown tweed jacket with leather elbow patches and brown trousers. The shirt was a classic tartan. Harry looked at himself critically in the threefold mirror. "You know Des, I look pretty good," His whole posture had improved.

"Pretty good, you look fabulous!"

He beamed and bought the lot, and as they dragged them out of Macy's Pandora took a turn left.

"Des, our cars are to the right," Harry motioned, engulfed in shopping bags.

"One more stop Harry."

His chest started to tighten as she walked into a trendy mall hair salon. Not her regular, but it would do. "Des, I go to a barber," He said it with almost a plea in his voice. And then for just one split second he thought maybe they were there for her.

"Yes, I guessed you did. But tonight you're going to get your hair styled," Pandora said it as nicely as she could.

She sat patiently reading fashion magazines while Robert, the stylist, took charge of Harry. The side burns went much to Harry's protests. The hair was shaped and cleaned up. Robert held up a mirror and Pandora jumped out of her chair to look.

"Harry! I can't believe it!" Harry looked back at a face he hardly recognized. He was wearing the Ralph Lauren denim jeans and sky blue sweater. He had debated whether to pack his original clothes, or toss them, but ultimately his practical side kicked in and he had the salesman bag them up.

His new hair minus side burns, and his subtle quality clothes made such an impression one of the young stylists came over to comment. "Looks great," She said with puppy admiration in her eyes. Pandora just raised her eyebrows at Harry and smiled, nodding in agreement.

They practically closed the mall, and as they headed toward their cars, Pandora began. "Harry, try again at Greater Expectations, and see if your first impression isn't better. You're a fascinating guy, and really kind of cute with that hair cut."

"But not for you Des?" He asked sincerely.

"Somehow I see us as friends Harry," And she meant it.

"You know I think I do too," Harry had to admit. He felt at ease with Pandora. And no one ever had given him any advice on any subject, let alone dressing. Before they went their separate ways Harry stammered out a thank you that Pandora knew was from the bottom of his heart. And she felt yes, it had been a good night, very good indeed.

As they parted, Harry headed to his car whistling.

***

Jillian had five more dates based on hits on their joint file. She stuck with her simple plan of meeting them at Barnes and Noble Café for a coffee, and determining from there if she wanted to go have dinner. They amused her, insulted her, bored her, but none of them tweaked her. It was just that simple. Jillian knew she'd know it, or feel it, when it happened.

But so far nothing.

As she got ready for one more date, she leafed through her closet. The basic black seemed to be the simplest answer. A Donna Karan knit sheath--plain, curvy, and sexy in a non committal way. "Just what I need," She thought. "Something I can pull over my head and go." Gone was the endless fussing over her outfit. Still, she went.

As she wandered to the Café bar at Barnes and Noble, the basically eighteen year old over--pierced counter boy smiled at her. His being there was as much a part of her Greater Expectations experience as the actual dates. "The usual?" He asked, meaning a low fat mocha latte.

"Yes." She smiled sweetly at him. "How are you today 'Jason'." She read his name off his tag.

"Great--hey, I was wondering if you were busy Saturday?" He read the odd expression in her eyes and hurried on, "No, no--not for me."

Jillian laughed a low throaty purr and smiled. "What did you have in mind Jason?" And she gave him a sincere look.

"Well, my Uncle is coming in town--actually he's moving here. And I thought I could hire you for the night. You know, to welcome him. That is if you're not too expensive." And Jason had the decency to blush.

Jillian's jaw dropped. Hire her, if she wasn't too expensive? Oh no, Jason saw her meet men here at the Café a couple times a week ... "Why he thinks I'm a hooker!!"

She was mortified! Amused, possibly even flattered would come later, but at the moment she was mortified! "Uh Jason-- you have it all wrong. I'm er not for hire." Jillian felt herself blush to the tip of her nose.

Jason just looked at her. "You're not?" He asked smoothly. More smoothly than she thought an eighteen year old had mastered.

"Jason, I joined a dating service to meet men. I'm not a hooker, I'm desperate!" She decided she needed to come clean. Be honest.

Jason's mouth dropped open. He was sure--so sure. She was glamorous. Better than glamorous, for old that is!

Tears formed in her big eyes and she fled the Café, leaving her low fat mocha latte cooling on the counter. As she started to rush out, she bumped straight into a short older bookish man. "Oh no, my date!"

"Excuse me, are you Des? Des Jones?" He asked hopefully.

Swallowing a snuffle, Jillian looked him right in the eye, "No, I'm sorry, I'm not," And raced to her car. She drove without thinking until she was safe in her apartment tucked in her bed.

Then she cried.

***

Devin sighed. It felt good to be back home and off that singles cruise. Back in his condo with his big screen TV, and his refrigerator full of beer. "I suppose I ought to call Mike and check in at work," But he got side tracked.

He booted up his computer. Using his Greater Expectations password, Devin typed in new applicants, female. The list started to scroll. Devin leaned back in his chair, thinking of all the bimbos from the cruise.

He sighed, "I'm pushing fifty. Maybe, just maybe I'm shopping in too young a market." It pained him to admit this to himself, but not as painful as the last two weeks had been. He typed in new applicants, female in their forties. He just couldn't type in any older--fearful; of what the computer would bring forth.

Just because he was pushing fifty, well fifty two to be exact, didn't mean he wanted to meet a woman in her fifties. Old, tired, wrinkled, fat, bad teeth, bad hair--his mind whirled with ugly images. No, no fifties for him, not that he even knew what the fifties looked like.

He would be the first to admit he had laugh lines that added character, women had crow's feet that that ... well, he didn't know what, because in all honesty, he'd never even thought about it. And he didn't want to. And he certainly didn't want to look at it.

Mind date it.

His idea of a beautiful woman was tall, leggy, with a great head of hair--preferably blonde, and a figure leaning to lean if anything. And, well that only lived in twenty something's. Shallow twenty something's. Or at least that's all he'd ever found, so far.

But he'd typed in the forties age bracket, and surprisingly several applicants scrolled up. He hit a few. "Uh huh," Heading toward his image of a fifties woman. A couple others had a little promise. And that surprised and encouraged him. And then the file for Des Jones appeared.

Dev couldn't get past the picture. He was caught--caught in it;

a picture of a leggy, slim girl, or woman. The sea was in the background fierce and wild, yet with this romantic woman bent at the waist with a puppy caught in her skirt like a little hammock. A couple other tiny dogs rolled in the grass. Her floral skirt was hiked up as she bent to the pups. Long lean legs were exposed.

The breeze had caught wisps of her long hair and an old fashioned straw hat covered most of her face. Only a provocative smile showed. A smile that seemed to say, "I've been waiting for you."

"Well, here I am," Dev said to the computer. He read on:

Name--Des Jones

"Hmm, Des, Dev--very nice together," He mused.

Age--forty six, hard to believe. Maybe he'd been wrong. Maybe he just hadn't tried hard enough. Forty six!!

Surely she lied! But then again, women lied to be younger, not older--unless they were twenty, and wanted to be twenty one. But not forty six!

Hair--Honey brown with auburn and blonde highlights. "Yes!"

Eyes--Hazel. Now what did that mean? Who cares?

He read on. She sounded very romantic. His heart started to quicken. Loves people, animals, and nature. Optimistic, sincere, loves sports. "Loves sports?" His heart leapt in his throat. Loves to bake, organize. Did that mean she cooked? Cleaned?

Well, what else could there be? His goddess was a sports loving, leggy, long haired baking dream boat!

Occupation—Caterpillar, "With a great job!" Dev's face broke into a foolish grin.

"Well whatever she's looking for, I am it!" He read on.

Looking for a sincere man. "Check."

With a sense of humor. "Check. Check. Check."

He was all of it; he was sure, very sure. This was his reward. Reward for the torture he'd been through on the cruise. Yes, his reward. Right here at home, on his computer, at his agency. He quickly typed in a hit on her file.

Trish sat at her Greater Expectations desk satisfied that she'd paired up fourteen couples that day, and a good ten of them sounded better than good. They sounded fabulous. Mike was in his office going over some paper work with Maggie, and Trish heard laughing--a great improvement over their initial meeting.

Trish knew once Mike got the hang of Maggie's system he'd be happy. Maggie was just that good at that type of thing! The ads continued to run, and the applicants continued to dribble in. Not floods, not at their prices.

But a dribble was good, and it gave her a chance to concentrate on the new applicants, and do her match making best. And of course what they did independent of her by scrolling the Greater Expectations internet site only added to their happiness.

She plucked at a red rose in a vase on her desk, one of twelve that the florist had brought earlier from a satisfied client--a thank you. Trish had started an album of the many thank you notes, and kind letters, clients had sent her. Mike had been impressed. She left it on the coffee table in the reception area.

Inspiration for new clients.

Trish sipped her tepid coffee, and decided she'd take a much earned break and check their 'site'. One new hit.

Typing in her code, she brought up his file: Patrick 'Rick' Jones. Now how odd was that? As Des's name was Jones and hers was Trish—Patricia, hmmm.

She stared at the picture; blonde hair a bit long, on a chiseled face with blue--sea blue eyes--eyes that held arrogance, and yet a twinkle at the same time. Eyes that held hers.

She scrolled on, reluctant to leave that face. Age fifty. Fine. Eyes--blue. She could see that! She skimmed on:

Occupation--office. Well, he worked.

Marital status--single.

Ever been married?-no.

Children--none.

It got better, no child support, or mooching adult children, as her soul mate book described. She finished reading and decided, he was hers, that simple. She didn't even consider her team members. She just decided he was for her. And she e-mailed him with her phone number.

And as if by magic, her cell phone rang. "Yes, this is Des." Yes, she'd seen his file. Yes, she wanted to go out. And no, this wasn't short notice to meet for a drink. After all it was Friday. Yes, she'd meet him at the Hilton bar in the lobby of the old hotel. Yes, she knew where it was, and would be there at nine o'clock.

Trish hung up and stared at the phone, and then replayed the conversation in her mind.

She clicked off her computer, dumped her coffee, gathered her purse, and started to leave. On impulse she pulled one red rose out of her bouquet. She stood at Mike's doorway. "I have to leave," She said hesitantly, and then caught Maggie's eye. "I, er, have a date." And she actually blushed.

"A date?" Maggie looked at her in wide eyed wonder. Really? This was a first. Not just since they joined Greater Expectations, but as far back as Maggie could remember. And her mind started to reel wondering about the details.

177

"Yes," Just one simple word.

"Well then Mike and I will close up when we're done. Won't we Mike?" Maggie said it so sweetly that Mike missed all the innuendo.

Trish's leaving was a blur. Mike turned to Maggie, "You know, now that she said that, I haven't known Trish to date--or at least not that I know of."

"I know," Maggie said, her eyes twinkling.

Chapter 9

Trish went through the ritual of getting ready--ready to meet a man, maybe 'the man'.

Her copy of 'How to Meet Your Soul Mate in Six Months or Less' lay forgotten on her bed. The book was still turned to a chapter called: 'Truth and its importance in a relationship.'

She flipped through her closet until she found her version of the floral skirt from the photograph. Only hers was silk, cut on a bias to give her that lean waist and hips look.

She scrounged past her blouses and sweaters until she found the pale blue cashmere camisole. Minimal was the only word for it. She'd bought it on a whim. It was a lighter blue than her eyes, soft, and clingy. She'd added the matching cardigan to her purchases. "Thank goodness." The cami was far too bare on its own--or at least to start the evening.

She pulled out pale heels that added a good three to four inches to her legs. Studying the picture of Jillian, she felt she'd made a good effort, giving it her own spin. Grabbing a tiny Prada bag, she was out the door.

The parking lot at the Hilton was crowded--of course it was Friday. As Trish angled into a space, she wondered, "What if I don't recognize him? What if I don't know what to say? I've been out of the game a long time." And she started to fret.

As she opened the heavy brass double doors, she saw him, not at the bar, but in the lobby--waiting for her.

He came instinctively toward her, reaching out two hands as he said her name, well her fake name, "Des?"

Trish just nodded, grateful that the initial contact was behind her. She didn't have to go to the bar and look all the men over, looking for her date. Looking like she was on the prowl for someone--possibly anyone. Or maybe she'd just stand alone and wait for him to find her. And look like, well she wasn't sure. She hadn't been to a bar in years--many years.

She swallowed and looking up into his sea blue eyes said, "Patrick?"

"Yes, but please call me Rick." And somehow they walked into the bar and found a cozy booth.

A waiter immediately brought them a bottle of white wine. Cliché possibly but Trish was grateful for the alcohol to slowly seep into her system.

They started out like two cats, afraid to come close, too fascinated to back away. But as their first glass of wine disappeared, so did their inhabitations, and conversation started to just tumble out.

Trish decided she better order a munchie, or with too much alcohol, she'd forget her profile. A platter of shrimp and cocktail sauce appeared, and as she nibbled, she stole looks at the best looking, and fascinating, man she'd met in years.

He was talking about a Black Labrador he'd had as a child. Then it dawned on Trish, the comment in her file, 'loves animals', and the photograph with the puppy in her skirt. "Of course I love animals ..."

"Why he's trying to talk about my interests," She thought, "How sweet." But what did she know about animals? The zoo! She'd been to the zoo as a child. That surely counted for something.

"You know Rick, I haven't been to the zoo in years, but I always loved strolling the park like setting, watching all the exotic animals watch me." And this was easy to say because it was true.

Somehow they had a date for breakfast to go to the zoo tomorrow, Saturday. What about that old standby rule of not seeing someone two days in a row?

It never dawned on her.

"Tell me about you," She managed to pick that much out of her brain. "I've got to stop staring," She thought, "And clear this fog my brain is in."

Dev took up the ball, began with a quiet boyhood, shy and thin--not terribly confident. "Now why am I telling her that," Dev thought? "She'll think I'm a nerd or who knows what."

"But then I discovered music and my world opened." Jim Hart was playing softly in the background singing about the long road home.

"Really, I love all music from rock to opera," Trish added. And that was another true thing so it was easy to say. And hopefully remember.

"Opera--no kidding. My maiden aunt used to drag me. As a child I was fascinated by the costumes, and drama, and the foreign sounds that just ah ..."

"Drifted over you and soothed?" Trish added and blushed. She loved exactly just that part of opera.

"Exactly!" Dev let out a small breath, wondering why he'd mentioned his fascination with opera--most unpopular with the usual girls he dated. Some didn't even know what it was. "La Boheme is here--maybe I can snag us a couple tickets?" He suggested shyly.

Trish thought about the wonderful love story and sighed. She sipped her wine, and looked up into Dev's endless blue eyes. "Yes, we could be together when Mimi dies one more time." And she pictured herself sitting next to him, maybe holding his hand while the main character breathed her last breath.

Touched by her response, and wanting to share the tenderest moment in all of opera with him, he squeezed her hand. Conversation went from serious to silly after that, and before they realized it, the lights were getting brighter in the bar.

Trish looked around, shocked they were alone. Two waiters leaned against a door patiently. Why, they'd closed the bar. She was stunned. Really, closed the bar?

"Look," She discreetly pointed to the waiters. "We've closed the bar."

Rick/ Dev laughed, not at all embarrassed, and just dumped a pile of money on their table, and held out a hand to Trish. He helped her back into her cashmere cardigan, and as they strolled out, he gently slipped an arm around her shoulder.

Slightly mussy from the wine, and still dazzled by his good looks, and sweet personality, she cuddled into his arm. As they approached their cars she started to pull herself together. Afraid she'd just abandon her car and follow him, she pinched herself.

"I had a wonderful evening," She said sounding sixteen as she fumbled for her car keys. He took them from her and unlocked her car door.

Just before she slid in, he ever so smoothly placed another arm around her and kissed her gently on the lips. Before Trish came to her senses the kiss deepened, sparks flew, and she knew if she didn't break the kiss she'd melt into him and become one.

She looked up into his blue eyes shyly, surprised, and yet pleased at the same time.

"I'll meet you at nine o'clock at IHOP for breakfast, and then we'll go to the zoo?" He asked it but hoped the answer was yes, because as he recalled, she had already agreed to go. Still he wanted to hear her say yes just one more time.

She nodded and drove off in wonder of what an evening she'd just had--a magical evening. Where had it gone? Time had just melted away. They had talked like the very oldest of friends, and also like they were both just discovering so much about each other. And she found everything he said to be fascinating, tender, poignant, and exciting.

She almost stopped her car. Exciting--it was a word she didn't use lightly. Yet her evening had been exciting. Well, not exactly her evening. It was Des. Des had been exciting.

Devin headed to his own car and wondered what had just happened to him. He'd spilled his guts breaking one of his own rules. And he talked about his childhood--something he rarely did, and certainly not to dates. And her Prada bag--he was sure it was Prada, yet he forgot to comment on it! In the past his dates loved when he noticed their designer accessories.

He drove home with images of Des floating in his mind.

Trish woke up at six in the morning still in a fuzzy place dreaming about a tall blonde man with a glorious tan, and sea blue eyes. They were sharing a bottle of wine and laughing like old friends ... but exciting friends. That combination she always wanted. As her mind started to clear, the dream started to dissipate. She tried to hold onto it but morning took over. Then her eyes flew open.

"I was at the Hilton's restaurant with a gorgeous, tall, sun tanned, blonde last night. A blonde with sea blue eyes! And I'm meeting him at the IHOP at nine o'clock!" She could hardly believe it.

Trish jumped out of bed and into her shower. "What will I wear? What will I wear?" She toweled off and mentally decided on a short denim skirt that pleated and had a little swing to it, and a coral cashmere sweater. And strappy little heels.

"Oh no, we're going to the zoo, and I'll have to walk," She moaned. "Make that a lower heel with a little bit of a padded sole." She swept her long hair up into a pony tail and carefully applied her makeup. It was eight forty five by the time she finished and raced to the IHOP.

"Foolish, I'm being foolish," Trish told herself. She took a couple of good deep breaths, looked in her rear view mirror, smiling at the image--perfectly made up, just the slightest bit flustered. "What the heck," She told the image and sprang out of the car.

Dev sat there dangling a menu from one hand, looking at his cold coffee. Maybe he'd imagined her? Maybe he just conjured up what he wanted--always wanted. He went to pick up his stale coffee and heard the door open.

She bounded in, just a bit breathless.

It took his breath away.

"Hi," She said, suddenly shy.

"Hi yourself, I thought I just conjured you up in a dream and you weren't real!" He laughed, not believing he let that slip out. Not his style at all.

"Me too!" She said too honest for words.

They both laughed.

"How about pancakes?" He asked, "The big stack?"

"Or French Toast with little sausages?" Trish found herself so happy to see Rick, she'd forgotten her diet. Her lifelong diet! How could she?

They devoured mounds of food, laughing like old friends. "How right this feels," Trish almost said out loud. When the last sausage link was devoured, and the last drop of syrup soaked into the last bit of pancake, they got up to leave. "I don't know why I don't come here more often," Trish said with a giggle, "It's so good!"

"Yeah, it'll be fun to walk it off at the zoo," Rick/Dev added.

"The zoo? Why I'd forgotten about the zoo!" Trish felt like a kid on vacation.

"Sure, we'll go wake up the bears, make faces at the monkeys," Dev joked. "Want to ride with me? I think your car will be safe here at the IHOP."

And they were off without a seconds thought to anything. Dev bought peanuts; Trish tossed them to the bears that ignored them. They laughed at the monkeys. Trish shrieked at the snakes.

"Oh look, cotton candy!" Trish raced over to the vendor's wagon. "I haven't had cotton candy since I was? Well, I don't even remember when!"

He bought her the gigantic cone of pink spun sugar, and they walked along holding hands, pinching off bits of cotton fluff and laughing.

Dev made a stop in the men's room, leaving Trish by an old iron bench. She sat, amusing herself watching the people go by, eating ice creams, pushing baby buggies. A tiny girl of about four ran by crying. Trish followed the little girls gaze--her red balloon had escaped, and was winging its way over the lion's cages.

Trish rushed over to the balloon vendor and bought another one. She was tying it onto the child's wrist when Dev saw her.

It was the sweetest sight he'd ever seen. He went from carefree and laughing to smitten. He'd never had feelings for a girl so strong so quickly. When she saw him she ran up to him in her short denim skirt, pony tail flying--looking like not more than a girl herself.

"Do we have time for the elephants?" She asked coquettishly. Because of course a visit to the zoo had to include the elephants.

"We have all the time in the world." And they headed down one of the flower lined paths to the pachyderms.

"You know I can't walk another step," Trish laughed, collapsed on a park bench, seemed as though even the flatter shoes had given up.

"Not even for the seals?" Dev teased.

"Not even for the seals," She smiled up at him, "We'll save them for another day." She said almost as though it were a guarantee they'd keep going out, laughing, and having fun. And she couldn't believe she said it, but it just felt so right she couldn't guard every word.

"You don't have to walk at all--if you can stay awake. I was able to snag us a couple of tickets to the opera tonight." Dev looked pretty pleased.

Trish knew they cost a fortune from a scalper, and she was touched that he would make the effort, and spend the money. She perked up.

"It is La Boheme," He assured her.

She laughed a gusty sound from deep inside her. "Rick, I can't think of a more perfect day starting with French toast, and ending with the opera, not to mention all the animals in between!"

"Does that mean you'll go?" He asked, suddenly shy.

"Absolutely, what time's curtain? I'll need to tidy up." Trish looked down at her little skirt, and tired feet, and sighed. She would need to work miracles to go out again tonight. And even more miracles to go to the opera.

"You're perfect," Dev said suddenly serious.

Trish caught her breath. Whoa---too fast, and sprang to her feet. "Not with cotton candy in my hair," She laughed and they headed out hand in hand. He dropped her at her car at the IHOP, and before she started the engine, she sat and stared.

A smile rose to her lips, "How odd to actually find a great guy, through a dating service." The irony of it all was just amazing to her. Yet she had chipped in her fair share for just this reason.

Just possibly underneath it all maybe she had been a nonbeliever.

Once back at her apartment it was impossible to think about anything but getting ready for the opera. There really wasn't time for a long soak, so Trish quickly popped back in the shower. As water sluiced over her, she realized she had that exuberant feeling of being carried away. A feeling she hadn't had in a very long time.

Thank goodness for the little black dress, Trish thought as she shoved pins in her hair, trying to get it up on her head. The buzzer to her apartment rang, and she had just enough time to slip into her heels, grab her little bag and go.

Rick/Dev was cute at the bar. He was darling in khakis and a plaid shirt at the zoo, but he was drop dead in a suit. He held a long stem rose in his hand as she opened the door.

Feeling school girl foolish, she took the flower, and as she headed for her kitchen and water, she reached for a pair of scissors and snipped the long stem to about five inches. She tucked the stem under the flap of her small bag, deciding on impulse to take it with her.

Dev noticed the gesture and smiled. He couldn't quite get his eyes off her long long legs and tiny hint of a black dress that clung to every dream he'd ever had.

"We better go," Trish said, feeling just a small bit self conscious. The lobby to the concert hall was crowded, and as they melted into the crowd, the lights flashed indicating ten minutes until curtain.

They found their seats as the lights twinkled out. The curtain rose. The conductor tapped her baton, and the orchestra wafted out to them as the story unfolded.

By intermission Trish remembered Mimi's life would soon be over. The arias had been breathtaking, the sets incredible. Even though she knew the tender story of the starving artist, and the beautiful Mimi dying of consumption, her heart split at the final scenes.

Dev gently pressed a clean handkerchief into her hand, and she dabbed away the emotional tears of being caught up in another world for just a few hours.

After endless curtain calls and applause, the lights lit, the people streamed out. Trish and Dev sat, watching the opera patrons hustle to the lobby.

Finally Dev spoke, "You know what's going to happen yet it still grips you." They made their way to the parking lot and Dev's car.

"Thank you--it really was a perfect day," Trish said in a melancholy way. "I can't believe we've been together since nine o'clock this morning."

It was late, most restaurants were already closed. They drove past the IHOP which never closed. "Do you want a sandwich or something?" Dev asked, slowing at the turn.

Trish laughed a lusty throaty sound, "Weren't we just here--a million hours ago?"

Dev pulled in and they found themselves in a booth looking at menus.

"I know they have a million things on the menu, but what sounds good would be scrambled eggs."

So, they ended their long day with more breakfast. By the time they got back to Trish's apartment, she was sated with comfort food, a beautiful evening, and exciting company.

"Can I see you again?" Dev asked, suddenly too shy to do his traditional moves.

"I'd like that," She said. No games--just a simple answer.

"Tomorrow? A baseball game? Late brunch at Jumers?"

She nodded sleepily, unaware what she was saying yes to. She slipped inside her door, before Dev had a chance to put a move on her, or she had a chance to debate.

And before Dev realized he hadn't even scored, he was back in his car, whistling.

"Baseball? Baseball? What do I know about baseball?" Trish woke up almost in horror. And then she laughed, three bases, a bat, a ball, a hot dog, what more could there be? And why in heaven's name would he want to take me to a baseball game?

Trish called Maggie, "Mags, you won't believe it. We need to all meet and talk. Well, not today, I've got a date--another date. Yep! From Greater Expectations! His name is Patrick Jones! I know. I went out with him Friday night and yesterday. Well, actually day and night."

Trish stopped to take in a breath and then went on, "Listen Maggie--call Pan and Jillian for one night this week. I've got to get ready. Can you believe we're going to a baseball game? What would possess a man to take me to a baseball game? I don't even know what to wear! Oh, oh yeah, the application. 'Loves sports.'"

Trish finally decided on a khaki skirt and her favorite silk floral blouse. If she added a cardigan--well maybe it would look like a ball game? At least it would pass for late brunch. "If this keeps up, I'll need to add to my wardrobe," She smiled as she said it, her two favorite things--shopping and men! At this rate she'd probably make it men and shopping!

Trish was definitely over dressed for baseball, but she didn't care because by the look in Dev's eyes, she looked perfect. It was actually fun, the crowd, and the excitement. She'd had no idea in her old rude ways why she'd always put down sports.

And of course Dev sat close to her, excited, explaining an action, grasping her during a particularly successful something. She cheered and grabbed him back. He'd bought her a baseball cap, and the gesture erased all embarrassment from putting it on. When he told her it looked cute, she blushed.

They dragged out of the stadium along with a million other people. "Are you hungry?" He asked knowing he was famished. They headed to Jumers Bavarian Lodge for the end of Sunday brunch. A jazz trio played softly as they entered. The scents of rich food filled the air.

The maitre d' seated them at a candle lit table for two far enough from the music to talk, close enough to let it envelop them.

As late afternoon spent into evening, Trish and Dev got lost in the newness of their relationship. After the final bite of torte and sip of coffee, Trish realized the day was gone. "I really need to go," She said with reluctance. "I have to be at work early."

"So do I." Dev admitted.

***

Trish drank one more cup of coffee, looking around the Greater Expectations reception area. "I can't believe it. I can't believe I have just had a whirl wind three days of dates with the most wonderful man!"

She twirled and then laughed at herself, "I'm acting like I'm twenty three!" She wandered back into her office and booted up her computer, knowing she had a ton of work to tackle.

The morning passed quickly as she took care of some stubborn files, and made arrangements for some newer applicants. It was quiet--just the way she liked it to get any work done.

She'd become accustomed to not seeing Mike on Mondays until the morning was well on its way. It didn't matter to her at all. As a matter of fact, Trish fantasized it was her dating agency, and the less he was around, the more she could do-- and do her own way.

Her changes had been drastic yet positive. And Mike had fallen in line with all of them. It had been easier for him to do when he started seeing, and hearing, all the great results Trish was getting. And of course, Maggie had turned his bookkeeping around.

So Mike was pleased. And he loved the fact that Trish never questioned where he was, or what he was doing. No, he loved the new set up--loved it a lot.

Maggie's changes to Greater Expectations had been nothing short of radical. Once the initial shock wore off, and Mike could see the huge savings, he'd come around. He was starting to soften around the edges already; quite soft--quite happy.

And now Trish was in 'like' as she called it--in 'like' with a wonderful man. She tried to review all she knew about him, yet once she got past their shared interests in activities, and love of food from Stadium peanuts, to candle lit dinners, well, the list was small. Trish knew his name was Patrick Jones. She knew about his childhood.

She knew she liked him. And she knew there was chemistry--loads of chemistry ... Chemistry for the first time in a long time. Her mind was on a little vacation on that area of chemistry when she heard the shouts.

"What has happened to this lobby!!?" It wasn't a question; it was a loud angry bellow. The next thing she knew her office door was slammed open!

Slammed open by the object of her day dreams! Slammed open by Patrick Jones! Trish shook her head, imaging she had projected his face on the screaming maniac. She got to her feet, tugging on her tiny Chanel pale pink suit. She actually tottered on her heels. And she started to shake. She started to speak but for once found herself speechless!

Dev stared at her, the color of rage drained to a ghostly pallor. He took a double take, lost in his own rage! It couldn't be! Of course it wasn't! There was no way!

As they stared, the front door opened again and Mike came in, for once actually a little early.

"Ah Trish, I see you've met my cousin," Mike was grinning as he made the introduction--or half introduction.

'Trish?' Dev mouthed.

"And Dev--I meant to tell you, I finally hired someone to er help us clean up the agency." Mike stood awkwardly as Dev and Trish just continued to stare at each other.

But Mike was oblivious to their standoff. He simply wandered into his own office and closed the door. The better to deal with it later, he thought. His thought was that Dev's look was resentment because he had hired someone.

"Geez, Dev can't complain. Recruits, er applicants, are way up, money looks better than ever, and Trish has a magical way of making all our members happy." So why was he hearing screaming from the other office? And it was quite loud. Even from Trish who he only ever heard polite and sweet things from.

"You deceived me!" Dev growled at the top of his lungs. His anger was past the boil. He'd finally met someone ... someone he thought might mean something--no a lot, to him. And she'd deceived him! How dare she? Impossible!

Trish was deathly pale and started to sputter out an explanation. Then she felt the rush of warmth and color return. "How dare you! You deceived me! Patrick! Rick! Or whoever you are!" And she stood with her arms crossed glaring at him.

They stood--a standoff and stared. His gaze took in her elegant office, the type of room that spoke beauty, and serious business, at the same time. She stood there in her tiny business suit, arms crossed, fire in her eyes. She didn't look like she was going to budge one bit. As a matter of fact she looked like she was going to start screaming all over again.

And then he laughed. The joke was on him. It really was.

And Trish lowered her crossed arms, let out a pent up breath and joined him.

At the point Mike heard laughter, he ventured out. He threw an arm around Dev's shoulder and tossed Trish a huge smile. "Cousin, why don't we let Trish get back to work, and I'll explain the changes." Mike dragged Dev off to his office.

He didn't want Dev scaring Trish away. No, he liked the new set up just fine, besides he had no idea when Dev would be gone again on some crazy adventure leaving him with all the work.

Once in Mike's office, Dev looked around, "But I don't have an office anymore!" Dev whined because obviously Trish had taken over his. The one that had been basically shrouded in plastic and not used for however long ...

"Sure you do, there are two desks in here." Mike's eyes darted to the one Maggie had been using for her accounting reorganization. The other held his putter paper weight, coffee mug from home, and a stack of papers Trish wanted him to review.

There was plenty of room, and when Maggie helped him it was a perfect set up. He didn't feel like he was sharing when Maggie was there, but as though he had his own important spot--his own desk.

Trish leaned against the wall not sure if she was angry or just this side of hysterical. She did know she'd been thrown for a loop--a big one. Still shaken she picked up the phone, "Maggie, I know you're busy but I need to talk, and I know Pandora can't answer a phone call in the kitchens." She paused still feeling rather desperate. "And I can't find Jillian." She spit this all out in rapid succession.

Maggie kept looked at a report in front of her and raised her eyebrows, "I can give you two seconds Trish, I'm swamped," She managed.

"Well you know I told you I had a date Friday--well actually three dates."

Maggie rolled her eyes as Trish rambled on.

"Friday, Saturday, and Sunday," Trish couldn't even believe she was admitting this. But it was true and part of the problem.

Maggie drummed her fingers. She really could not talk; she really had work piled up. "And we're going to meet Wednesday night to talk about it," Maggie cut in. "We can meet tonight instead."

Trish ignored her. "Maggie, I'm found out. He told me his name was Patrick Jones, and this morning he showed up here at the office. He's Mike's absentee cousin Devin." Trish just blurted it out. She needed help and support now--was desperate for it now.

"And you're not Des from Caterpillar," Maggie made it sound like a little slogan. But it was a statement that basically said she wasn't who she said she was either.

"No I'm not," Trish admitted with a defeated sigh. Of course she wasn't. But she never figured anyone would find out. She just had never let her mind go that far because in her heart she just never thought anything would go that far, or this far, or anywhere really.

"Let me think Trish. I honestly have to go," And Maggie was gone, hung up.

Trish held the dead phone and stared. She was counting on Maggie to give her a one liner to solve it all, not tell her she had work to do, and had to hang up. Slowly Trish set her phone down and realized she was on her own. And she rather hated it.

Mike and Dev stayed closeted in his office. Trish eventually got tired of holding her breath, and got back to work. A new divorced client age forty-three, shocked by her husband's wild affairs and now alone. The new client wanted to date. But of course, she didn't know how to begin. So, she'd come to Greater Expectations for help to get her back out there. Help her heal or just start over.

Trish pondered. This client needed someone gentle, kind, possibly a bit older. She started her search on the computer--

maybe a Cancer. Always gentle. She read on, lost in matching heaven.

Trish didn't even see Dev standing in her doorway.

He watched her concentrating, occasionally making notes. He was as taken with her there at the office as he had been the last three days. And he couldn't quite believe this about himself.

Once Dev had digested the deception, Mike explained how good Trish was with their clients. "Clients--Mike, we don't have clients. We have suckers who give us ten thousand dollars, and we give them a computer program for them to tune into," Dev almost laughed at Mike until he saw how serious Mike was.

"Well, we have clients now Dev. Satisfied, very satisfied clients--clients who are referring friends as new clients. She has a way with them." Mike was oblivious to Dev's jabs. Especially now that they had turned a corner and business was, well, booming.

Dev had stopped by Trish's office to tell her they weren't match makers. But of course they were. That was exactly what they were. What had happened to his cushy business while he was gone? And as Dev looked at her long sweep of gorgeous hair, he wondered what had happened to him?

She was dialing the phone and started to talk by the time she noticed him. She waved him to a chair. She went on talking on the phone, "Larry, this is Trish from Greater Expectations. I was reviewing our files, and I found someone not only do I think you'd enjoy meeting, but who I feel would be very compatible with you. Her name is Marilyn #1139. Take a look at her file, but remember photographs are never as good as the real thing,"

She paused and smiled a little embarrassed at Dev. She wasn't used to having someone listen to her little talks she had with her clients. Her clients? Well, the Greater Expectations clients.

"I think you should take her somewhere quiet for dinner. Not too expensive and intimidating." She listened and added, "Yes, that will be perfect. I'm going to give her a quick call and tell her to expect your call. Today? Great. That's exactly the right thing to do. Thank you. Let me know how it goes."

Dev just stared, and of course listened. He wondered who this Larry was to get such special treatment.

Trish disconnected, caught her breath and dialed, "Marilyn, this is Trish from Greater Expectations. I've given your file considerable thought. Yes, I understand. I think you could share some happiness with Larry #841. I've spoken with him and he'd like to take you to dinner. No no no--nothing formal. No, nothing expensive--just quiet, where you can talk. Yes I do feel he would be ideal for you. Of course you should think about what to wear, maybe go shopping if you think it would be fun. Now let me know how it goes. No need to thank me Marilyn. This is what Greater Expectations is all about."

She hung up, slightly embarrassed even though she had these conversations repeatedly with clients. She looked up at Dev nervously, "What can I do for you?" After all she was working, even if it was for him.

He'd forgotten what he was going to complain about. "Uh, nothing I guess. How often do you do that? Put people together, I mean?" He was fascinated. It never ever dawned on him, or his cousin, to match people up--never. And yet after listening to her setting Larry and Marilyn up he realized how special it sounded — personal, caring. The kind of treatment he actually wanted himself.

"Oh, all day," She said it rather absently wondering just what else was on his mind.

"Any complaints?" He asked wryly, raising an eyebrow. Because really, what made her think she could pick them, could match-make, could figure it out better than his clients could themselves.

She handed him the beautiful album on her credenza--the album full of happy letters from satisfied clients.

JACQUELINE GILLAM FAIRCHILD

Dev opened it gingerly and started to leaf through. The letters were glowing, emotional, and yet he'd been gone a total of three weeks, two on his cruise and a week to rest up for the cruise. Could all this have happened in three weeks? Was the album fake? Had she made all this up just to … whatever?

As he read the album, the phone rang and Trish answered, "Greater Expectations. Why hello Mark, so nice of you to call."

Dev's heart tripped. She was dating someone named Mark.

"Your date with Amy went well? Yes, I'd call perfect well!" She laughed into the phone, "You're bringing her home to meet Mom and Dad? Oh Mark, I'm genuinely happy for you. Thanks for calling." And she beamed at the phone, pleased.

Dev stared. He'd never received a letter, or phone call, that wasn't a complaint--ever. And he owned the business.

"How do you do it?" He asked in way of a peace offering for all his early reactions.

"Oh, I just keep reading the files--looking for interesting qualities, and trying to match them up," She hedged, not mentioning her aid from astrology. Well she was doing what she said …

"I've got a psych background, human nature has always fascinated me--maybe we could, well, work together." He smiled and Trish began to relax.

So, she wasn't fired. She still had a job. With all the benefits she had wrangled out of Mike. "I think maybe we could." And she gave him full wattage.

***

The girls met at Jillian's apartment. They'd nixed the pizza idea. Dating was getting to be too fattening. They'd all brought salads, which they set in the center of the table.

"Okay," Jillian began, "Tell us Trish."

"I don't know where to begin," Trish stared off into middle space. "I mean, I hadn't been interested in any of our hits, so I just divided them up among the rest of you. But well, when I saw Rick's, I mean Dev's file, well something just clicked and I said 'mine'. It never even dawned on me to share him."

"And the minute I met him I felt a connection, like meeting part of myself. But I didn't want it to be the sneaky deceitful part of me." Trish looked distraught, and yet the happiest the others had ever seen her. She described her dates that seemed to go on and on. It was as though she had packed a whole season of dating in just a few days.

"Actually, we did more together in three days than I've done in months, maybe years, with a man. It was like a cram course on dating. We just couldn't seem to get enough time together," Trish sighed.

"When he appeared at Greater Expectations Monday, I just freaked. I couldn't believe it. And then it sank in, he'd lied to me! I was so mad, and hurt--oh, I don't know what I was!"

The girls nodded in support.

"But as the day wore on, he heard me fixing up some of our clients and he offered to help."

And all three of them raised their eyebrows surprised at this turn around. The girls continued to eat, and discuss the agency, and eventually as the support of good friends sank in, Trish felt better.

***

The next morning Trish stood in front of her closet. "I don't know what to wear."

"How stupid am I," She thought? "Is this a date or work? It feels like a date ..." She settled on a pale grey little suit, similar to the pink one she'd worn Monday. It was work, and even though her heart fluttered, she had to treat it that way.

Dev was there when Trish arrived at eight thirty. How long had he been there? He looked nervous, and well, she felt it.

"So, what's on the agenda for today?" He asked in an attempt to sound business like.

And she took this as a good sign. At least he didn't have a list of chores for her.

Trish settled her Kate Spade bag in her drawer, and turned on her computer. "Well, I always like to check for messages--see if we have any potential new members or problems on our voice mail."

Dev squinted at her. Surely she was kidding around, "New members? How often do you think we get new members?" Dev asked astonished.

"Well, since I've been here, we've gotten fifteen--so I'd say about five a week." She had several interested in joining, they were saving up, and Trish was pretty positive they would come through.

Come through once she invited them to come and talk. Once they saw the exquisite reception area they were tweaked. Once they read her albums of happy testimonials they weakened. And after that it was just a matter of finances. But of course as all the ads said, they took all major credit cards.

Dev couldn't believe it. He couldn't do the math fast enough.

"After they call, I usually invite them in for what I call the initial meeting. I show them around. When they feel a little settled I boot up the computer, let them scan their age bracket, just so they know we have a lot to offer. Then I show them our albums of happy testimonials--that usually gets their attention. And then there's this." She waved over at the beautiful reception area.

"First impressions with businesses are as important as first impressions with people," A line she had practiced for Mike. Only now she was using it on Dev.

Dev had to admit it looked impressive. Classy, as though it held the same magic and style in a secret client file.

"Besides, I think we've paid for the new furnishings with our new members."

Well, Dev couldn't argue that one. And as his brain started to do the math on the price of the new office interiors he blanked, sure Trish was wrong. Nothing could cost that much. And who exactly approved the expense of all that glamour, or class, or whatever he wanted to call it? His cousin? Surely he had no clue what was what in the decorating world.

"Then I have them sit down with the questionnaire and start to fill it in. After that I give it a quick skim, while they enjoy a cup of coffee, and another look at the happy client albums. I try to make a snap match just to sort of get the whole process jump started. I print it out for them and together we review it. By this time I either have their check or VISA card." She dimpled with pride as she took a breath.

"I see." Of course he didn't see at all. How could she do all this? They never had done anything like this at all. As a matter of fact, they were hardly ever in the office. If people wanted to sign up they did. If not, well maybe the next one. And besides, weren't his ads enough?

Obviously not.

"I wasn't sure how it had been done, but this method seems to work just fine. That is unless you have any other ideas?" And she dimpled at him, knowing of course he did not, that they had no system at all—none, that they were con artists, ripping off the public. She knew it and she had a feeling he knew she knew it.

"No, no, I think you've got a good system." Mentally he added great, unbelievable system. "We'll just stick with it the way you've set it. And tell me Trish, just how is it you make what was it you called the 'snap' match?"

"Oh, I er just have a knack," Now she hedged.

He looked at her critically, but she started to make a cup of coffee, mentally congratulating herself for not saying, 'Oh, I type in his birth date to my astrology quick match program, and do an instant search for compatibility.' No, no word at all about astrology, the most misunderstood science out there.

As they sipped their coffee, it dawned on Trish that there really was no protocol--certainly none she'd seen, and Dev probably didn't know what to do with himself. So, she had a feeling he wasn't only curious about what she did but what he should be doing.

"After I review the voice mail, I sort the problems by urgency. Then I like to take six to twelve clients from our files, either older ones, or ones with little activity, and set them aside and try to find them a match."

He nodded, surprised at her initiative.

So they started with the phone messages. Three angry clients couldn't find anything on the computer that appealed to them. Six clients felt they just weren't connecting.

"Let's start with the not connecting ones," Dev suggested, because he wanted to see her in action again.

"Er, don't you have things that need your attention?" She asked gingerly.

"No."

It didn't appear he was going anywhere.

And Trish guessed he meant it. He had nothing to do. "Well, let's each take three and see what we can find on the computer, and then we'll compare notes."

"Let's make it more of a challenge," Dev began. "Let's each take the same files and compare what we find." His expression was challenging.

Trish bit her bottom lip; life was so simple when she ran the agency alone ... her agency ... "Okay." What else could she say? Technically he was the boss--her boss, of the new world she absolutely adored.

So they headed to their computers.

Number one was Katherine a fifty-three-year-old shoppe owner. Trish read on. Katherine worked in her tiny dress shoppe with occasional holiday help. Basically, a one woman show with long days. Vacations were used for trade shows. Evenings were used for alterations, or displays in her shop, and of course the endless cleaning that her shoppe needed. And paper work. Katherine would alternate cleaning with bill paying.

Katherine's hobbies were: her shoppe, sewing, and reading. "Surprise, surprise" Trish mumbled. Gee, a lot of chances to meet people there. Katherine sounded single minded, yet she seemed to enjoy herself. Possibly single minded by choice.

But Katherine was lonely. She'd obviously spent a lot of years dressing the public. Probably helping people get ready for that special event or romantic dinner. And still Katherine wasn't complaining, probably a care giver in her own way. Yet Katherine was lonely.

Katherine left most of what she was looking for blank. She didn't know, Trish was sure, what she wanted. Katherine just wanted to end the quiet solitude that stretched before her, lingered behind her.

Trish guessed--Pisces. She read the birth date, sure enough, natural care givers, very creative, and with the right moon, workaholics. Trish stared off into middle space. Although a Cancer would be compatible, she thought of the needy parts of their personality and decided against it. Her first choice for Pisces usually was a Scorpio. Usually, if there weren't any problem planets, there would be instant empathy. The two signs were magically drawn together by means of a forceful and yet quiet understanding.

Trish typed in age fifty five plus male, Scorpio, to see what her computer would spit out.

Only one entry appeared on the screen. She held her breath. Maybe she'd been too limited on her requirements, but she knew what she wanted. "Okay, let's see who it is. Ken, age sixty one, retired department store executive."

Trish felt a tingle go down her spine. She read on: background: women's ready to wear. She thought she remembered when this department store was bought out by another department store, and guessed that was when Ken took early retirement--forced out more than likely, yet too young not to work. Hmmm. Probably misses those trade shows, and the excitement of new merchandise coming in.

"Wouldn't it be nice for Katherine to have company at the trade shows, possibly stay at a nicer hotel, and take time for a quiet dinner? Of course it would be."

Trish was excited. Everything else seemed to fall in place. From what she could read between the lines, Ken seemed just a little bored. "Well, I think I can fix that romantically and professionally!"

Trish tackled the next two files with equal gusto! There was a tapping on her door and she looked up to see Dev leaning on the frame.

"Should we order in some lunch and compare notes?" Dev suggested, looking confident and just a tad too pleased with himself.

Trish smiled but behind the grin thought "Oh no, I think I've found perfect dates--really perfect ..." She let that thought hang there and nodded. And of course she wondered exactly what Dev had come up with.

As they unpacked Caesar salads Dev began, "Let me tell you what I have in mind for Katherine."

"Katherine," Trish thought. "Katherine is done, perfectly done. All I have to do is make the calls."

She took a deep breath. "Tell me what you had in mind," Though she didn't even really want to hear.

"Well, first of all, Katherine works far too much," Dev began. He knew the type. Worked round the clock, obsessed.

"Maybe she loves to work?" Trish injected. After all she loved to work.

"No one loves to work that much--did you read her file? That's all she talks about," Dev smirked.

"Maybe it's her life," Trish countered.

"Yeah, right, that's why she plunked down ten thousand dollars--to get a life," He tossed out sarcastically.

Trish started to bark and purposely breathed slower to control it.

"Katherine needs to play," He said it like an authority. Like playing was the most important thing in the world.

"But what about her business?" Trish worried her bottom lip for Katherine.

"Don't worry about her business." Dev blew it off without a second thought.

But Trish did worry about her business. It was more than likely Katherine's baby, nurtured and growing by her own hand. Just as she, Trish, was doing here at Greater Expectations. "Only," Trish admitted reluctantly, "This isn't my business."

"She needs a younger man to take her out, and liven her up. She's nice looking. I think we can pull it off. So I found her Barry." He handed Trish the profile.

Barry was forty-one and had been married twice. He loved to party. He was a Gemini. He was bad for Katherine. He was Gemini the twins--bad twice over; too young for starts, and married twice, -- also bad. Katherine would never relate--ever. True she was a workaholic, but she was fragile. And Barry was trouble.

"Oh no Dev, I don't really think so," Trish started to protest. She couldn't believe this was Dev's idea of the perfect date for Katherine. What was perfect about it, and what in heaven's name made him think this Barry was going to be attracted to Katherine? Right there he was wrong.

Dev looked like he'd been slapped, "You don't think so? Trish, I'm the psych major remember," He said it with authority. "What did you find?"

Trish proceeded to fill him in and her reasoning.

"But it's based on more work Trish!" He couldn't believe it. More work? Come on.

"Well, if they connect, I think she'll not only have companionship but a potential business partner." Trish could see it as though she was actually right there. Perfect.

"Yes, I suppose," Dev had to toss her that much. But he didn't want to. He wanted to be right. It was, after all, his agency, his brain child.

But even though Trish knew all this she also knew he'd let his brain child starve. Trish could tell it made sense to him but he didn't want to admit it. They reviewed the next two files conflicting like rivals. They finally agreed to call the clients and give them both choices. And as Trish said, "Let Mother Nature do the rest."

Chapter 10

Jinx took a moment at her shoppe Fairchild's to just sit. It was late in the day and she was tired. She nibbled mindlessly on a Protein bar, then purposely tossed it in the waste basket, and reached for a Cadbury Flake. "Better."

She opened her newspaper, scanning for competitor's ads and maybe a sale at one of the big department stores when she saw it.

'Greater Expectations

You're not in this alone
We use scientific methods
To match you with your perfect companion
Our files are endless
So are our skills
$1 - 800 - 555 - D\text{--}A\text{--}T - E$
All major credit cards accepted'

She thought of Trish, now manning the computers, so to speak and grinned. "I wonder if she and the girls have met anyone yet." And she wondered just what these scientific methods were.

***

As Trish went through her 'men' inventory, as she had taken to calling it, she thought about Dev. How could they be working, and now competing together? The challenge became personal--not just to satisfy her Greater Expectations clients but to show Mr. Psych she could do it.

She could match people together. Well she knew she could do it, and do a great job of it. But now she had to prove it to him.

It gave her great satisfaction to tell Dev that Katherine just felt she couldn't even consider a younger man, and then had added, she wasn't a party animal.

Dev hadn't taken it too well and gone into a snit. The snit became a sulk when days later Katherine called to say she and Ken had been out every night, and he'd been at her dress shoppe just sort of helping. It was the kind of news that made Trish's heart swell. It was why she did what she did.

Trish and Dev continued to work on the problem files, but Dev had to admit his psychology methods just weren't producing results. Mike was doing the ads now, with input from Trish. Both men felt obligated to show up at work once they realized how devoted and hardworking Trish was.

But Mike continued to daydream about the golf course--he was losing his season stuck at work.

Dev started reviewing Maggie's accounting plans, since his match making skills were not producing, and he found not only did Maggie's ideas make sense, but that he had a bit of a knack for them.

He stared over at Trish's closed door. How could he be so attracted to someone only a few feet away, and yet so uncertain as to what to do? It baffled and annoyed him both at the same time.

He'd lost his zeal for shopping for women through their files, and yet he just didn't seem able to ask Trish out again. Dev wanted to date her, but work with her? Confine in her? Share his business? Well, this was all new territory. Not that he had much choice.

She was already there, already on the pay roll, already in place, sitting at her desk in one of her tiny suits with a bouquet of roses on her desk. Roses. It was too much. And he didn't like that she seemed to have a better knack for this match making than him. He, after all, was the psych major, and she was, she was--why she was just a lonely woman over forty.

If she was so good at this match making, why was she alone? The fact that he was alone was entirely different. The fact that he couldn't get her out of his mind was another matter, an entirely annoying one.

He'd yet to bring up the fake name on her file situation. Of all the nerve ... it still grated on him. Of course, she hadn't brought his up either. But it was his agency, and he had the right to do whatever he wanted. He tried to dismiss it all, and went back to the spread sheets.

They continued dodging each other politely yet with an electric attraction that seemed to hang in the air. Trish dressed everyday as if it were a date, but just didn't know what to do to break the tension. She didn't want to bring anything up ... so she retreated to her office and just plowed through work.

Finally Dev wandered into her office. Trish was deep into one of her Astrology books, looking for answers to a stubborn case. "Uh hmmm," He began, "Am I interrupting?" He forgot why he'd come in, enraged to see her pleasure reading on his dime.

She quickly banished the book, "Oh no. What can I do for you?" Trish felt flustered, enough that Dev softened.

"I, er, had some nice compliments come in, and thought you'd like to know." Then he gave her his slow smile. "You really do have the touch."

Mike was at the golf course and Trish realized they were painfully alone.

"I really want to work with you Dev," She began nervously; "I've never had a job I love as much as this one. I'm not trying to second guess your judgments; I'm just trying to do my best." That was the best she could offer because it was the truth.

Dev realized his ego was getting in the way of all the progress the agency was making. "Well, maybe you could show me how you do it," He began as a peace offering, not really sure if he was serious or not. After all, his background was in people and their personalities. He did know he wanted peace in the office, and maybe, just maybe be able to rekindle what they'd started with.

A bead of perspiration trickled down her neck but Trish thought it was now or never. This strained atmosphere was making her crazy. She reached in her desk and gingerly held up the Astrology Encyclopedia.

Dev looked at it blankly. "I didn't mean to holler at you for doing a little reading. Geez Trish, you've made us more money in the short time you've been here than--well, you've done a great job."

He couldn't believe how many new clients she had signed up. And even more impressive was the way she took care of their existing clients, especially the tough ones. And some days they all seemed like varying degrees of tough.

"No, you don't understand Dev," She started nervously, wondering if she was making a mistake. Maybe she was. Well, it was who she was. It was time--time to come clean. "This is how I do it, and well my astrology computer program. I match our clients by the stars."

There she'd said it. How bad could it be, after all, it was working. He said so himself, repeatedly.

Dev's mouth dropped open. He looked carefully at the book she held. He had heard what she said. He thought he had. No, surely he was wrong. But a closer look at the book told him it was about astrology. Even the subtitle of matching your love life by the stars was right there for him to see. It hit him like a slap.

Jim Hart played in the back ground. His newest CD 'Find a Way'. Jim Hart was segueing into 'Love Me Fear Me.'

"Witch craft? I can't believe it!" He was practically yelling at her. Okay, he was yelling.

"No," Trish scrunched her eyebrows. She knew he was stubborn, but she was sure he was open minded. "It's not witch craft at all, why it's one of the oldest sciences known to man."

He gave her such a doubting look she almost lost it herself.

She paused, in for a penny she thought, "That's why I decided to go out with you. You're astrologically perfect for me." Then she blushed with just the glimmer of a thought that maybe she'd said too much. Just a little too much. And with his temper, maybe the stars were wrong ... but of course they weren't. Never were. She could take on his temper.

"You checked the stars before you answered my hit? I don't believe it!" Dev was seriously yelling now. A vein in his fore head was starting to pop.

"Which part?" She asked quietly.

"All of it! I don't believe any of it! You mean to tell me you felt there would be a a a ..." He was losing it--quickly.

"Connection?" She supplied. Because that was exactly what she had thought? That was why she had responded.

"Okay--A connection before we went out?" He was horrified. He looked at her with new eyes. The look was cold, it was calculating. And it was powerful.

"Why yes, I ran our charts. Not only are we astrologically ideal, we have the Mars Venus connection." Trish couldn't keep a tone of pride out of her voice.

After all, it wasn't everyday you found that ideal combination; that combination that put the sizzle in the attraction, that combination that just capped it all off making it pretty ideal.

It was too much! Dev stormed out of her office and out of the building! "Ran our charts! The Mars Venus connection! And to think I was attracted to her!" He muttered to himself, not that it helped anything.

He didn't even know what this Mars Venus connection was! He resented that they had it, and worse yet that she was able to find it, and actually take advantage of it. It was an unfair advantage ... no power. No, it was just wrong.

All wrong.

He drove aimlessly. He was attracted to her more than he wanted to admit. But it was impossible to fall for her foolishness! Why she was making a mockery out of his business! His very serious, albeit, stagnant business. And a mockery out of him!

Surely she was joking, though she looked pretty serious. Maybe she was laughing right now. And pretty proud when she mentioned she'd run their charts ... How could he lust after someone with that logic?

Then he sighed, maybe it was the Mars Venus connection — whatever that was! Because he hadn't been able to talk himself out of her ... as a matter of fact, she haunted his every waking and sleeping, thought, for that matter.

He continued to seethe unable to believe her answers for her success. There must be something else: some night classes in psychology, women's intuition, something. He drove until he ended up at Dinks Roadside Diner.

The scents of fried foods engulfed him with comfort. A TV hummed quietly in the corner. A CD player seemed to be playing the same Jim Hart music he had just heard in Trish's office. Dev sat at a small table and just stared, and tried to calm down.

Eventually Dink wandered over, "What can I get you?"

Dev looked up from his fog of misery, "A woman. That's what! A perfect woman! Who doesn't talk or have opinions!" That was exactly what he wanted.

Dink grinned at him, "Hey man, you got it bad--how about a loaded burger and a beer?"

Dev nodded absently.

Dink came back with a half pound sirloin burger on a grilled bun in a plastic basket--smothered with Texas Fries. He held a frosted beer mug in the other hand.

Dev looked at him in surprise, and then tried to clear his head. Dev guessed he had ordered. "Sorry--have you got a woman?" He asked sullenly.

"One to spare, or one of my own?" Dink answered good-naturedly. Before Dev could reply Dink filled him in, "I haven't got either, and by the looks of you, you've got one that's causing you some grief." Dink had seen it a million times, and he knew it right off the bat. Some woman was making this poor soul miserable.

Dev nodded and sank his teeth into his burger. Mustard and ketchup oozed down the side. He caught some with a fry. It was heaven. "I needed this." And he took a gulp of his icy cold beer.

"Hey, what you need is that fancy agency!" Dink tossed Dev the newspaper with the day's Greater Expectations ad glaring at them. "You know--you 'pays' your money and the perfect woman appears!" Dink laughed at himself, because if he did say so himself he was pretty clever.

Dev choked, "I own that agency!"

Now Dink's attention was caught, "You? You own the agency? You own Greater Expectations?" Dink was shocked! This sad sack of a person owned that intriguing agency? The one that continued to run the most interesting ads? Hard to believe.

Dev nodded sadly but kept eating. His burger was fabulous. He'd have to remember to come back here.

"And you're having woman problems?" Dink almost started to laugh at him but decided maybe he better not.

Dev started to nod, "Well, one woman. One in particular," Dev said it sadly, like it had really gotten the better of him.

"Well now isn't that just always the case." Dink looked around at his empty restaurant and pulled up a chair, "Tell ol Dink." And he settled in.

"You mean you found her in your files, and she's perfect, and then it turns out she works for you?" Dink couldn't begin to believe it. It was the stuff of dreams.

Dev nodded miserably.

"Well you're one lucky fool man. Pay attention here. You've got her where you want her--right there at work." And it flashed through Dink's mind all the hours he put in at work--endless hours.

And when he wasn't working, he was sleeping--literally. Why if his dream date worked for him, at least he'd get to see her, banter around with her, and well, just enjoy her while he was still awake.

Dev groaned and finally spoke, "You don't understand. She's good — very good at what she does. She's organized, and she has a way with the business--it's growing by leaps and bounds, and the clients love her." Dev sounded miserable. He drowned it in his beer.

"And the problem would be?" Dink asked fascinated, and then let out a deep breath. "Oh man, your ego. You own the business. You leave, she arrives. She improves it ... your ego. Your ego can't take it!" Dink wanted to laugh, but held it in. It was getting to be a habit for him with this character.

"No! It's not that!" Dev almost yelled. He took a gulp of beer. "Well, maybe it is, sort of. Okay, it is." He looked like a wounded animal.

"So, this woman of your dreams, in all her gorgeous glory, is right there every day, and she's making money for you. And I assume working hard. And?" Dink was trying to get the point of all this, the heart of it that was making this poor guy so miserable. Other than the one he'd already come up with: his ego.

Dev looked exasperated. He really didn't have an answer.

But Dink had one for him, "And you can't force yourself to adjust man?" Dink was flabbergasted. This was what employers dreamt of.

"I don't approve of her methods," Dev said meekly. "I'm a psychologist--well not a practicing one, but a trained one none the less and she she ..." He couldn't go on.

"Uses intuition?" Dink asked with a bit of a smirk on his face. After all he was around a lot of people ... a lot of women. He saw it all--all the time.

"Oh yeah, she uses intuition alright and and ..." Dev took another drink before he pronounced the horrid word, "Astrology!"

Dink almost split a gut; he laughed so hard, "Astrology?"

Dev wasn't sure if he should be genuinely annoyed by Dink's reaction but he felt too miserable to get it together so he nodded again.

"Man, astrology isn't all that much mumbo jumbo--why, it's a science, the oldest science, an ignored science! It's kind of fun." Dink looked at Dev critically in his expensive suit. "And an insult to your trained mind! Where were you in the eighties through the nineties man? Harvard?"

Dev nodded and Dink winced.

But Dink wasn't put off. "Well man, have some fun. You've got to lighten up! My guess is you're a Scorpio. When's your birthday?"

Dev raised an eye brow and replied, "November 3."

Dink laughed out loud. "Ha! I knew it! I'm the bull--every inch of me. Now, you--you're the scorpion. Swallow your pride, figure if it's working ... a ctually it is working, so go for the ride. Now I bet your lady is a Pisces--very intuitive! Very clever of her to turn to the stars! Why man, you're perfect for her. I have a feeling this just might be a perfect match." He poured Dev another beer.

"If she's as good at this match making as you say, if you don't keep her, she'll go somewhere else or worse yet, open her own agency." And with that said Dink headed to the kitchen.

Chapter 11

Thank goodness it was the weekend. Trish was at her wits end with Dev--wanting him, and wanting to wring his neck. Not a good combination.

"I need to get away." Trish told herself, half fantasy, half reality. "I went right from Caterpillar International to Greater Expectations. I need a break. I need what the rest of the world gets--takes. I need a vacation!" And as she said it out loud she felt a layer of stress dissipate, just a layer. And it felt good.

She dug out her stack of travel magazines and lost herself. Interrupting her daydreams was the wail of her phone.

"Trish, its Jillian. I just wanted to let you know I'm heading back to Southern California to take care of some loose ends. Oh, I'll be there I guess a couple of weeks. I need a break, and actually I want to see an old photographer friend, and get his input for starting up a photography studio here, and maybe a little R&R, not that I've earned it, but I want it. And I'll see my Aunt in Coronado." Jillian got it all out in one whoosh.

Trish made a snap decision and pleaded her case.

"Sure you can come. I'd love the company. But can you get away?" Jillian knew with any new job you couldn't just up and go simply because you were having a bad day, or because you thought you deserved it, or, worse yet, because you were disagreeing with the boss. No, that's not how the business world operated.

"Can I get away?" Trish thought, "I almost can't get away. But if I don't surely I'll go mad. And Dev will just have to adjust. Or fire me, or whatever." She made the decision then and there--she'd go to California with Jillian. Check in to the Del Coronado Hotel, that glamorous old Hollywood resort, and veg. And think.

Dev got to work early. "I'll get there first." This was his method. "I can, and will, work with Trish. She'll see my way. I'll convince her. This astrology thing surely is a joke. She surely will try using my logic and give up her foolishness. Besides if our clients ever found out how we matched people they'd be horrified."

The truth was his clients probably no more cared what method the agency used, as long as they got results. Of course, Dev wouldn't know this. And then he added, "Maybe, just maybe, we can work together. And if we can work together, we can date."

Not quite ready to give up on the dating aspect of Trish. His three day date with her still haunted him. He let himself in and flipped the lights to the elegant reception area.

There was no coffee brewing, no scent of roasted beans to assault him as he headed to his office. No CD music softly playing in the back ground. He slammed his brief case down on his desk. "And I can make coffee! And I can turn on the CD player!"

Once this was accomplished, and he was forced to admit how nice the quality coffee maker was to operate, he settled at his desk and hit the messages.

He started on some difficult files, one ear to the door. By noon he'd assured a despondent client that he could find Mr. Perfect just like the ads said. Ads he'd written. The phone rang, piercing his thoughts. "Trish?" He almost hollered. Catching himself he switched to "Er, Greater Expectations." He was losing it, just a little.

Still he was losing it.

"Hey, get a grip, its Mike, Trish not there?" Mike sounded worried. Trish basically lived there.

"Uh, no, not yet anyway. What's up?" Dev ran a hand through his hair, exasperated.

"I'm not coming in," Mike started. It wasn't a question. It was a statement.

"And what else is new Cous'. You know we hardly need you," Dev started to joke, "Just to collect a check now and again, and spruce up your social life."

Mike let out a breath he didn't even know he'd been holding, "Exactly." And then he got up his courage. "The Club has offered me a job as a golf pro, and to head up some golf clinics this winter, and well, I took it." Mike felt good, no great, to say it out loud--to tell his cousin.

Silence, absolute silence.

"Dev--you there? You know golf has always been my life, and as you said you hardly need me. We hit it rich when we stumbled on to Trish! She's worth ten of us." Mike laughed good naturedly. "I start today. I was going to come in and talk to you but I didn't make it, and hey, not only did I know you'd understand--you've got Trish. So, consider yourself in for free golf time from me—use of the course, clinics, you know," and Mike grinned, excited to begin his new world.

Dev stared off into middle space, lost in thought. He'd just said he and Trish could work together--could handle anything. And she had single handily turned around the agency; now all he had to do was accept it.

"I'm happy for you Cous'. Real happy! And you know you'll always have priority on the files." They talked further, and as Dev hung up he was flushed with the idea of working with Trish--just him and her, doing it all. Together!

He settled back into his files. It was three o'clock before his stomach called out for a sandwich. Opening his desk drawer, he found the remnants of a bag of Oreos and ate absently.

His watch told him it was five o'clock, and as he looked at his desk, realized he'd gotten a lot done. The new series of newspaper ads were written. He'd matched up a few mild cases, much too their satisfaction, and stacked up the stubborn ones for Trish. Funny, she hadn't come in--or called.

He went through the motions of closing up the office. Flipping a light here, closing a door. He stopped at Trish's office. The lights had never been turned on. She'd never shown up.

He flipped them on idly, and the pretty crystal lamp on her desk glowed. A faded bouquet of roses sat next to her phone. It was sweet how she fussed over her flowers, always bringing in a fresh bouquet. These were dry; petals had fallen on her blotter. The water looked murky. He picked them up to dispose of them and soak her vase when he saw the note. It was propped up in front of her computer.

He froze, dead flowers still in his hand and forced himself to read.

"Dear Dev: I've decided to take a little time off. I need a break, having come to work here directly from Caterpillar International."

A cold chill ran down his neck and he read on.

"I need time to think about my future here at Greater Expectations and you. I'll call when I'm ready. Trish." That was it. No more, nothing else.

Dev stared in disbelief. Gone? For how long? Needs a break? Needs to think? About her future with Greater Expectations--her future with him ... He stared at the flowers still in his hand, and started to go through the motions of cleaning them up.

A trail of blood red petals floated to the carpet as he walked to the trash. He gently set the vase and roses in the trash can and stared off into another dimension: One where he and Trish were at the zoo feeding peanuts to the elephants, snuggled together at the opera.

He shook his head, realizing he'd put her crystal vase in the trash--pulled it out, and took it to the bath room. Carefully he dumped the green water, scraped the crud off the edges and washed it clean.

"When will you be back?" He asked the air.

And remembering the note, his mind echoed, "When I'm ready."

Dev drove home numb. He'd never ever been the one to not call the shots.

In anything.

Ever!

He'd been a bully in the third grade and a lady killer in college. And since then, he'd done as he liked--always.

Picking up the phone he called her home number.

"This is Trish, leave a message."

He held the phone and just stared.

He hesitated and then spoke, "Trish, its Dev. Can we talk?" Feeling foolish, he replaced the phone. How could he feel such anguish for her when he'd known her how long? Gone out with her how many times? Why did he feel they had a history? Where had their connection come from? He put his phone away and started to sulk.

The next day he started the routine again only to find stale coffee still in the Krupps machine. He flipped on all the lights, and got down to the business of answering his messages.

Difficult clients piled up. The snap ones were just that, a snap. Was he finding them the best companion? He didn't care, as long as he could move them from one pile, the problem pile, to the finished pile. That was all he could do. That was all he had time for, or energy.

That's all he wanted to do. He had his own problems.

Carrying the tough files to Trish's office, he stared at the stale coffee, went over and cleaned it out. "This isn't my job," He muttered only to hear his own voice echo. No Mike. No Trish. "I guess it is my job." And the bitter reality tasted awful.

***

The days wore on, and the stack of difficult clients was piling up. Repeat phone calls were coming in demanding solutions--solutions that he didn't have the first time. "I'll tend to you," He said to a hung up phone.

But he knew piling the problems on Trish's desk wasn't tending at all. What if she never came back? The thought gave him a chill. What would happen to his agency?

He wandered back in to her office and took back the tough files. He sat at his desk scrolling the computer trying to make rhyme or reason out of their requests, trying to evaluate their personalities.

Night fall came and he continued to work, talking to the files as if they were warm bodies sitting across from him. "Just because you want a younger woman file #86," he said as he looked at the picture of the aging hippie, "Doesn't mean one wants you! How about a younger thinking woman?"

He picked up another file. "You want a doctor and you have six kids? Now you should know a doctor will never be home, and you'll have all the work of those kids on your shoulders. Maybe you want a man with a good income, and a man that wants a large family."

Finally exhausted, Dev turned off his computer, started to flip lights, and turn off his mind. As he stood in Trish's office, he eyed her small library of books. 'The Stars and You', 'Astrology for Today', 'Perfect Companions from the Heavens.' He was hungry, exhausted, and tired of trying to guess what people wanted--or worse yet, figure out what they needed.

He walked over and pulled a volume off her shelf and tucked it in his jacket pocket, turned out her light and left.

As Dev finished his pizza in front of his TV, he saw Trish's astrology book winking at him from his jacket pocket. He slipped it out and took it to bed with him. How interesting could this mumbo jumbo be, he thought? Laughing, he crawled under the covers and looked at the cover of the book.

Thumbing through he read Scorpio: October 23--November 21. Well, he was November 3. So, Dink was right, he was a Scorpio. The first blurb said: 'Scorpios are intense, forever mysterious, and passionate about love and food.' Right--Dev thought. I have no love life and I just ate a frozen pizza. And of course he also ruled out intense and mysterious. He closed his eyes, rubbing them.

He read on, 'This man makes decisions based on careful analysis of facts, always balancing opposite points of view. He can be as cranky as a croc with a hang over, and his idea of rationalizing everything including love will drive you crazy.'

"Well, so much for astrology, I knew I was right, this doesn't even almost sound like me!" Dev laughed out loud. Then he noticed he was reading 'The Libra Man'. Had he flipped a few pages? Hadn't Dink said he was a Scorpio? He flipped the pages.

'How could anyone with so much obvious self--control be passionate, let alone dangerously so?' Dev readily agreed. He considered himself Mr. In--Control, always on top of everything and very reasonable. It just was who he was.

Dev read on. 'He's only bluffing with the surface cool. Inside his passions are as hot as the stove you burned your hand on as a child. His feelings run deep and true. He is more easily wounded than causing a wound, and has developed a deceptively controlled manner. He'll bewilder you with his twin Scorpio traits of passion and reason. He's master of both. Intellect and emotions rule him equally. His passions are part of his soul--his reasons are more than beliefs to him--they are his very core. Scorps have explosive tempers, some seldom seen but still deadly. He not only enjoys winning he has to win. Something inside him dies when he loses even in small ways.'

Dev stopped, shocked. Why this was written for him. How could it be? How could they know him? Who were they? Exhausted he drifted off to sleep with Trish's astrology book lying on his chest.

***

Trish walked up the grand front staircase at the Del Coronado Hotel. Built in 1887, open in 1888, and today a national historic landmark, the hotel referred to itself as one third sand, one third sun and one third fairy tale. And indeed it was from the red peaked roof and endless Victorian railings in glistening white, to the fifty five million dollar restoration that brought the word luxury right up to today. A luxury that made a guest feel the opulence of another era while quietly supplementing all of today's 'for granteds'.

A history of celebrities from Marilyn Monroe when she filmed Some Like It Hot, to L. Frank Baum, author of The Wizard of Oz, who considered the Del his second home, added to the Del's mystique.

The plane ride had been fidgety--fraught with guilt over having left her job and Dev. Jillian was lost in her own thoughts, plans for a photography business back in Illinois. Just as well, Trish could only hash this all out so many times, and she certainly didn't want to burden Jillian with it—again.

No, Trish needed some quiet time to sort it all out, to make some sense of it, and to come to some conclusions.

Aunt Jilliana waited at the top of the steps--arms open. "Girls!" She cried and they both rushed into them. Aunt Jilliana was grandly resplendent in a jewel tone caftan, her silver hair bobbed in a fringe. Aunt Jilliana looked like the aged movie star she in fact was--retired, semi—reclusive, and a permanent guest at the grand Del Coronado hotel.

"Now tell Aunt Jilliana all--I have tea in my suite waiting." Two porters stood beside her, and with a nod tended to their things.

"Bring me their keys when their suites are ready." Both porters nodded and Jilliana whisked the girls through the grand lobby to a brass elevator. The door opened to another world--of black and white photographs, a silk fringe scarf draped baby grand piano, plump velvet furniture, faded oriental rugs. It truly was an elegant eccentric Aunt's home, yet it was a hotel.

An old Sevres tea service sat on the coffee table, next to a three tiered china stand with tiny sandwiches, delicate petite fours, and chocolate dipped strawberries. "I'll pour girls and you talk," Aunt Jilliana declared.

And as they nibbled the delicate goodies, and revived with Earl Grey, the girls each told their stories, pouring out their hearts to the loving, and sympathetic, Grand Dame.

"I'm just staying a couple of days Auntie and then I'm off to Los Angeles. But I'll be back before I leave again to say good bye." Jillian looked like a younger version of her aunt, dramatic and beautiful.

Aunt Jilliana raised one eye brow and looked at Trish.

"I'm here to rest and think--maybe two weeks, maybe longer. I just need to gather my thoughts and calm down." And Trish didn't know what else to say.

But Aunt Jilliana nodded, and at that moment the porter tapped on the door, "Dougy--thank you dear." She discreetly handed him a bill, and he handed her the girl's keys.

"Everything is ready Mam." And he disappeared as quietly as he'd appeared.

"I do so love living here," Aunt Jilliana sighed. "People think I'm eccentric, and well, perhaps I am, but it cost the same as a good nursing home--which of course I'm not nearly ready for. And they treat me like Royalty, not to mention room service, and the ocean outside my window." She waved a jeweled hand in the direction of a small terraced door, and sure enough the ocean loomed bold and resplendent, beating to the shore.

"Why I'd pay what I do just for the sunsets over the water," Aunt Jilliana said romantically. "Enough about me girls--now off to your rooms. We will have plenty of time to talk, and do whatever needs to be done."

And, keys in hand, they were ushered out.

Their rooms were miniature versions of Aunt Jillian's, full of priceless antiques, and equally as grand views. Trish looked out at the ocean and sighed. Someone had unpacked her things, reminiscent of an old English estate. Even her makeup was all set on a small vanity.

Trish lay down across her mahogany sleigh bed basking in the luxury and found herself drifting--drifting softly away.

The next morning Trish found herself gravitating to the Del Coronado gourmet buffet breakfast--indulging in fresh mangos, crusty croissants, and fluffy berry stuffed omelets.

Jillian, she assumed was sleeping in, or possibly up early, and hard at some task, regardless, Trish sat reading the local paper, The Coronado Eagle and Journal, nibbling on a huge blackberry, or maybe it was a Huckleberry. It certainly was like nothing she had back home. And a far cry from the diet breakfasts Trish had eaten at Caterpillar.

Caterpillar seemed like years ago, before she ditched them, and plunged into Greater Expectations, a bold, or maybe reckless, move on her part--maybe both. Her mind wandered back to the agency.

Trish thought of Dev with a pang of depression--not exactly sure if they'd had a real riff or just a slight clash. Couldn't they work together? Possibly be together? These were questions she asked herself as she walked along the beach, her news paper rolled up under her arm, her toes digging into the wet sand, as she watched the waves roll in and out, and in again.

The very pattern seemed reassuring somehow. Breathing in the salt air cleared her head. And she knew taking some time off was long overdue.

Trish whiled away the days in this fashion--usually stopping up to see Auntie Jilliana, as she'd taken to calling her, late afternoons. Sometimes Jillian would join them, just as often she would not. They'd share a Mimosa, and Aunt Jilliana would tell her stories of her Hollywood days gone by, and give her advice about men in general.

"They're difficult, there's no question," Aunt Jilliana said one afternoon with a sigh, "But oh so heavenly when you find that balance."

That balance was what Trish was looking for. Most evenings Trish would stroll to the shoppes, stop at a café for a salad, letting her mind ramble. It usually rambled back to Dev. "I wonder how he's doing without me?" She said to her arugula. "I wonder if there are any new recruits. I wonder how the agency's doing--doing without me. If there are any tough files that need me to solve them, any complaints that need smoothing over."

She kept poking at her salad, finally abandoning it all together. Leaving a small pile of money to pay her bill, she got up and started to walk aimlessly. She realized one thing--she missed the agency. And she missed Dev.

***

Dev woke up the most clear headed he'd been in weeks. He'd been reading bits and pieces about himself in Trish's astrology book--quite amazed. At first he actually entertained the idea that she had summed him up, and somehow printed in her book--with the plan that he'd find it and see himself.

Then he confessed his ego was as big as it described, and that as unique as he always felt he was, he was simply a classic Scorpio.

He fought the idea at first, but late at night as he'd read a little more, he knew he was looking in a mirror. After a while, it became comforting, her magical book that described him.

And he stopped scoffing at the whole astrology theory. The one where he called it hocus pocus. And maybe it was hocus pocus, because it somehow had him pegged--perfectly.

He headed into Greater Expectations accepting the now empty scene, and flipped the lights. Dev actually had the hang of brewing the coffee, usually remembering to wash the pot at night, and keep the gourmet coffee Trish liked on hand.

It was better. Better than the junk he used to buy. Out of habit he flipped on her lights before he turned on his own office--maybe subconsciously wanting it ready in case she returned today. Hoping she'd return today.

Dev hit the phone and started sorting the messages. As he looked at the stack of difficult people, his mind wandered back to his own astrology description. He hated to admit how frustrated he was becoming. Few of his matches seemed to resonate with his clients. If he didn't make them happy soon, there was a possibility they would give up ... or worse yet, demand a refund. Out of desperation he picked up one of Trish's books on the stars, booted up his computer and looked at the first tough file.

And read: a head strong sounding man at Caterpillar International. He had one interest other than work that he listed, and that was he enjoyed theater. That was it? Couldn't he make his applicants give out a few more clues? The applicant was an Engineer. Probably always right.

Dev scanned down the file for the birth date. April 23. He leafed through one of Trish's books--Taurus. A strong silent attitude prefers to attract people to him—often thinks he is right. "Hmmm," Dev read on, "Ideally suited to a Virgo or Capricorn."

Dev looked at his male Engineer's age: forty six, and typed in ages forty to forty seven, Virgo, female, hoping for any kind of match. The computer did the rest of the work. He was amazed. Fourteen files appeared. As he read through he found a forty one year old accountant at Caterpillar who loved theatre. No reason to look any further.

He placed the call to #614 the Taurus engineer, introduced himself, and said he highly recommended file #461 and that in his expert opinion a date for the theatre this weekend would be ideal. He also said he was calling #461, the Virgo female, and letting her know she should expect the engineer's call tonight.

Both parties sounded thrilled and promised to get back to him. It was the most positive response he had since he opened the agency. He wiped his brow in amazement.

Dev tried another only keyed right in to their sun sign, a lonely Aquarium music professor at the local college. He found an intriguing Gemini that played piano and sang--why not? Gemini was the twin sign which might account for the piano and singing.

He didn't know--this was all new territory for him; still ... He trusted the computer and placed the call, suggested the symphony, hung up, and grinned like the Cheshire Cat.

He could do this.

He was doing this.

The afternoon turned into evening; the beginning of the week into the end. And the pile of client's files needing help disappearing before his eyes. And he was having fun. So much fun his own dating was forgotten, or at least put on a back shelf in his mind. His success rate was winning over his loser rate. And he sincerely thought his new matches were good.

Sound.

Saturday he left the offices of Greater Expectations whistling. He headed back to his condo pleased with his weeks work. Pleased with the relationships he set in motion. The lives he knew he was changing. He wanted to call Trish and tell her she was right, there was something to that astrology thing after all. He could admit it to her.

Admit she was right. But she wasn't there.

Maybe he'd been a little harsh at first. It was only because he hadn't known any better, had never looked into it, couldn't look into it. It was far too 'out there' for him. He never would have even given it the time of day if Trish had stayed. No, he had picked up one of her books in desperation--and opened it in more desperation.

Maybe she'd be there ... so he dialed. Her phone picked up and gave the same vague message he'd gotten before. Discouraged, he wandered from room to room. Spying his computer, a light bulb went off. He booted it up, and brought up her file. 'Des Jones'.

"I wonder if we're astrologically compatible." He asked the quiet apartment. Trish had said they were, but now that he had a bit of a system, he wanted to see for himself. As he paged down he noticed that an age was typed in but the actual birth date was blank. He studied the picture of Trish with a puppy caught in her skirt and his heart did a small flip flop.

He read, and re—read, the bio. Finally he typed in a hit on her file and added his phone number. Did Trish even know his phone number if she saw it? Maybe she'd respond, where ever she was ... Well, he'd see.

Pandora was surprised to see a new hit on their file. She checked it constantly; sure that Mr. Perfect was just a click away. The file looked interesting, and rather than share with the others, she simply dialed the phone. "This is Des Jones."

Dev couldn't believe it, he thought Trish sounded a bit strange or strained or both but he thought he'd play along. He gave his code name and they agreed to meet for a drink.

Pandora fussed with her clothes, took her pony tail down, swept her hair behind her ears, went for a side part and ultimately put it back in a pony tail. She got out the 'Des' uniform floral skirt but matched it to a blue jean jacket, and added her favorite floral hiking boots. Well, it did say nature lover, and the idea of heels after a long day at work in the kitchens was just out of the question.

It was seven o'clock; the bar was dimly lit but Pan kept her eyes glued to the entrance. Eventually he walked in. He was cute, definitely not her type, but cute none the less. She mustered the courage and walked over.

"Hi," She started shyly.

"Hello," He answered absently. He continued to stare at the entrance as if waiting for someone.

Pandora was sure it was him--she had memorized his file. Well if she was brave enough to come out, not to mention chip in to join Greater Expectations, she certainly wasn't going to just stand there.

"Patrick?" She asked.

He continued to stare at the door.

Finally she tapped him. "Are you Patrick? Patrick Jones?"

Dev looked at this auburn pony tailed tiny gal and said, "Uh--Patrick Jones?" Then it dawned on him of course, his code name--his file name--his Greater Expectation's name.

"Uh, yeah, I am." Why was she asking? How did she know?

"I'm from Greater Expectations." Pandora was so nervous her knees were rubbery. Still she persevered.

He stared, his mouth dropped open.

"From the agency Greater Expectations--you put a hit on my file." There, she got it out.

He stared in amazement. Of course he hadn't put a hit on her file. Why he really couldn't stand short women, they always seemed too childlike, and besides made him feel too tall and gangly. She was cute, in a round, pony tail sort of way--not at all his type. Not even close.

He scrutinized her jeans jacket, and glancing down, was horrified to see she was wearing combat boots--with flowers on them. No, no, no--not his type at all. No he hadn't put a hit on her file. Of course he hadn't.

"I'm Des. Des Jones," She barely got it out. This wasn't going too good--no, not at all.

"You couldn't be," He was defiant. He thought Trish was back.

Pandora's eyes started to water. This was everything she hated about dating: the put down, the subtle, or not so subtle, insults. She turned and fled. It was humiliating enough to basically buy dates--but begging, well that was out of the question. So she ran.

Dev stared after her as she fled but she had obviously jumped in her car and escaped. Discouraged, he followed her out and went home. He got back to his empty condo and looked at his computer. "Traitor," He said. The phone rang as he headed to the refrigerator.

"Patrick?" A sweet voice asked.

"Yes."

"This is Des. Des Jones. I got your hit and if you'd like to meet for a drink--well, I know its short notice, but I'm rather shy."

Dev couldn't believe it. Okay, he thought, what's Trish up to?

Eight thirty found him at the same bar. An odd feeling enveloped him but he pushed it aside, ready to see Trish.

"Patrick?" A cute girl with a bouncy streaked cap of curls asked.

He decided to play along, "Yes. And you're Des?"

Maggie smiled coyly or as coyly as she could manage because that really wasn't her thing.

"Yes--Des Jones," She tried for a little confidence. Very little came through.

Dev's curiosity was up, "Let's grab a table, shall we?" He steered her to a corner booth and ordered a bottle of white wine.

"So Des--tell me a little about you." Dev thought he needed to know more.

Maggie stared at him frantically. What had that stupid application said? "Well, I love nature, and I uh work at Cat, and well, it was all in my file, tell me a little bit about you." She said this all in one long fast sentence and started to chug her wine.

This lying, well deceiving, well, yes lying just didn't come easy to her. And this Patrick just wasn't her type, handsome, yes, but well, just not for her. She'd let one of the others have him.

He reminded her of someone.

Trish!

This man was tall, and lean, and blonde--very Trish-ish, in a male sort of way. Yes, she'd let Trish have him. She'd have Trish put a hit on his file. Trish, she thought, I miss her--broken hearted or at least confused by some jerk--poor Trish. She continued to drink, not hearing a word Patrick said.

Dev couldn't quite decide what to do with his date. Obviously there was no joke with Trish popping out of the ladies room, and as nice as this Des was, well there just wasn't any chemistry. Again, she was no one he would have ever looked at twice; mind put a hit on her file.

"You know Des Jones is a rather unique name," He began. "I actually had a date earlier this evening with another Des Jones." And he watched her closely.

Maggie felt a trickle of sweat roll down her neck. She poured herself another glass of wine, and kept her eyes down as she downed it. Finally she managed a "Really?"

"Yes, a short girl with a pony tail." He tried to watch her face but Maggie remained neutral looking. He thought he saw a glimmer but it was too faint. "And flowered combat boots!"

"No! I told her to never wear those boots in public!" It just slipped, honestly, Maggie thought. "I didn't mean to open my mouth. It was the wine! Too much wine."

Dev's eyes glared. "Oh, so there are two Des Jones and you know each other?"

Maggie looked like a deer caught in the head lights. "Uh, I didn't say that," She paused, "Did I?" She started to panic.

Dev nodded.

"Well, I er, didn't mean to." There. Did that help? She had a wine dazed feeling that no, it didn't.

Dev laughed in spite of himself, and Maggie laughed right along. What else could she do?

"Okay, you caught me. But you know how expensive that agency is! There's no way a working girl like me could possibly afford to join." She stopped to catch her breath and went on, "Let's face it, it is highway robbery! And just for the record, I do work at Cat!" She looked defiant as she added that last bit. "And so do the other Des's." There, that was telling him.

Dev couldn't believe his ears! "Other Des's, how many of you are there?" He tried to sound as gentle as possible. He couldn't believe his ears. Not to mention the rip off to his company.

"Well," Maggie bit her bottom lip and then thought, why not, "There are three officially, four unofficially. We cut Jillian in since she posed for our picture." Maggie actually felt relieved to get it out in the open. "We just pooled all our qualities, and well, we share the men. I mean we take turns on who gets who;

we don't actually share the men. I'm not sure what happened tonight. I, er, forgot to check with the others."

She looked a little guilty but plowed on, "Usually it's obvious. The men seem to fit into categories, or styles, and we rarely conflict on who gets who. In fact, you're not my type at all." At this point she let loose a little nervous laugh, "Nothing personal." And then she gave him a truly sincere smile.

Dev had the decency to try and look hurt, and then laugh.

"Well, actually it's very personal but anyway, I think you'd be perfect with ..." She caught herself before she said Trish's name, "Uh, one of the other Des's."

"But not the one with the pony tail?" Dev asked with a twinkle in his eye. He knew he could get it out of her.

"Oh no--not at all," Maggie was sure Pandora would be all wrong for him, and he for her, for that matter.

"And this other Des--can I meet her?" Dev slipped it in as smoothly as possible.

Maggie had already had more than her token one and a half glasses of wine, and was feeling a bit free, but she managed to pull her thoughts together. "Uh, no I don't think so."

"You don't think so?" Dev was starting to get riled. "But you just said I'd be perfect for her."

"Did I? Well, actually ..." And she cleared her head and gave him a hard look. "She's, uh, sort of seeing someone, or at least she'd like to be."

Dev let this sink in. Was it him? Was it someone else? Or did this Des have him in mind for the number four Des? And wasn't that Trish in the photo? He'd have to re--look at the file tonight. He'd thought it was. He remembered the sexy yet innocent picture of her with a puppy in her skirt.

He looked over at Maggie. She seemed to be wearing the skirt from the photo. And actually so had the Des with the pony tail he'd met earlier! What about the puppies? If it was Trish in the photo, well, she'd have those puppies.

"Does the Des you think would be good for me own those puppies?" He asked innocently.

"Puppies?"

"Yes you know, the puppies in your photo!" He couldn't believe it! Give this Des a drink and she forgot who she was! At least she wore the skirt!

"Oh, the puppies," Maggie started to worry her bottom lip again. "Actually, the puppies were just props."

"Props!" Dev couldn't believe it. "You mean that picture was staged?" Now Dev was starting to get riled.

"Uh, yes, I guess you could say that." Maggie felt as though she was losing ground quickly. "Look Patrick, I enjoyed meeting you, but I really have to go and oh yes, good luck to you." She started to gather up her purse, looked longingly at her one half glass of wine and thought better of it. As she rose, Dev grabbed he hand.

"But what about my Des? I want to meet her." He probably should come clean, but he couldn't. "Couldn't you just give her a quick call, and ask her if she wants to meet me?" He tried his sweetest approach bordering on begging.

"I'm sorry Patrick. Even if I wanted to, number three Des is out of town, and she didn't leave any of us the phone number where she'd be. She, uh actually took a trip with number four Des--to get away." Maggie paused, afraid she'd said too much. "To think, about this man--the one she's not really seeing--and her job." With that said, Maggie escaped already convinced she'd said too much.

Dev sat and stared as she left. He couldn't believe it. He'd been so close--so close to finding Trish again. He emptied his wine glass and got up to leave. He didn't know what was going on tonight with multiple Des's but he did know he wanted his Des, number three, back.

He couldn't go home, he was too strung out. He headed back to the Greater Expectations offices. He flipped on Trish's light and stared at her desk. There must be a clue here as to where she went.

He started opening her desk drawers, knowing it was a breach of her privacy. He didn't care. He finally found what he was looking for: a brochure for the Del Coronado Hotel in California. Notes were made in the margins. He was sure she was there. He picked up the phone and called the hotel asking if she was registered.

"Yes she is sir, shall I put you through?" A friendly voice offered.

"Ah no, no thank you."

He hung up the phone and called the air lines, and rushed home to pack.

Chapter 12

Trish kicked up a little sand and stared out at the ocean. The water was beautiful, that went without saying, but she'd seen the surf roll in and out now for almost two weeks. She'd nibbled on delicate fruits and indulged in exotic sea food, and shopped a bit.

She wandered back to her suite. Her lap top stood staring at her from the desk. She'd resisted turning it on for two weeks, and checking on the agency.

She fingered the keys, and then booted it up. But she didn't know what to do. She pulled up Dev's file 'Patrick Jones' and read it slowly and carefully. Some of it she knew was a lie--not unlike her own file. Other little bits she found insightful. Things people wouldn't make up--they were too trivial. She scrolled down and read on, picturing his piercing eyes and crooked smile.

And her heart longed to be home. Her heart longed for Dev.

She saw the E mail address for Greater Expectations and began to type.

'Dear Management: It has come to my attention that file #401 for a Mr. Patrick Jones needs to be deleted from your system. He is no longer available for your client's perusal. He is involved, and in the process of making a serious commitment to one of your employees. Said employee would like to change her status, and buy into the business as a partner.'

'Financial arrangements could be 1) Taken from her wages or, 2) Gifted as part of a permanent contract with file #401. Conditions of such arrangements could be ironed out as long as the word 'equal' appears in every sentence.'

'Said employee is willing to devote all working, and personal time, to the betterment of this union.'

Before she could change her mind, she added her E mail and hit send.

Dev sat in a taxi with his duffle bag and lap top. The cab was crossing the bridge to Coronado. He may as well check his computer--it would help pass time. As he brought up Greater Expectations, he saw the agency had mail.

He stared in disbelief as he read--and re-read.

He typed quickly, 'One stubborn, yet love struck Scorpio, is willing to risk all for one creative and very wise Pisces. All details could be arranged with a walk in the moon light.' And he hit send.

Trish looked over at her lap top and saw her mail box winking at her. She opened her mail, tears streaming down her face as she heard a knock at her door.

At this hour?

She peered through the peek-hole and threw the door open.

Dev held out his arms and she fell in. "I believe we have a date for a walk on the beach."

***

Auntie Jilliana stared out her window lost in thoughts of her youthful days, when she saw the couple. They walked along the beach. He had on an over coat, she appeared to be in pajamas.

The next thing Aunt Jilliana knew, the man in the over coat was kneeling in the sand, and the girl in the pajamas was embracing him. Aunt Jilliana walked back to her canopy bed and sighed.

Chapter 13

It was late at Fairchild's gift shoppe, and Jefferson was getting ready to close up. "Jinx--you never got to the newspaper. Do you want to take it home tonight?"

Jinx nodded and tossed it on top of her huge tote bag. As Jefferson hit the lights, the CD player started to fade. Jim Hart was singing about the long road home. As he faded away Jinx saw the paper had fallen open to the back section. Her eye caught the ad in bold type.

'Greater Expectations will be closed

For two weeks in honor

Of the marriage of

File 401 and 264'

Grabbing the Pekingese's leads, and all their daily minutia, Jefferson flipped the shoppe sign to closed and Jinx tripped the lock.

About the Author

Jacqueline Gillam Fairchild writes cozy fiction stories that are escapes to countryside settings, and also on Nantucket Island. She writes of women who are ready to take the leap into starting their own business, or who just want to start over. At the heart of Jacqueline's writing is the belief we all want a life that is just a little bit prettier and maybe a little bit magical.

Jacqueline owns and operates Her Majesty's English Tea Room, and her British store Fairchild's, in the middle of the middle with her Scottish husband, and their Pekingese, Piewacket. A former Interior Designer who studied pastry at Le Cordon Bleu, her business was a finalist for Gift and Decorating Accessories Magazine's Retailer of the Year award. Her business won the coveted Icon Award from Americasmart Atlanta. Youtu.be/HK3_bUCqbWE. Jacqueline is also a script writer and is a cast member of the Grand Hotel Murder Mystery Troupe. Youtu.be/CO5bCckAEUs.

Enjoy her daily blog at jgfairchild.wix.com/tea-room-life, and on Facebook at Her Majesty's' English Tea Room.

Maggie's Story

Sneak peak of Maggie's Story, book two of Greater Expectations.

Introduction

"Jinx, why are we so late this morning?" Jefferson hollered to his wife as he dashed out of the car to unlock Fairchild's Ltd, their tiny British shoppe. Located in the middle of the middle of absolutely no where, their store was chocked full of English tea from Yorkshire Gold, the one the Queen drank, to Twinings Pumpkin Chai, like a slice of pumpkin pie in a cup.

They stocked delicate china teapots, and cups and saucers, from the United Kingdom, so you could have tea at home. Along with McVities Digestive Biscuits, a cross between a shortbread and a graham cracker, 'Digestives' were the essential Brit snack.

And Jinx's essential afternoon snack. Well, sometimes even a bit earlier. She usually ate any packages that looked a little 'hurt' and if there weren't any, she was known to drop a roll of 'Digestives' on the floor and figure it couldn't be sold.

All under the guise of quality control.

There were princess crowns, and wands, and dressy clothes for young, and not so young, princesses. Jewelry that really was a bit different--okay rather odd at times, but still tempting.

Books, of course there were books, from volumes on where to go in England to the latest cookie cookery, and entertaining volume--and for sure tea time books, because they were a natural with the tea and tea cups.

CD's. Somewhere along the line Jinx decided to sell the air, and then proceeded to always play her favorite music. It changed, of course, because she had a short attention span. But right now she was favoring Jim Hart's jazzy, bluesy rock. It went from mellow to upbeat, and she found her customers liked it as much as she did.

There were items for dogs because Jinx had two very spoiled, and rather lazy, okay very lazy, Pekingese and she felt someone should carry cute dog stuff. The word 'stuff' could be translated from doggy sweaters that of course matched the big girls sweaters, to goofy toys that she was sure dogs wanted. Of course her Pekingese didn't want them. But then again, they were Pekes. They had an attitude.

Still she carried cute items for dogs and dog lovers. And besides who didn't love dogs? Who didn't always want a dog of their own? Jim Hart's newest CD about Man's Best friend sat next to her stack of cute dog dishes. Well, dogs needed cute china too …

Jefferson hollered out again. He hated to start the day behind, even a little. "Jinx, really why are we so late today?"

But Jinx didn't answer. Her mind was a million miles away, to Coronado California to be exact. She absently got out of the car, dog leads around her neck, newspaper rolled up under her arm turned to the Greater Expectations ad and stopped.

It was not at all what she was expecting. She headed through the garden at Fairchild's, their British shoppe, and ambled in, flipping the closed sign to open. Jefferson was already inside with the dogs. The CD player started up with Jim Hart's music waking up their store. He sang of fears and changes. It was soft and subtle. But the words were pretty poignant.

The Pekingese found their own beds, realizing they were being ignored. After all, wasn't that their job--to ignore Jinx? But Jinx didn't even notice. She was preoccupied. She was on the phone. And still the Greater Expectations ad just stared out at her:

'Greater Expectations will be closed

For two weeks in honor
Of the marriage of
File 401 and 264'

Chapter 1

Maggie couldn't believe it! Her friend Trish was married! "Married? Really? The first one to go of our little group!" And the group was herself, of course, Pandora, Jillian, and Trish.

Well that had been the plan for all of them, the very expensive, join—the--dating--agency plan, to find their soul mates, and ultimately marry them. They were all too old, and far too sensible, for just carrying on. Not that anyone had offered to carry on with them …

Didn't that always imply it would never be permanent, and then they would have to start again, with a shard of their heart cracked? Well, it did to them. Besides they were all having trouble just finding someone to have a coffee with, mind a dinner.

So, the idea of an affair was so far out of their realm, well they knew it. And they also knew that if they got past coffee and dinner, and cared for someone enough to keep seeing them, they wanted the whole package.

They all wanted what they assumed most of the country had. The things they saw as they would drive by subdivisions of tidy little houses with two cars in the garage. They assumed there was a husband and a wife.

It was a quest not limited to the ultra rich, or the super famous. Not exclusive to Royalty. It was what the average person had. And that's what they all wanted, were ready for-- to be the average person … with their soul mate.

Married.

Maggie sighed, "But Trish surprised us." It was that simple. It was true Trish had been dating, and it was true there was a bit of drama, well, drama they had to listen to. "And that Trish did seem serious, and okay, smitten." Well maybe there was more to it that Maggie had missed in her own busy life.

Or jealously she had not paid much attention to. Could be either, or a bit of both. But it still caught them all off guard when Trish called from California. Called to say Dev had come looking for her, and that Trish had in fact gotten married--married to Devin, from the agency--from Greater Expectations Dating Agency.

And Maggie hadn't even met Dev--well, not really. She had met one Patrick Jones, Greater Expectations dating agency file member when he had put a hit on her file. But that had been his fake name so he could cruise the Greater Expectations files and remain unanimous. As a matter of fact Pandora had met him also, under the same circumstances.

And Dev wanted to remain unanimous because he owned the agency. Well, technically he and his cousin owned it. And didn't this just imply that they were using their own business for their own social life?

It did.

Still, Maggie was a busy accountant for Caterpillar International, and she also did some side accounts, including the Greater Expectations books. So, she guessed it was probably okay.

Probably.

And as to her own file at Greater Expectations, well, it was actually a composite file 'Des Jones' made up of Pandora, Jillian, herself, and of course Trish. Composite file to pool their assets, but most of all divvy up the ten-thousand-dollar fee. "Because let's face it, who had ten thousand dollars lying around just to meet men?"

Obviously enough people did, because the dating agency was thriving. But Maggie and her friends Trish, Pandora, and

Jillian didn't. Not even close. Pooling their money had been hard enough.

Still they were all thrilled to be part of the Greater Expectations family and have access to those coveted files--the files where all the gorgeous men and potential soul mates lingered. Or at least she assumed they were all camped out in those files.

And if that wasn't sweet enough, Trish had taken a job at Greater Expectations to get her hands on all the inner goodies. But when Trish actually got to Greater Expectations she realized the place was a scam, and a dump. Not a good combination.

Well, Trish had given up the security of her human resources job at Caterpillar International--security yes, but oh so boring. And besides Trish's heart had left human resources and moved on ... to match making. So, Trish single handily started to turn the agency around; first with a makeover of the reception area and then the files.

"Inner files," Maggie thought, "Trish certainly had gotten into them." Trish started dating Patrick Jones who turned out to be co-owner of the company she worked for. But the Patrick Jones was his alias. Alias to Devin Streetmatter, owner of Greater Expectations, and now husband to Maggie's long-time friend Trish--funny how that all happened.

Devin flew to Coronado, California to patch up their relationship and somehow was returning not with a placated girl friend but a wife. Dev claimed he wasn't leaving without putting a ring on Trish's hand. And to his way of thinking that meant marriage not just engagement.

***

Trish said it was all very sudden, a moon lit ceremony on the beach. Jillian's Aunt Jilliana, permanent resident at the Del Coronado Hotel, was her matron of honor. The concierge was the best man. The flowers had been Bougainvillea and Birds of Paradise.

Her trousseau purchased in the gift shoppe. Well, obviously more than a gift shoppe, but still, Trish managed to find all she needed right there at the hotel. Because as Trish explained on the phone all she really needed was Dev.

The passion carried on for days, and the decision to do an intimate ceremony--well, as Trish described it, there really wasn't any decision--it just seemed right. The wedding just happened. Because Dev was determined to add his ring to her finger before they left.

The romance of a committed man was its own steam powered machine. After years of organizing and planning everyone's lives from her Cat job to her work at Greater Expectations, Trish basked in the simplicity of 'I do'.

And Trish had been amazed how extensive and high end the Hotel Del Coronado's shops were: ivory silk just waiting for her, along with Manolo Blahnik silk shoes, delicate undies and sensual perfume.

But now Trish was headed back home to her friends, a husband in tow. Back home to a small reception Maggie, Pandora, and Jillian were whipping together at Estate of Mind Bed and Breakfast and Orchards. Back to her job, where she would be assuming the title of Mrs. Greater Expectations, where she could continue to refine the dating agency that she loved so very much.

***

Trish twisted her diamond and gave Dev's hand one final squeeze as the plane departed and she drifted off to sleep.

***

Maggie went over her list again. Birds of Paradise and Bougainvillea check, delivered to the bed and breakfast. Maggie said a silent prayer of thanks that Randi and Angus

MacTamara, proprietors of Estate of Mind Bed and Breakfast, had become not only her free lance accounting clients, but friends as well.

The grand old home with its gigantic porch, and stately rooms, would be perfect for their party. Party? What she really meant was reception--wedding reception. This was way more than a party. Or if it was a party it was THE party.

Dev's cousin Mike was bringing the champagne.

Randi was doing the dinner, well actually her gourmet adopted Aunt Biscuit and Biscuit's friend Jingles were doing the dinner. Lobster tails and shrimp in puff pastry, designer salads (whatever that really meant), tropical fruit--Maggie couldn't remember it all. When they went over it all with Pandora and Jillian they all simply agreed, because it sounded wonderful, and well, done.

There was a part of all of them that was just too shocked to come down to earth enough to ask what all the tropical fruit mix contained or exactly what a designer salad was. So they'd nodded, agreeing to foot the bill.

Pandora, her dear friend who baked cookies for Caterpillar's restaurants and cafeterias, was bringing heart shaped oatmeal cookies.

The cake was a concoction of cream and strawberries. Jillian had found a vintage bride and groom for the top.

Maggie had simply nodded to all of it, and well, what had she contributed? She didn't really have a specialty like Pandora did in baking, or Josie, Randi's sister in law, did in flower arranging. No, Maggie would simply show up, and be supportive, and try to let the whole thing just sink in.

Whatever else needed doing; she was sure Randi and her sister--in--law Josie had under control. Maggie's job was to get dressed. She slipped into her floral skirt and pale pink cashmere sweater.

Jillian and Pandora had agreed to wear their version of the outfit used for the photographs for their Greater Expectations composite file. The pictures actually were of Jillian, posed to discreetly hide her face, with the plan they could be any of them. And they thought if it was the floral skirt that had been part of their early plan, well it was the best choice for the wedding reception.

Maggie slipped on her ivory heels, checked her bouncy highlighted sable curls, and grabbed her gift. A crystal frame she was sure a wedding photograph would look divine in. Was it very creative? Well, no not really. It was just the best she could do or was going to do.

When they'd gotten the phone call it seemed everyone went in to creative mode and Maggie shut down. A gift? Maggie was clueless because she refused to think about it seriously. What would Trish like? Love?

Well, with a pang of jealousy Maggie guessed Trish would love a husband and now she had that. So, Maggie put off gift hunting, and then last minute had to run into Hallmark and made due.

And still at a loss, the kind clerk had suggested a frame, and even wrapped it. With a twinge of nostalgia, Maggie headed out to her car, to her dear friend's wedding reception.

As Maggie pulled in the drive and caught a look at the house, her heart skipped a beat. Josie, Randi's sister in law, was on the porch tying the end of a floral garland to the rails. Clusters of yellow and purple Statice, baby's breath, and golden yarrow, formed the basis for the swags that were caught every three feet with gold and silver French wired ribbon. It was dramatic and warm at the same time.

"Oh Josie, I'm going to cry!" Maggie blubbered as she got out of her car. "No wonder your everlastings business is booming."

Josie, and her husband Jamie, lived at the bed and breakfast orchards in a converted stone barn. The front section was Josie's everlastings business where she created topiaries, wreaths, dream pillows, and any wonder of floral arrangements. And of course, the orchards sold their apples in the fall.

"I've finished arranging the Bougainvillea and Birds of Paradise," Josie said as she tied the last bow and headed in with Maggie. "And I made her a small nosegay."

A crystal cake stand stood on the ancient reception desk. On it was a tiny bouquet of tissue like Bougainvillea mixed with off white Statice and pale pink straw flowers. Ivory French ribbon streamers trailed along with baby English Ivy.

On closer inspection, Maggie realized there were in fact two diminutive bouquets back to back, "Two Josie?"

Josie blushed, "I thought she'd want one to keep and well, one to throw."

Maggie looked ready to weep. What had been meant, or at least in Maggie's mind, to be a casual party was turning into a traditional reception.

"I tried to work in the dry flowers so when the Bougainvillea goes, the bouquets will still be a wonderful keepsake." Since Josie specialized in dry everlasting flowers it was a natural for her to mix them in with the fresh ones.

"Oh Josie ..." As Maggie fought for composure, she heard cars starting to arrive. The party was starting and she couldn't believe the first of them was getting married. Correction--got married. They were no longer four single friends. Trish was married, paired off--gone. Now there were three--just three.

"I think its Pandora and Jillian," Josie said peering out the door.

As they came in, the tears, and oohs, and aahs started all over.

"You haven't even seen the house yet," Josie laughed and tugged them into the dining room. The endless table was set in the old family Imari china, crystal, and candles.

Randi was fussing over a trailing ribbon from one of the crystal candle holders. It looked magazine perfect. It was perfect. "Thank goodness you're all here," Randi sounded frantic. "I feel as though my own daughter is getting married!"

At that Randi's precocious four-year-old daughter Annie appeared, wearing taffeta. The child had on her good white tights, and her pink velvet ballet flats. "Do I look like a princess?" Annie twirled for everyone, her golden curls bouncing, her petticoats billowing.

Then Annie added, not waiting for anyone to confirm her princess status, "Bart has to wear a tie but he's waiting to see if the other men do."

Bart was seven, up in his attic room playing with his trains, oblivious to the girls endless planning and fussing.

And much to Annie's surprise no one seemed to care if Bart wore a tie or not. They had more important things to worry about. "I thought we'd put gifts in the parlor," Randi went on still fussing.

Jillian, Pandora, and Maggie walked around as if in a trance, fingering a blossom here, oohing over a candle cluster there.

Gifts, of course there would be gifts. Maggie hadn't even thought about guests bringing gifts. Of course, she had one, and she was sure Pan and Jillian did. But the others … And suddenly it really was a wedding, with packages to be opened and shared. And a place to put them and … well, Maggie didn't know what all. It just started to hit her.

The door opened and Mike, Dev's cousin came in. "Where should I put the champagne?" He hollered out, anxious for the party to begin, holding a case of expensive champagne.

Randi was still in panic mode. Her eyes darted to her accountant. "Maggie, could you get Angus. I think he's in the kitchen. Mike--could you bring it all in the kitchen through the French doors," Which meant back outside to the kitchen door. So Randi could worry about the foyer and front of the house. She left to direct him, and Maggie headed to the kitchen.

As Maggie opened the kitchen door she was assaulted with the scents of sea food simmering in white wine and cream. Angus, Randi's husband, and Mr. Jingles were at the stove gently stirring huge copper pots.

Aunt Biscuit was gently taking little rounds of puff pastry off cookie sheets. Jamie, Josie's husband, was slicing strawberries. "Uh, the champagne's here," Was all Maggie could say? The makings of the wedding dinner were in full swing. Everyone seemed to have a special job but her.

Little Annie had followed Maggie in now pirouetting a bit. No one noticed. "We're not supposed to bother anyone in the kitchen," Annie explained in a rather parental tone. The child was used to her mom and dad entertaining at the bed and breakfast, used to the kitchen being in party mode, and time being short.

Annie knew the drill. It included her not getting in the way, and not even considering whining about anything, until the event was over. And usually by then the little girl was too tired to carry on. "Let's just open the outside door," Annie informed Maggie with great importance as she did a little twirl and pointed to the door.

Maggie stood in awe at the feast that was underway, and suddenly felt she was watching a movie--a movie at an elegant set, where her oldest friend was having her wedding reception.

There was no time for melancholy tears because the crunch of drive way gravel told Maggie cars were approaching.

Little Annie took her hand and said, "Let's man the front door." This was something Annie did when the bed and breakfast was expecting guests. Annie even had a coloring book under the counter to keep her busy. And today was even better than checking in guests to the bed and breakfast. This was special, and Annie didn't want to miss one minute of it all.

The little girl wanted to see everyone when they came in, and she wanted them to see her. This was her first wedding reception at the bed and breakfast, and she felt like she was the star.

Maggie stared as people got out of cars. Josie's Aunt Bix and her husband O.T. came in with Margaret O' and Royal (Angus's cousin), followed by Hale (Royal's brother). Jinx and Jefferson, from Fairchild's, were coming up the walk as Trish and Dev pulled in; too many people, too many names to remember. Faces Maggie knew, but it was all so emotional she just couldn't piece it all together.

"Who's that?" Little Annie asked Maggie from her perch on the reception stool. She was looking at the glamorous couple that looked like movie stars. Of course, Annie knew everyone. Well almost everyone. The child usually went where her mom and dad went, and if she behaved, she was included. So, the little girl behaved. Why chance being left out?

"That's the bride and groom," Maggie said softly.

Annie looked carefully, no big fluffy white dress, no tuxedo--nothing formal. Was Maggie sure? They didn't look like a bride and groom at all. No veil cascading down the porch and on to the driveway, the way little Annie planned hers to be.

Maybe the bride was going upstairs to change. Maybe that princess dress was up there waiting for her to put on ... Annie could only hope. There was no gigantic bouquet with ribbons trailing down to the floor.

Then Annie stopped, Aunt Josie had made a couple of the world's smallest bouquets she called nosegays. They were on the check in counter on a cake stand. But Annie had been sure; well pretty sure, they were just for looks. They couldn't be the real bridal bouquets ... could they? Was this really a wedding reception? Annie was starting to have her doubts.

Maggie sighed the words bride and groom. And as the words came out of Maggie's mouth she started to feel that prickle of tears fighting their way. She said it, "Bride and groom." It was real, very real.

Trish had gotten married.

Made in United States
North Haven, CT
05 December 2023

45099888R00143